MW00937383

Driving in
Second

Marietta J. Tanner

ISBN: 1547200839

ISBN 13: 9781547200832

Library of Congress Control Number: 2017909132

LCCN Imprint Name: CreateSpace Independent Publishing Platform

North Charleston, South Carolina

Contents

Introduction

The story is based on a motor trip that four Black women in their early twenties took in August 1954 from New York City to Mexico. Its avowed purpose was to ascertain whether the Supreme Court Decision, Brown vs the Board of Education of May 18, 1954, was having any impact on their own lives and the lives of Black people in the states they visited.

Black people were suffering Jim Crow laws and customs throughout the States; the Decision elicited a mix of responses. Negroes themselves in some cases opposed any change. This dilemma provides the conflict in the true story which has been expanded and supplemented with fictional additional incidents, personages and encounters to define certain points and give the reader greater insight into the trauma Black people were experiencing.

The narrative is in the first person. For the narrator, it was a trip of self-evaluation and discovery. She has broken up with her boyfriend and is suffering because of it. The trip was to provide escape and a new beginning for her, but she is constantly reminded of her lost lover. While she tries to cultivate new interests to lessen the attachment, he is always present, dominating her thoughts so that she has no release. Hers and his attachment centered around their deep understanding of the residual psychological effects of enslavement that were a part of their upbringing and continue to impair their functioning as whole persons. They had reached a point in their relationship where they knew they were deeply in love, however, an unfortunate incident drives a wedge between them and brings out behaviors that had been subverted but not overcome, separating the two.

The story ends without reconciliation, but the narrator has gained new knowledge, insights and ways of behaving that might bring her inner peace and strength to carry on as an independent, free and equal woman. Whether this will be enough to sustain her is left for the reader to ponder.

Marietta J. Tanner, 2017

Dedication

To my mother, Mary Dickens Jones

Acknowledgements

I waited years to tell this story, therefore it meant I needed not only to search the dusty files in my memory but jog those of my companions too. Unfortunately, most of them were deceased, and those still with us had only slight recollections of the places, events and people whom we encountered all those years ago. One companion, Evelyn Batts, the main driver, Eve, in the story, survives, and offered every shred of recollection she could muster to help propel the narrative. I am eternally grateful to her. There was research too at the Schomburg Center in New York, the Free Library of Philadelphia and the Library of the Americas in Washington, D.C., on-site visits to some of the places, plus the internet, a right handy resource.

My mother, Mary Dickens Jones, passed years ago but her graciousness and love are still with me. She would disapprove of much that I actually did in this story and the telling of intimate details she would never have mentioned in public. But life has changed greatly since her straight-laced upbringing; many of the strictures stemming from our enslaved past which hobbled her are no longer evident, or at least are subtly practiced, and in some cases, are eradicated as a matter of law. I wish she could have seen some of the mountains that I have climbed and the people I have met, and enjoyed the adventures my audacity has allowed me to experience.

I thank my family of five siblings for their part in weaving the fabric of this work: Charles T., Thelma, Elayne, George and Dorothy; I extend appreciation to my friends who were there for me, Louise Singleton Pugh, Edith Thomas Dent and Cynthia Vance Coleman. They may not recognize themselves in this tapestry, but they and many others were my inspiration, especially the men whose names I have not mentioned but for whose presence I say, "*Vivé le difference.*"

And thanks to the folks at Goodwin House Bailey's Crossroads, Falls Church, Virginia who spurred me to action to finish a languishing project, to Paul Blackburn for his conscientious editing and proofreading, and to Dr. Ben Wilmot who designed the cover.

Part 1

I'm going to be late again, and I hate that. I'm running out of my crummy one–room apartment, hating it, but oh so glad to have it. I searched so long for it, and really didn't think I would get it. At least it's in the village – or East Village; I couldn't get near Fifth Avenue, but I can walk to NYU and all the events, and it's just a hop to First Avenue and the bus to work. I know why I got the place – there was already a Black guy in here, a famous author -- his white wife must have done the search, and they admitted her. The landlords had made one mistake so why not go with me and have two of us. What a cruddy room it is, but my decorating has done something for it, putting down those black and white tiles before my kitchen bar, and making the covers for the bed with matching pillows everywhere, I really do have a flair for decorating, it's almost comfortable. I guess I'm especially bitchy this morning having seen Freddy's new place. Don't let me think of that, I behaved terribly about it, but then I can't always squelch what I feel, I'm so repressed, and getting more so. Just to get along, and not be on the outside looking in all the time, I find myself just smiling and being mum; are people beginning to think I'm losing it?

I've made it aboard and if this bus doesn't lumber I'll get there before nine. I'm just going to hold this strap and watch the scenery, admiring all the beautiful factories blocking the view of the tranquil, brownish-gray East River. I'm thinking, "Don't think about anything for a few minutes and stop flagellating yourself, you made the decision to ask Freda to go with you to the opera; you're jealous of her, you always have been, you resent her, yet you crave her company – what kind of insanity is that?" I think I'm going to discuss the whole thing with Ella; she's Jewish enough and smart enough and honest enough to give me her opinion and I shall value it.

I am rushing again to get to work at my editorial assistant job in the Carnegie Endowment for International Peace building, just across the street from the United Nations. I love the location, probably as close as I will ever get to a dream job in the place; they wouldn't be hiring any liberal Americans during the Eisenhower administration, and certainly not one who is Negro. But I'm grateful that I can get time off to go to the General Assembly building for important sessions, working among people who were deeply involved in world affairs, seeing Secretaries General on the street like Dag Hammarskjold or Trygve Lie and even having a chance to meet and talk with Eleanor Roosevelt in the elevator. It wasn't all bad, and quite a step up from my old jobs transcribing phonograph discs and being a secretary with the educational testing people. Here I am working on publications, meeting the authors and participating in editing and development sessions. And there are people I like, especially Ella, really an old maid, who found

Dan, her love when she was over 40 and married him, lamenting that it was too late for them to be parents. But embracing me, inviting me into their life whenever I was dragging.

Which is often these days – I admit, I am really missing my old boyfriend; I keep saying to myself, he was a drag, too demanding; cut too much from my father's cloth for me, just didn't see things my way. Okay, that's not exactly true, he was beginning to be more open and …. but rid of him I can experience some of the world. He was so provincial, there are other things beyond the Black church on Sunday, his mother with her admonitions about being careful, she seemed to want to look through me every Sunday asking whether we had been intimate, and if I were pregnant. Oooh, I do get so lonely sometimes, I must admit, I am often dragged these days with melancholia, thinking of him. Although I am always meeting new men, they are either on the make, or maybe I just feel that way. It seems that no one really wants to get to know me. Why doesn't one of them come as a complete package – each has a little piece of what I'm seeking, but none satisfies the whole person.

Then there was Freda, ensconced in her Riverside Drive apartment. Can you imagine, in this country two years, a Jewish refugee from the extermination camps in Austria, speaking in her soft, cultured, heavily German-accented English, already enrolled at Columbia, already working in the travel industry, making *beaucoup* cash, with an adoring boyfriend to boot. It seems like every synagogue has rolled out the red carpet for her. I had no idea she had amassed everything when I asked her to go to the opera with me – we were both job hunting when last we met, and although we had spoken frequently on the phone, she never for a moment let on that she had found that fabulous apartment, while I, a Black person with a history of struggle in the building of this nation, was lucky to live in the bowels of New York City among the pushcarts and slums near the lower East side.

I invited her to the opera because I knew she had a love-hate thing with Wagner, and her former financial state could never have afforded those loge-level tickets. When I mentioned Wagner, she gushed forth with how anti-Semitic he was and how much Hitler loved him. Yet she had been reared on his music, understood everything about it, and ached to hear it well-played. I had thought we would have dinner somewhere around 40th Street and walk to the Met and she would explain everything to me, since she was a very fine pianist, and I couldn't play a note on anything. My boss gave me the tickets; I knew none of my Negro girlfriends would go with me – they think I'm way out in my tastes anyway; it would just add fuel to the fire of their contempt for what they consider my overreach.

My boss was always giving me tickets to the finest music at Carnegie Hall, to chamber music concerts, to hear a soloist she knew personally, like the people in the Doily Carte Gilbert and Sullivan troupe, or her nephew who himself was a concert pianist. I do have an odd relationship with Freda; she seemed anxious to get to know me too, even though she said she never saw a Negro person until she came to the United

States. When talking with her I sort of accept her innocence about the place of Negro people in this country – but I never let her get away with saying things that are absolutely unacceptable coming from any white person, like pointing out how certain low-level jobs seem to be especially appropriate for the mentality of Black men. I would say look here, you just arrived in this country; you don't know a thing about how Negroes have been defiled in mind-numbing jobs like picking cotton for three centuries, so lay off. I in turn can make her squirm – I told her about transcribing those phonograph discs for United Jewish Appeal social workers and how angry I would get when Jewish concentration camp immigrants from Germany said they felt they were being disgraced by having to live or work with Negroes. They had some nerve, I said; while Negro soldiers died to free them from the death camps, somehow they had learned that they were better than the Negro and should have greater privileges. She would redden, asking me to forgive that person; that he had suffered so much shame and degradation that he was scapegoating Negroes in this country, finding someone he could degrade as he had been degraded. Then she would speak so highly of those Negro soldiers who had helped to liberate Europe. Although she had never seen them, she knew they were there. I must say, she's a smooth operator, with her soft, accented speech, her cultured demeanor, her hand resting lightly on my arm.

I was explaining my anguish to Ella that morning when the phone rang. It was my good friend Lou, who was making more money than I doing social work. She wanted me to teach school, a job which I had sworn not to take. I was going to crack the publishing industry, go to the Columbia School of Journalism, travel the world, etc., etc. We all used to live near each other in Harlem, she at Convent Avenue and 147th and my roommate, her brother and I nearer the river. My room-mate had returned to Washington, D.C., and her brother had gone to the Korean War. So we had split. I first roomed with my landlady, Golda, on 102nd Street and I am now in my horrid kitchenette. Lou was an old friend from college with whom I had experienced much maturation; we learned to smoke to-gether, drank our first rum-and-Cokes together, and yes, it was Lou's boyfriend Tom who had brought my boyfriend to the Savoy that day...oh God, there I go again.

Lou was proposing that I go with her and two of her friends to Mexico. I laughed. I was broke; I just got this new apart-ment. Her idea was that we would help Eve with the driving on the highway, through the Appalachian Mountains, down to Texas and through the high Sierras to Mexico City.

I have done very little driving since my boyfriend and I broke up, and although it seemed like something I would like to do, I couldn't get a month off to do it. Furthermore, the last time I went on a motor tour through the South with my family, it was hell to find food and a place to stay. She assured me that it wouldn't be that expensive, we'd be driving in Eve's car, mainly buying the gas, and remember, this was 1954 -- the Supreme Court decision had just been passed desegregating the schools and making the whole country safer for Negroes.

What a laugh; that last line was the height of ridiculousness. Didn't she read the papers; hadn't she seen all those soldiers lined up around those little Negro children being spat upon trying to go to school? She said she was shocked that I would be expressing these doubts – wasn't it I who had watched Thurgood Marshall and the lawyers run across Fifth Avenue to Grand Central to get the train to DC to fight for that case? The last time we talked, it was I who was ready to picket, to go to Washington, who went to those meetings on 125th Street, and hung around the NAACP office waiting to hear the news about the progress at the Supreme Court. I admitted that it would be a worthy trip, and I should make my actions match my rhetoric, but this comes at a time when I am going through a few things. But maybe I could think of something, I said. Don't count me out. She said I should come up to her place tonight and talk it over with the other two women.

I sat for a while thinking of Lou and Tom and then reverted to my melancholia. Yes, it was they who brought my boyfriend to the Savoy that day....

◆ ◆ ◆

Sunday at the Savoy

One of the things our bunch of singles who lived around 145th Street in upper Manhattan liked to do was to go to the Savoy. It was the only integrated ballroom around. You could go there any evening or on a Sunday afternoon and hear Lionel Hampton, Count Basie, Duke Ellington or any of the hottest jazz and swing artists. The music was continuous, and the floor spacious and polished. We would crowd into the booths and order rum-and-Cokes, or just Cokes, since none of us drank very much. This Thursday, my roommate, Kit's sister, Marg, was with us. She always came loaded with cash, and insisted on making all the rounds. Their brother, Fred, was a music maven, and knew what was happening musically everywhere. He adored the Black band leaders but was into several white musicians too, especially Stan Getz and Woody Herman, whose music he played endlessly at the apartment. Lou was with us and a few minutes after we arrived, her latest boyfriend, Tom, came with two friends. One of them was a young man I knew from our college campus, but not very well. He didn't associate with us much; he was bookish, and had a job off-campus, so he wasn't around very much. He also had a steady girlfriend.

Immediately there was controversy about the music. Tom wanted to stay at the Savoy and listen to swing and stride piano. It was Fat Waller's birthday, May 21. Fred was OK with that for a little while, but he wanted to go to 52nd Street where Charlie Parker was playing, and maybe the latest sensation, Miles Davis, would be there.

While they argued, this friend of Tom's asked me for a dance. The Count was playing an old censored Fat's Waller number. My partner's first comment was, "Why did they ever censor this, what he is saying is that 'Everybody's Truckin'. It was to commemorate the latest form of trans-porting goods, supplanting the freight train to some de-gree. Filthy minds, don't you think?" "Indeed, it's a cute number, although I never learned to 'Truck' and it seems like everybody is doing the two-step, not bothering to shuf-fle along 'truckin'." "Look over there in that corner where the best dancers are, some people are doing it," he said. We danced over, and the dancers started singing, including my partner and me:

> "We had to have somethin' new, a dance to do up here in Harlem, so, someone started truckin'. As soon as the news got round the folks downtown came up to Harlem, saw ev-erbody truckin'. It didn't take long before the high hats were doin' it, Park Avenuin' it all over town. You'd see them hustle, and bustle and then truck on down. It spread like a forest fire,

our heart's desire, and so in Harlem now, ev-erybody's truckin'."

We were laughing and singing in unison, he in his hoarse, off-key voice, as we tried to follow the expert's steps. He gave up and held me close in a two-step so he could say in my ear, "It's my business, so I like to promote it in song so more people will consider sending cargo in trucks. Why, once Ike gets those highways built, that will be the hottest commercial enterprise out here." "Oh wow, you are really into trucking, you mean you'd like to drive those big rigs across the states?" I said. "Oh no, I want to run the company; that's what I did in the Army. I know the business, and we have a start-up in Brooklyn," he said. "We who, I don't believe they're letting any Negroes get their hands on an enterprise like that. I just read about this Negro man who started gathering up the met-al left behind overseas from the war, thinking he would have a great business in scrap. He could gather it, but they wouldn't let him have the ships to transport it to the U.S."

"You have to have a white front man, there's no way they will let us have the whole thing, even if we supply the money and the know-how. You got to have them front and center," he said. "Miserable, so you have a white front man?" "Yeah, my Italian captain from the quartermaster days in the Army; he and I were inseparable in Italy. Our teamwork got the cargo through. We said we could do the same thing when we got back to the states. It has taken us seven years to get things up and running, and if we can just keep the race thing at bay,

I know we can be successful." "I do admire your optimism, but I think racism pervades everything we try to do, even on a minor scale like having a day-care center. Having a business that is profitable, that employs hundreds of people with machinery and plants, that just seems impossible." "Some of our guys are working with the big companies now, like IBM and Coca-Cola. ..." The music had stopped, but we were still dancing, so immersed were we in the conversation.

When we returned to the booth, Kit and her siblings were ready to depart for 52nd Street, and since I had come with them, I decided to go too. Lou was going to stay with her new boyfriend; my dance partner asked me to stay, saying he would take me home. I thanked him, but, not wanting to be a pick-up that night and seem too anxious for a date, I declined. He asked if he could see me again, and I said, "Why not? There might be a song about sailing or fishing, something more practical that we could dance to." He laughed and scribbled down my address and phone number, and I departed in a waiting cab.

◆ ◆ ◆

The Planning

I picked up my steno pad and went to my boss's office. I worked for two editors – one had a son who was at Harvard Medical School. I had a date recently with one of his Black African friends – more of my survey, and my determination to go out with guys who ask me, to test all waters and see whether we were on the same wavelength. He and I most certainly weren't. All the way downtown on the subway, he was diagnosing people, telling me they had liver problems or were malnourished, or suffered some communicable disease. He had sickened me by analyzing my case before we reached 59th Street.

Anyway, that boss was away, and it was Miss EL, boss two, for whom I was working this morning. I wanted to thank her for the tickets, and she wanted to know what my response to the music was, whether it had made an impression, whether I was beginning to understand the saga, appreciating the beauty of the music, despite how ludicrous the narrative was. I told her about Freda's hatred of Wagner, and asked her whether she shared those feelings. She said she was completely enchanted by the artistry, that it transcended the one who produced it, although she could never admire Wagner the person because he was disdainful of Meyerbeer disparaging his Jewishness, not a very nice person. But she wasn't ready, so soon after the Holocaust, to listen to him. She was determined that I should study some music, I had the hands for it, and it was too bad that I had been denied a musical education.

Just as we were finishing looking over a manuscript, I mentioned the offer to go to Mexico. I was amazed at her reaction. Miss EL walked with a slight limp, she was not an attractive woman, and idolized her sister, who had the handsome, rich husband, the good looks, and children. Miss EL was a spinster, talented, but marked by ill health throughout her life. She reveled in the possibility of such an adventure. Immediately, she said I should visit EF, a Black artist who was her protégé and lived in Morelia just outside Mexico City. She always knew somebody, she always had a connection, and her money reached everywhere. "Go, go," she said, "you will never regret it." "You know I can't go; first of all, I just got a new apartment, and am spending my last cent to fix it up. Furthermore, I don't have a month's vacation left."

"Well," she said, "I think the time off could be managed. Summer is our slow season, maybe I could arrange for you to get the four weeks off. Anyway, you need a change, I can see it; sometimes it seems you are losing your zest for life." Ella, passing by, overheard, and nodded in agreement. "You too! I'm doing fine – you Freudians, always doing armchair psychoanalysis. I am not your patient," I said.

I was overwhelmed by Miss EL's offer, yet I knew how generous she is, how much affection she had shown me; the great restaurants I had gone to with her and learned to eat a horrid *fromage* I had ordered as I tried to read the French menu. She would do everything except get me an apartment in one of the downtown buildings her family owned. Maybe not in a building as fine as hers with its doorman, a marble lobby, an elevator of wrought iron and brass, which whisked you up to her front door. Lovely indeed were its parquet floors and floor-to-ceiling windows that overlooked the Hudson. I had asked, but she had reddened, and said that the clientele was restricted, that the buildings had boards, and they would not allow Negro tenants.

She assured me that was not the way she felt, but she was just one person, trying in every way she could to change the mindset that so many people had. She was confident that change was coming, and she and her family were doing everything humanly possible to speed desegregation, etc., etc. The upshot of all this was that I lived in a tiny walkup on 6th Street that cost as much as Freda's luxurious apartment that her synagogue friends got for her on Riverside Drive.

So Miss EL said she would give me a gift – she had never given me one, and she greatly appreciated my having come to her parties, where I sometimes felt like exhibit A. I went because I wanted to meet those intellectuals, musicians and politicos. She was especially pleased at the last one where I had talked so freely with her British corporate candy friends about how I experienced segregation in this country. The discussion had made that cocktail party quite a success, really giving everyone there a new perspective.

She never asked me to serve food; her Negro maid would do that. That maid was the snootiest person at the parties, obviously resenting the fact that I was a guest and not helping her with the dishes. Never for a minute did EL suggest such as thing; I was her young, college-educated, well-informed guest.

I protested mightily, but then accepted the cash, promising to finish all the work around the office before my departure.

Lou still lived in Harlem with two other women in a large apartment, not at all elegant to say the least, but more than adequate. Upon arrival, I was introduced to one of the women, Theta, very tall, with a loud and sarcastic laugh; Lou had invited Eve to the New Year's party so I knew her. She had the car and had been driving for years. She was an only child of a doting mother and had a certain sophistication, a cultivated worldliness, constantly smoking her cigarettes, and speaking with authority about everything. She was younger than Lou and I, but considered us country bumpkins. She had lived in New York most of her life and knew the ropes, or so she thought. She was recently married, and we were stunned that her new husband had agreed to let her take this trip without him. But once you met Ben, you understood why: he was completely enamored of her, and she could persuade him of the wisdom of almost anything.

We sat down and looked at the maps she had gotten from AAA, tracing our path through the U.S. to Mexico, deciding what we wanted to experience along the way. We should have but we didn't have the "Little Green Book," a recently published guidebook to tell us where Negroes could get gas and eat throughout the South. There were relatives in Pittsburgh for Lou and sites like Little Rock that were in the news for me, and mileages to consider, as we talked about distance and time. Theta had an uncle in Memphis whom she would write to so we would be offered free lodging for a night and see Beale Street. She also had folks in Galveston, Texas. Eve was the only one who had lived in the South. She had relatives in South Carolina and Florida, and told us that we had to understand the ways of the South if we were deliberately going to the hot spots of prejudice we had cited.

We would have to practice how we would talk to white people. We could be arrested if we had confrontations with the wrong people. She was going to be the expert on decorum, because I could see from the start that Lou was not ready to kowtow to anyone. Eve said that submissiveness was absolutely essential, even being willing to say, yes sir or ma'am.

Our objective was to see if *Brown vs. the Board of Education* had made any difference, or if we were still second-class citizens, still not eligible for equal protection as promised in the 13th Amendment. Well, I was sanguine about that whole thing – I lived in the North all my life; had I seen anything tangible happening here since the decision on May 17? Even the schools seemed to be getting more segregated every day. I was sure there might even be a backlash in the South. My aim would be to speak with Negroes who lived in those places, who were putting their lives on the line to get equality, and I would steer clear of confrontation with white folks, since I wanted to come back in one piece. One of the places I wanted to see was New Orleans; all agreed to spend some time there, and let me eat the pralines I had once tasted. We agreed to give ourselves at least a week in Mexico City and visit the pyramids and silver country. All things considered, it seemed like a congenial and enlightened group.

I decided to take a quick trip to the library to get more information about Mexico itself, brush up on my Spanish and get a phrase book. I also had to pull together a wardrobe, maybe sew two snappy dresses without Golda's help that were wrinkle-free and easily laundered in the few weeks I had to prepare.

I called my mother to tell her about the trip – she was not at all happy with the plans. "Don't think for one minute that travel through the South in 1954 is much different than travel in 1936 when we drove to Virginia, with food and water in the car as we dared not stop along the way except to get gas," she said. We were *persona non grata* at the roadside restaurants. Her concern too was my motion sickness – did I forget that I had puked all over my sister on the Virginia trip? "Mom," I assured her, "I have traveled quite a bit since then, flown in a plane, traveled frequently in trains and driven in cars all over New York. I am not a child, but a grown woman, able to take care of myself. Furthermore, things are a little better, certainly in Pennsylvania and Ohio; we'll stock up on food before we get to Tennessee and Arkansas."

My mom, a person who wanted adventure sometimes, tried to do some courageous things, but only with her autocratic husband's permission; completely submissive to the brute she married, asking us always to forgive and remember, "He is your father, and the head of this house." She had encouraged me to get an education, have fun before marriage, because, as her life attested, it was drudgery thereafter. "I will call you regularly long distance and ask for myself," I told her. "The operator will give the name of the town where I am. You will know that I am safe. But don't say that I am at home as I will have to pay for the call, and I don't have much money." Of course, my mother never got that straight – she would start yelling, "Where are you?" and the jig would be up.

My mom. My Mom. Her story was crowding my brain as I prepared for the trip. I laid down on the bed to rest for a while and think of all she had endured; how her life laid the foundation for my anger and annoyance at being second-class, riding in the back of the bus, sitting near the steam engine on the train, superseded by every new immigrant who came and took first place in line for the best jobs, and would soon own the houses we were reduced to clean and the stores where we were reluctantly served.

I scoff at the Freudians in my office psychoanalyzing me, but quote Carl Jung as I try to explicate the baggage of my past; I am dragging a ton of it. Jung spoke of a fateful link between himself and his ancestors. He had daguerreotypes of his ancestors and antique Bibles that recorded his family line from centuries past.

My ancestors had been snatched away from the home-land, chained ankle and neck in the bowels of a slave ship, scattered willy-nilly over Barbados or Haiti or Jamaica, and brought to rest near the Chesapeake and James River in Virginia. A few grainy unmarked photos in *The Ark*, our family album, and some first names of property in the 1850 census make up my sketchy record. Yet, like Jung, I feel I "am under the influence of questions left unanswered by my parents and grandparents and more distant ancestors…." I know that I am the composite of these unknowns: a mole here, a nostril there, a widow's peak, an especially large big toe may be visible re-minders, but the carriage, the demeanor, the voice, tempera-ment, the intelligence or lack thereof are there too.

I'm named for, but never knew, my grandmother. But her elderly friend used to shake her head, as I would hold my face between both hands while searching for some solution or oth-er, and say, "My God, you are your grandmother incarnate." Those ancestors' lives are an essential part of who I am, as the few episodes from my parents' lives that I pen below will show. We would be driving to Mexico, through our homeland, but we could be subjected to insult and possibly injury for the sin of being Negro.

The Back Story

Gratz Street

Life was tough around Gratz Street, where emigrant former slaves settled in Philadelphia after fleeing sordid conditions in the South. Folks from Culpeper, Leesburg, Charlottesville, Gladys and all over Albemarle County, Virginia, settled there; relatives from Jamestown, South Boston, Danville, Paces and Halifax County crowded into the tiny row houses, without porches but with marble stoops leading out to brick sidewalks and cobblestone streets. These old two-story houses were the refuge to which my grandfather brought his wife, Susan, and their five children.

He had lived in the North for years, having come as a water boy for a Yankee general at the tender age of nine. He had worked on the construction of the Brooklyn Bridge in New York, watching many of his co-workers go down beneath the Hudson and emerge shaking, then trembling, then dying from having risen too quickly from the deeps with what became known as "the bends." He had gone back to get his wife, first bringing her to live in Newport News, Virginia, where he thought he might make a living among his relatives building canals. Then he got wind of opportunities in Philadelphia where much construction was taking place, where they were hiring Negroes in all capacities of the building trades, and he could make a better living. He bundled up his family again, his wife having just given birth to twins, a bouncing baby boy and a sickly underweight girl with a curvature of the spine, so small that they put her on a platter and kept her warm in the oven. She was named Mary.

Susan would take in washing to supplement the income. Every Monday morning at 5 o'clock her two older boys would take their wagons up Germantown Avenue to gather dirty clothes from wealthy German families, and drag the loads back home. Susan would have tubs of water boiling on the wood stove; she would have soap she made from lye and pork fat, she would have blueing and corn starch and she would scrub on her wooden board (soon to have a tin front) to remove the spots, and she would soak and rinse the whites and darks and blacks in separate tubs, making sure nothing faded. Then the boys would go to school; Harvey, scholarly and determined to read every waking minute when his hands were not engaged in toil; and Herman, stronger, taller, more handsome, more athletic, able to get the job done with muscle and agility. In summer heat or wintery cold, clothes had to be hung on the lines crisscrossing the back yard to dry. Mary helped to hang and gather in this laundry, wrenching the clothespins from the frozen towels, warming them before she could neatly fold them in the basket.

Tuesday was the day to iron every linen, cotton or silk garment. Even though each sheet, each slip and handkerchief had been carefully folded, it must have a few licks of the iron for finishing. At an early age, Mary and her sister Ethel were enlisted in this job. They learned to wrap the flatiron handle in rags and place it on the red-hot stove, test its readiness with a wet finger and rub the surface first across the cover of the board to make sure there was no residue that would scorch. Only then would they smooth out the garment or sheet. There were special irons for pleating and ruffles, which were all the rage in the early 1900s. This delicate work was left to Susan, because each pleat had to lay in place, and each ruffle had to stand up perfectly. On Wednesday the boys returned the completed laundry and raced back with their empty wagons to get to school on time.

On the way to school, they had to punch a few white boys who would be taunting their sisters or yelling, "Dark clouds arising," as the Negro students wended their way to the schoolhouse door. They would often have to fight their way home too, especially at times when Mary reported that a certain little red-haired white boy had wiped his feet on her pinafore, leaving an ugly stain. Mary loved school, learned to speak German and was good at math. One of her German teachers took a particular liking to her, helped her learn to play the piano, and treated her with kindness and respect. She could be found with a book propped up against the sideboard as she ironed her quota of the washing until darkness fell after school.

Often in the cold winters, Poppa would come home with saliva frozen on his beard. Mary would sit on the floor tugging at his boots, which had frozen to his socks on those January days. He worked at the Felin meat processing plant up above Pike Street on Germantown Avenue. He began as a hauler, unloading carcasses of beef and lamb from the wagons as they came down from Wayne Junction. Hogs were purchased locally and slaughtered on the spot. He butchered, too, but soon Europeans took over that job. Because of his knowledge of horses, he was promoted to teamster, driving the wagons and making more money. His connections at the market made it possible for his family to come on Friday and get tubs of hog innards: livers, hearts, ears, feet and chitterlings, which an enterprising Susan would make into delicious meals, or into delicacies like scrapple, head cheese or souse made of various ground-up hog parts, and sell.

About this time, Eli's youngest brother, John, had written from Danville that he wanted to join them. John was dwarfed, never grew over four feet ten in a family where most of the men were at least six feet. John had been a rather celebrated jockey on the tracks around South Boston and Danville in Virginia, but had been thrown from a horse, suffering a broken hip that ended his horse-racing career. Eli welcomed his brother into his crowded residence on Gratz Street, but they knew they needed larger quarters and began to look around. John limped, but was soon employed by Hunting Park as a stable boy for the carriage horses. His reputation for horsemanship soon got around and jockeys wanted his expertise. He bought himself a little surrey so he could travel the five miles to the Cedarbrook Racetrack in Glenside. Soon he was grooming and evaluating horses and riders for entry on the tracks. With this added income, the family was able to move to Butler Street, a newly opened neighborhood for Negroes, nearer both of the men's jobs, with a larger backyard for hanging clothes, an alley for delivering goods and a porch on which to sit in the summertime and watch the world go by.

The move also meant that Second Baptist Church was just two blocks away. Here was the gathering place for ascendant Negroes. Butler Street was named for the family who owned much of this territory and huge plantations in the Carolinas. Pierce Mease Butler, heir to the cotton family fortune, married a beautiful English actress, Fanny Kimble, who was appalled by the working conditions of the slaves when she visited the plantations in the South and became an avid abolitionist. In 1863, she wrote a scandalous book "*Journal of a Southern Plantation*," which angered her husband, but told the story of the deprivation and cruelty of enslavement. She also suffered the assignations of her husband, believing one of them to be a slave mistress he kept at the farm. After the divorce and death of her husband, she and her daughter were instrumental in opening some of the Nicetown area to Negroes as well as supporting the church and supplementing the salary of a certain John Davis who became the preacher.

John Davis was an exceptional man; schooled at Howard University, tall, erect, dark-complexioned and handsome. He talked scholarship and culture, he taught ethics and health; he brought into the building professionals of all stripes to speak to his congregation. Everybody learned to read; there was a lending library. He promoted the arts, bringing singers like

Sissieretta Jones to sing opera arias as well as spirituals. He took bright boys like Herbert J. and Harvey under his wing and helped them with their studies. He sought scholarships and urged their college attendance. Harvey ardently sought one of the scholarships and attended Howard University. Herbert attended Lincoln University, but found it too far from the gaiety he craved in the city, and soon enrolled in Eckels embalming school. Herbert and Harvey were intellectual rivals, a competition Reverend Davis promoted, believing such debates and arguments stimulated creativity and erudition. Harvey was the more diligent, the more ambitious, the more devoted to a career in medicine. He resented Herbert as a dilettant, a playboy, a wastrel of opportunity, and soon found to his dismay that this boy had eyes for his sister.

Reverend Davis promoted the "New Negro," the "Talented Tenth," educated, cultured, politically aware Black people, as espoused by a young WEB DuBois. He questioned the proposals of Booker T. Washington who was embraced by white supremacists as he lectured for racial separation and trade school education, admonishing Negroes to learn skills and work with their hands. Children read and practiced the etiquette taught in "Floyd's Flowers," and other books and newspaper columns teaching rigid behavior and moral precepts especially for girls. He wanted the congregation at Second Baptist to be dignified, educated, well-mannered, and not display behavior from their enslaved past when especially Negro women and girls were considered wanton, crude ignorant and undisciplined. In reality, this perception evolved because the enslaved had no control over their own sexuality or that of their wives and children. Whites railed against miscegenation, blaming it on seductive Negro women. Largely, it occurred because lusting masters imposed their will on innocent enslaved girls, making them compliant and "prematurely knowing" in the Biblical sense, often becoming teenage mothers of mulatto children.

Eli, Mom's father, was a deacon of the church. One daughter and son sang on the choir, his wife was a member of the Women's Auxiliary and the Dorcas Sewing Circle, another daughter played the piano, a second son served as a trustee and the third taught Sunday school. The family's social life revolved around Second Baptist; it was a vibrant, enlightening escape from the six days of hard labor comprising the rest of their week.

Emigrant Negroes fleeing the South were the main source of labor, and work was plentiful from the end of the Civil War until the 1890s. Midvale Steel was processing iron for wagons and the new motorcars. Fleisher invented a yeast that could be stored in cakes, which made the production of bread possible as a commercial enterprise. Freihofer opened a bakery near Hunting Park, which employed Negroes initially, but soon this industry, like other factories around the bustling area, began to limit jobs to the new immigrants who were arriving from Eastern Europe. These people unionized as artisans, bakers, journeymen in steel production or as clothing workers, preventing Negro women from working in the sewing trades and men from learning the artisan skills including the cutting and measuring of fabric for garments.

Philadelphia was a fashion hub; the department stores were advertising ready-to-wear Gibson girl dresses with stylish flounces and ruffles in the *Philadelphia Inquirer.* At $10 each, ordinary girls could find a dress similar to Alice Roosevelt's blue gown. They could buy boots with buttons at the ankle and patent surrounding the instep and heel at Lit Brothers, or at the innovative John Wanamaker's that would let people try clothes on and even return them, if they found they didn't like them. A Negro man had invented the shoe last, which made mass production of shoes possible, but Negroes found themselves locked out of this and other flourishing trades. They were relegated to the most servile and arduous jobs: hauling bolts of fabric, pushing racks of clothing down Market Street, scrubbing the splintery floors, working as maids and butlers, servants to the new immigrants who looked down on them and considered grudge work the proper work for what their religion and government sanctions told them was an inferior race. Blacks found themselves redlined into ghettos, restricted from starting a small business, except as cess haulers, undertakers or preachers, while new arrivals from Italy, Ireland or Poland were free to build industries and buy land wherever they wished.

A backlash was building against freedmen of color even in Philadelphia, the Quaker City that had given them their first taste of freedom and equality.

Eli struggled to make a living. He had his own horse and wagon, did light hauling for various industries, but now he found contracts scarce and competition cutthroat. Jobs were given to immigrants from Europe who had formed guilds there and knew how to organize into unions to protect their jobs and keep Negroes out. Susan was weakening physically from her intensive domestic enterprises. Ole missus used to say, "Nigger don't need but five hours sleep," and Susan toiled like her mother before her, filling her hands with industry every waking moment. Mary and her sister had to quit school at 16 and go to work outside the home. After working as a laundress, and several other similarly menial jobs, Mary found a job at Wanamaker's. Although she was stylish and well spoken, and understood fabric and clothing construction, she worked as a stock girl, never a salesgirl, and at the lowest level of that job, clearing and cleaning up. Being able to work at a department store was unusual, and in itself a step up for a Negro woman.

Harvey was living off a hot dog a day as he completed his studies in dental school, conceding that there was just not enough money to make it through medical school to become a physician. He pushed rickshaws down the Atlantic City Boardwalk every summer, he bussed tables at restaurants during the school year, he took semesters off to work full time to earn enough for tuition the next year; he and his family pinched and saved at every turn to help him earn his degree. Finally, he was able to graduate from Howard University Dental School with honors in 1915.

Jack Johnson and the Fight of the Century

One of the things my father liked to do was to have parties in the yard. We lived in an old stuccoed farm house with 12 rooms. It was *jerrybuilt*, my mother would say, requiring steps up to the dining room as the kitchen, pantry, laundry room and two upstairs bedrooms were added as the family grew. There was a large lawn surrounded by lovely shrubs and flowers Mom planted, with blossoms and fruit hanging from trees at various seasons of the year. Every Fourth of July was an important day and 1935 was no exception. The children placed flags in the flower beds and swags from the rafters overhanging the side entrance and the garage. The garage was emptied of cars and sawdust strewn on the floor; a Victrola was set up and connecting wires strung for lights and power. Much preparation was going on in the kitchen: Mom and her neighborhood helpers had killed a few chickens, which were popping and exuding their fragrance all over; potatoes had been boiled in the big pot, and now it was filled with potato salad. The children had been instructed to go to the garden to collect early tomatoes and ears of corn, small as they were, but having the silk just brown enough to have produced a delicious kernel. There was even a whole pig in an outdoor brick fireplace being hand-turned and basted on a spit over a hickory wood fire. The men dedicated to the barbecue would leave just enough room for some hot dogs to be placed on the side, especially for us kids who would be running around asking for their rolls to be toasted, before they slapped yellow mustard, relish and even some chopped onions on the luscious sandwich.

This day was warm and sunny and folks were driving up before noon to a space designated on the hill, parking their cars under my brother's direction. One of the first to arrive was Miss Viola and Mr. Archie, her husband and my father's stepbrother. She was one of my mother's oldest friends, but scorned by Mom as she smoked and drank along with the men. We kids thought she was fascinating; she was sophisticated, her dresses were always the latest accented by lots of jewelry, her hair "crocked-and-oiled" (wavy and oily), her cigarette in a holder, her hoarse voice full of laughter as she hugged and kissed us one by one. She was childless, but she seemed to love being around us, inviting us to her home with its hardwood floors, oriental rugs, large vases and shelves full of crystal. She was a staunch Republican, couldn't stand Franklin Roosevelt, dwelled on the memory of Teddy, and could hold her own in arguments with my father and his New Dealers. Mom always looked askance at her achievements as being slightly immoral, in cahoots with some Republican politicians, making lucrative deals that brought her prosperity but sold somebody out, most probably the colored poor struggling nearby her fine house on Norris Street.

By 12 o'clock, Eddie C, my father's dearest friend who had come the night before to help, already had a few beers and was chastising Father about even celebrating the Fourth of July. "You know Rev. Davis preached every Sunday about having all this drinking and picnics and fireworks on the Fourth. He told y'all that this was not our day; he said that Frederick Douglas had spoken: What have we got to celebrate? Juneteenth is our day." Viola laughed and took a long drag on her cigarette. "Look at you, Eddie, you been celebrating the Fourth since you were old enough to light a firecracker and hold a beer, and now you gettin' race-conscious. Put down that beer mug and prove how righteous you are."

Everybody was laughing, toasting, and somehow the conversation reverted to the July Fourth of 1910 when they were all involved in a life-threatening situation. Eddie, Archie, Viola, my father, Johnnie, Louis, Dora, all the friends who were sitting at the tables or in the lawn chairs, lifted their glasses; even my mother saluted the luck of their survival with a glass of iced tea. We kids were baffled as they all became a little somber after that, so my big brother asked what happened. Viola said that was the night of the Jack Johnson fight, when he KO-ed Jim Jeffries in Reno, Nevada, and destroyed their "great white hope" in the ring. White people got mad and fought Negroes all over the country; 84 Negroes got killed in Philadelphia alone. A lot of head-shaking and hugging followed, but soon the music started and the crowd moved to the garage or to the pit where the pig was crisping as it was being basted in its juices, or the tables now weighted down with food and the kegs gushing forth beer were ready.

I sidled up to Miss Viola and prodded her. "What happened that day?" I asked. She put her arm around me and said, "That was the day your mother fell in love with your father and would adore him forevermore." "Well, what was so bad about that?" I asked. My mother sat down beside her on one of the large Adirondack chairs as if she would temper Viola's too-vivid explanation. They rambled through the story contradicting each other, then finally agreeing on a coherent, fascinating episode in my mother's life which neither she nor my father had ever talked about:

Strolling in the park was the thing to do on Sunday after church in 1910. Negroes around Nicetown, the upscale Black neighborhood where my mother's family had recently moved, were allowed to go to Hunting Park. It was built on the old Stenton Plantation, which belonged to John Logan, a secretary to William Penn. It was first a race course that in 1824 became a public park. Negroes couldn't ride on the merry-go-round or in the handsome carriages driven by liveried drivers atop shining horses sauntering down the wide lanes of the spacious park. They couldn't sit in the cafes in the summer and were restricted to a tiny corner of the ice pond for winter skating. Mom wanted more than anything to go to Woodside Park, opened in 1897, which permitted Negroes to ride on the roller coasters and buy orangeade crush and sit outside the cafes and eat it. It was a long way from Broad and Butler Street to West Philly, where the park was situated on 18 acres at Monument Avenue. It was an adventure just to get there on the open-air trolleys.

Fourth of July 1910: She would be going as a chaperone with her older sister, Ethel, and her fiancé. She had made her dress of white lawn with a tiny Gibson girl waist, the pleated blouse exaggerating her trim form; the skirt falling just to the ankle and revealing a white and patent leather pump with a two-inch heel. Her hat had come from Lit Brothers, where they trimmed them for free with the feathers or flowers you purchased. Hers had ribbons which she had sewn with some of the remnants of her dress, as the store-bought decorations made it too expensive. She did look lovely; there would be lots of boys there, and her Sunday school class had agreed to gather by the pavilion at 4:30 p.m. to listen to The Fight.

They could not go inside the pavilion, which was strictly restricted to white diners, but they could be served outside and sit on the wooden benches. Woodside had arranged with the *Philadelphia Inquirer* to get the blow-by-blow report. The *Inquirer* had a set up with the *New York Times* bulletin press which would, for the first time, display information on a large reading service outside its building the moment it was transmitted over the wires by Morse code. Woodside would transmit the news flash by megaphone to the eager listeners gathered inside and outside the pavilion. The periphery around the pavilion was packed, as was the inside. You would think it would be empty as so many people white and Black had fled to the shore to escape the 89-degree heat. Crowds were in front of the *Inquirer* building itself on Market Street clamoring for news of what was billed as the fight of the century. The telephone was 34 years old, and newspapers reported that "there was a direct wire if you dialed Filbert 2505 where you could hear a graphic picture of the mighty struggle between the white man and the Black man under the burning Nevada sun."

Mom's friends from church were there, and so was a dapper young man named Herbert, who had shown an interest in her at Second Baptist. She gave him a come-hither smile. At church socials, her brother, Harvey, had discouraged his attentions, saying he was one of the fast guys with whom she was not to associate. Today he looked smashing in a tropical worsted suit with a stiff white collar at his throat that seemed to bother him not in the least as he strolled with his entourage, tipping his straw bowler hat to all the girls. She couldn't deny a special interest shown in her when he walked over and asked if she would like some refreshment. Both her sister and her fiancé said no, and moved away from Herbert, saying they were going on the roller coaster and she would have to go with them. Herbert persisted, saying that he would like to escort Mom on the ride, but they insisted that the three of them could sit in the seat together. They both knew that this was the young man with whom her brother had nearly come to blows in esoteric arguments about biology and science that devolved into issues of values and character. Harvey resented Herbert's flashy extravagance, and had admonished his sisters to be wary. Herbert had a reputation for recklessly riding motorcycles from Philadelphia to Boston. He was the well-paid assistant to a wealthy white undertaker with whose son he was attending embalming school. His mother, who operated a farm and catering business in Willow Grove, indulged his every wish. Mom's interest in this boy was heightened by the rebuff. She was incensed but could do nothing, because she had strict instructions from her parents that she was to obey Ethel and go and come home with her and no one else.

Herbert's friends commiserated with him, but were pleased to move on making other conquests and being sure they would get a ride home in *the car*. Herbert had one: a 30 horsepower Mercer that cost $1,250. True it wasn't the top of the line, but for them it was a limousine -- a 50 horsepower Mitchell-Lewis with six cylinders couldn't hold a candle to it. They all worked on it, shining up the exterior and adding the latest Ward Leonard electric system with batteries installed on the running boards on each side of the car. With the touch of a button you could turn on those headlights, side lamps and taillights and operate the electric horn. When the car moved over 10 miles per hour, the lights stayed on because there was a generator mounted under the hood. They had piled into the car and driven down Broad Street and across Girard Avenue with the isinglass flaps tacked up so they could look out at the streets of expectant Negroes, exulting the prowess of Jack Johnson. For weeks, their boasts had been stirring up the dander of the white guys, who had been reading the newspapers with writers like Jack London doubting that the "great white hope" could win.

The groans from the white guys inside the pavilion could be heard from the first bell. Jeffries, older and despondent, was unsure of himself. Only the enticement of money had made him agree to combat this young, ever-smiling Black Texan. Johnson climbed over the ropes at 5:30 p.m.; he did not shake hands with his opponent. The loud megaphone at Woodside repeated this and every action round by round, move by move, detail by detail, so that the rapt crowd got a vivid picture of the struggle.

Not a single blow by Jeffries ever grazed Johnson, neither a left nor right landed on the cool-headed Negro. Whites had declared that the Black man, in fact all Black men, had a yellow streak. Johnson disposed of that myth as he pounded Jeffries at his leisure wherever he wished. Johnson was a stylish fighter, noted for wearing down his opponent, and then delivering a telling blow. Jeffries was described as a ferocious giant, with a hairy-chested cave man persona. Johnson was not intimidated; he beat Jeffries down until he lay helpless before him in the 15th round. Jeffries' seconds threw in the towel so he would not actually be knocked out by Johnson. The commentators reported that it was not a great fight, but Johnson was declared the heavyweight champion of the world and all hell broke loose.

Negroes were jubilant, shouting and dancing all over the lawns and avenues of Woodside Park; whites inside the bar were seething with anger. Intoxicated, hyped up and red-faced, they burst out of the pavilion determined to get some *niggers* who had the nerve to think they were now as good as white people.

Mom and her friends fled for the trolleys as fast as they could. At first, she held her sister's hand. Her fiancé was steering Ethel and steadying her across tree roots and around huge oaks, through the thick forest rather than on the paved roads that led to the streetcars, to avoid the howling mob that pursued them. Mom was not much of an athlete, a city girl who didn't like roughing it outdoors; she never learned how to dodge thickets, so soon lagged behind, dropping her sister's hand and stumbling alone. She ran in the direction of her sister's voice, who was plaintively calling her name; she strained her eyes, staring ahead, but she couldn't see her. Not watching carefully what was underfoot, as trekkers know they must do, she tripped on a tree root, tearing off the heel of her shoe and twisting her ankle. Now she hobbled along as runners she knew passed her, telling her to hurry, which she couldn't do, leaving her helpless as the white mob drew nearer. She found a large sycamore tree that was hollowed out at the bottom, leaving space for her to crawl in and pull her legs up under her. Ants were crawling over her legs and up her arms; she had the creeps, but knew she must remain silent in her hiding place. She rubbed her ankle; the whole foot was swelling and aching inside her shoe. She had visions of her cousin Pauline, who had told her of the days right after slavery when she would be running through the thickets in Newport News, Virginia, trying to escape the white boys who would gather every evening as the Black housemaids made their way from the James River boats to their homes. The boys would yell "Poontang," which meant that Negro girls were ripe for raping if they could catch them. She shivered as she thought of those drunks dragging her from this place, and pulled her injured leg deeper into the hollow, writhing with pain and fear.

As tears streamed down her face, she heard a familiar voice: It was Herbert and his friends who had lagged behind, trying to fend off the mob to allow some of the women and children to escape. She wiped her face and peeped gingerly around the trunk. "What in the world?" he said. "What happened to you?" He saw the swollen foot and without another word, he bent down to scoop her up in his arms. He found that he could not do the job alone. He told Eddie that they would hold elbows and she would sit on their arms as they made their way as fast as they could to the car. He had parked in a nearby posh white neighborhood in the driveway of a home owned by a friend of Eckels so that the white boys, resentful of the fact that he even owned a car, would not deface or destroy it. Eddie grumbled about the danger of this additional burden but Herbert was adamant. "Help her up, use your left arm to propel yourself as fast as you can, man, save your breath, run." Archie led the way, discerning the quickest, safest way to dodge the mob. Breathlessly they arrived at the car and plopped Mary down in the front seat, pulling her now-swollen leg in behind her. Eddie, who was inebriated, began mumbling, "Well, you finally got her, now whatcha gonna do?" Herbert jumped into the front seat and started the engine. "Shut up, Eddie, this is serious, we've got a helluva journey just to make it through these streets to get her home. Archie, you guys gotta keep the flaps down so they won't see that we're colored. Can you peep out? As best you can, both of you keep your eyes peeled; those white boys are killing Black folks tonight."

It was a perilous journey; they could not ride across Girard to Broad. Men in sweaty undershirts were in the streets with chair legs for bludgeons. They crossed as far as 17th Street and took the trolley route, winding across the bridge that had just been built near the new Shibe Park Stadium. Still they had to dodge angry whites, who, as soon as they saw Herbert at the wheel, threw garbage at the car, or tried to stop them by hanging on the sides or jumping on the running boards. Archie and Eddie pushed them off, or hit their fingers with the wrenches or hammers they used for car repair. Mary was getting carsick from all the swerving and gear stick jerks as Herbert reversed the car. They decided not to try to make it all the way to Erie Avenue where they knew crowds would have gathered, so they took a detour to the densely populated Black ghetto around Gratz Street where Mary used to live, and decided to wait until it was dark. Some of Mary's relatives still lived there; they found Cousin Silas and his wife, Nona, who took Mary into their house, removing her shoe and putting ice and a poultice on her ankle. Nobody had a telephone in this neighborhood, and even if they did, her parents didn't have one, so there was no way to contact her home.

Herbert and his friends were standing guard with the men in the neighborhood; marauding gangs from across Broad and Alleghany Avenue were carrying torches as darkness fell, throwing firecrackers at Negro homes and families, and generally causing bedlam. Herbert decided not to venture out until things calmed down. Silas was happy to see his niece and fed the whole group with leftover chicken, potato salad and collard greens from their afternoon celebration.

They prepared a bed for Mary so she could lie down on the sofa. Herbert took the opportunity to talk with her as she ate and drank her iced tea. She told him how grateful she was that he had rescued her. "I don't know what I'll say about this when I get home; it sounds too miraculous to be true, but I'm going to do my best to let them know what a gentleman you've been. It's going to be a hard sell." "Yep, I would say I am pretty much misunderstood, to say the least, at your house. To make things worse, I am going to deliver you after midnight; no matter what, I'll take you to your door. Maybe Silas will give you a note to let your mother know that you spent the evening at his house. That might help."

She was smitten, it was clear. She admired how kind and patient he had been through this ordeal; how soft and concerned his voice was as he spoke with her, how he had whispered words of comfort to allay her anxiety as he put the car in reverse, or made quick turns to avoid gathering rioters all the way from West Philadelphia. That ride was a hair-raising, stomach-churning experience. She had not ridden in a motorcar before; her father had a horse and wagon which he used mainly for work, but into which the family would pile to go on short trips and she had ridden in Unkie's surrey.

Fires were smoldering and smoke was in the air, but only a few stragglers lingered on the curbs after midnight as they made their way up 17th Street, across Erie, and turned right onto Butler Street. Her mother was on the porch, rising as the car approached. She called her husband, and they came down the steps to gather around the car. Herbert got out, and went around to the passenger side to open the door and help Mary out. Her father rudely brushed him aside; brusquely he asked, "What do you mean keeping my daughter out so late?" "Excuse me sir, but you can see that she is hurt. We had to ride through danger to get her home, it wasn't easy," Herbert said apologetically. Mary held onto his hand, clutching her patent leather pump in her right hand with the broken heel inside. Then she leaned on her father's shoulder and said, "We stayed at Cousin Silas' house because of the mobs around Erie. Please Poppa, I am thankful to this gentleman who showed such kindness in bringing me home when I couldn't walk." Her mother was still fuming, not ready to hear any explanation. She opened the front door and tried to usher Mary inside quickly. Mary turned and took Herbert's hand, "Thank you so much, please, I am eternally grateful to you for this. Goodnight." Herbert tipped his hat to the parents and stammered a warm goodnight with wishes for a speedy recovery to Mary. He waited until they were all in the house before revving up the car and taking off.

Ethel, who was holding back the curtain watching the delivery, rushed toward Mary, with tear-stained face, offering apologies for having left her in the park. Her mother wanted more explanation, but her father said, "Let her go to bed, Susan, she must be bone-tired; get some more ice for her leg. I'm gonna carry her upstairs so she can rest. She'll talk about it tomorrow."

Ethel helped with the undressing, binding up and icing the injury. Mary fell into bed, closing her eyes, pretending to sleep immediately. Her heart was pounding, her senses were wide awake; she had met him, a man who had touched something inside her that no one else had ever come close to reaching. She couldn't wait to see him again.

Miss Viola

Lou was right. I was the one who would go to the lectures or listen to the street speakers in Harlem as they mounted a soap box to declaim the misadventures of the white man and how the Black man must unite.

The rhetoric of Marcus Garvey could be heard on 125th Street and Lennox Avenue in front of the Micheaux bookstore, where you could buy paperbound lectures by prominent Black revolutionaries, the left-wing papers and Communist books. One of my Jewish friends and constant companion was Leah, whom I had met while working as a secretary at an office on Broadway near 57th Street. She and I went to free musical events at the churches, rehearsals at Carnegie Hall, art shows at the Art Students' League just down the block where some famous artists who used to be students would come by for informal talks, and impromptu recitals at Steinway Hall. She was avowedly socialist and knowledgeable about Negro literature and concerned about the mistreatment of our people. She introduced me to *The Guardian*, a newspaper that carried articles by Ben Davis, a Socialist who was elected to the City Council, and William L. Patterson, who petitioned the United Nations with his pamphlet, *We Charge Genocide,* about the deliberate statutory killing of Black people in the United States by neglect and racism. We would listen to them lecture at a hall on Upper Broadway near 96th Street, and go to a movie theater nearby that would show *avant garde* films from Europe on revolutionary subjects or classic films like *Nanook of the North* about the plight of the Eskimos. We would go to

City College to Lewisholm stadium in the summertime and hear outdoor concerts with the New York Philharmonic or the NBC Symphony. Leonard Bernstein might be there or any fine soprano from the Metropolitan Opera. I was amazed at the intellectual excitement available for free or minimal cost in New York City and was determined to take in as much of it as I could.

I have to acknowledge my mother, who made us listen to classical or religious music on Sunday, no jazz. But also I credit my mother's friend, Miss Viola, for having instilled much of this hunger for culture in me. As children, we would be invited to Viola's house for dinner, or we might just drop by on the way to visit my grandfather. To me it was the epitome of elegance, with pictures of Booker T. Washington and Frederick Douglas on the wall. Her sofas were deep and the windows hung with lace curtains and drapery. She had a fine Victrola and a collection of thick 75 rpm records that included Caruso, Melba, Jenny Lind, Lily Pons and any number of famous white singers. Viola didn't go to the Academy of Music much to hear the operas because the seating for Negroes was up in the high balcony with narrow steps and lots of pillars blocking the view. She had gone to the Metropolitan Opera in New York and gushed over the glamor of it all. She had worn white gloves and a long black velvet coat over a white satin gown and her husband, Archie, was in a tuxedo. They went with one of Philadelphia's city councilmen and his wife, had dinner at a fine restaurant, promenaded and socialized with no sign of prejudice. Her eyes glazed over when she reminisced about that night. She loved the music, and could sing some of the arias and reach the high notes right along with the coloraturas. She would call up my father and tell him there was a play or an event that she wanted us to see, and he would take us to her house early on a Saturday morning so we could attend the matinee. With her I saw the original cast of *Porgy and Bess* at the Walnut Theater. I don't remember whether our seats were segregated, but I know I was in the first balcony overlooking the stage; the view was spectacular and I was mesmerized by the play and the music.

Viola loved to sing the arias; she had a recording which she played endlessly. Some of the melodies were on her player piano rolls. I would sit beside her on the piano bench and she would pump the pedals in rhythmic beat to the music. We sat at the keyboard as if we were the pianist, running our fingers along as the keys moved up and down for each note. She could sing several opera arias with complete abandon from memory or she would use her song sheet, which she had marked phonetically. She wouldn't sing the English translations because she said they didn't flow right, or the harsh Germanic sounds interfered with the melody. She was friendly with some of the families on Butler Street where single Italian men, who were imported to work as stonemasons but couldn't bring their women, had married Negro women. They had a regular song fest celebrating Verdi. She reveled in singing with them doing *Aida* as its Ethiopian princess. She worshipped George Gershwin because he had resisted the clamor to have Al Jolson play *Porgy* in blackface, declaring that the cast would be all Negro singers or else. She would explain everything; she talked about how superstitious the people were on Catfish Row, how afraid of white people, how poor and isolated from the rest of society. She wanted to make sure we were not that way; that we would study in school and learn how to be a part of what white people were doing in this country. She told us about the people she met at City Hall, how they ran the government, making the decisions about taxes, real estate, who could live where, and who could have a business. She would put in her two cents trying to ameliorate the condition of our people, but she didn't have the education, she didn't know the legal words or hadn't read the literature that gave them the edge in decision-making.

Each spring, she took us to the circus. This day we went with my big brother, 12 years my senior, to help her because she wasn't feeling well, but did not want to miss the excitement of the big tent. My sister, Dorothy, hated it; she couldn't stand the animal dung stench, she was not in awe of the lion tamer, nor the feats of the acrobats. I enjoyed everything, stretching my neck to see the aerialists and watching the clown antics. This time they had an actual Negro clown, not one in blackface with huge white lips like the minstrels. He was ebony-complexioned, with maybe some cork to darken his face, and was dressed in baggy pants with a checkered vest and caved-in stovepipe hat. He entered bowing and waving with something under his coat which he was obviously trying to silence. We were laughing along with everyone else as he leaned over nearly touching the ground with his long shoes to help him keep his balance, and we saw that his bundle was a live chicken. A white fellow hobo came up and gave him a pat on the shoulder and a cigar. The cigar exploded as his white partner lit it; everyone laughed and the chicken shifted noisily to the back of his coat. The two began to argue, with the Negro declaring by wide gestures that he had nothing hidden under his arm. The white clown grabbed him by the collar, tried to pat him down, but he skillfully juggled the chicken so that it never appeared for him to see, although the audience peeped at the bird when the Negro man turned his back. He fell backward from a slap then a kick (sound amplified), but never touched the ground. In the scuffle, he dropped his pants, grabbing the bird by the head to quiet it, and stuffed it into the pant leg as he fastened the long belt around his waist. The white man stood back, hands on hips to survey the scene, and deduced that there was a chicken back there. With funny mime, he made a deal. He ran and got a big pot and a bag trailing an onion, some carrots and other vegetables, and with exaggerated hand motions convinced chicken man to share the fowl. The Black man accepted. After being kicked in the behind and taking all that punishment he comes up smiling, waving his hat, dropping the noisy chicken in the pot and walking arm-in-arm with his white partner as they left the ring. The Black man once again was the fall guy.

We were so caught up in the show that we failed to see that Miss Viola was weaving dizzily. My brother put his arms around her and she fell against his shoulder. He summoned for help and two guards came up; they spoke for a moment and then they summoned two men with a stretcher. They would take her by ambulance to the hospital. My brother could not go with her because he had to see to the rest of us, and asked what hospital she was going to, hoping it would be one nearby. "No," they said, she would be going to the Negro hospital, Mercy Douglass, in South Philly. My brother took us to my grandfather's house in Nicetown, which was north of the stadium, and drove frantically back to the hospital, instructing my cousin to contact Mr. Archie, Viola's husband. Miss Viola died of a heart attack on the way to that hospital. We always believed she would have survived had she gotten treatment sooner.

♦ ♦ ♦

The Journey Begins

One suitcase, that is all that I had, and a cosmetic bag, a pillow and a blanket – we would be sleeping on the side of the road part of the time to save money. We were talking about a 6,000-mile trip, and none of us was flush with cash.

Eve drove up in her 1953 Maroon Buick sedan; she and Theta would sit in the front and Lou and I in the rear. It was hot and sticky that Sunday August morning, so we started out with the windows rolled down. No air conditioning, so plenty of grit was flying in as we made our way across the George Washington Bridge, southwest, along The Garden State Parkway, I-78 to Route I-81 South through New Jersey and onto I-76, the Pennsylvania Turnpike through Western Pennsylvania, about 400 miles toward Pittsburgh, Pennsylvania, our first stop.

I sought to avoid the subject as Lou probed constantly, trying to find out more about what had transpired between my boyfriend and me, what had caused the break. She had seen him, noted that he still had that "ole feeling" and wondered about reconciliation. I shrugged the conversation off with a casual, "I'm looking over the field," and talked about the latest news – what President Eisenhower was doing to improve the roads, noting the additions and the detours as

construction proceeded; the talk about the upper roadway for
the George Washington Bridge, and an expansion of Route I,
or a new road entirely down the East Coast. I pointed out how
few Black men were working, except on the pneumatic drill;
its vibrations shook the whole body, making it a short-term,
dangerous assignment. And even when I talked about the
roads, I thought of him and his trucking business; how many
nights I would listen to his optimism about the gargantuan
struggle he was attempting; how he would welcome the new
highways, how gently he was teaching me to drive. I shook
my body as if warming from a chill, but no use, he was omnipresent; I smiled as I remembered the day I realized he was
the guy for me; the day he took my mom and her friends to
the Rainbow Room:

◆ ◆ ◆

Lunch at the Rainbow Room

My mother and three of her middle-aged friends were at the NAACP Convention at the New York Hilton in late August. I told Boyfriend that I was going down to visit them, and he said, "Why don't we take them out to lunch?" "What?" I said. "These women are my mother and her friends, you really wouldn't want to take these grandmothers to lunch, would you?' "What do you mean? Of course, let's take them somewhere where they've never been, say to the top of Radio City to the Rainbow Room." "Oh, come on, that will cost a fortune." "I'm not exactly a pauper, and this is your mother. When, what time, and let's make it a great day for them."

I was absolutely flabbergasted. He could be rather tight-fisted; he had talked with me about how he budgeted for whatever he needed, how he learned to mend his socks, and didn't waste food, often warming leftovers for himself. He had put himself through NYU School of Business while helping his mother and skimping at every turn. One of the reasons we didn't see each other much after our meeting at the Savoy, I learned from a mutual friend, was that he said frankly that he couldn't afford to take me out to good restaurants. I supposed, now, that during the hiatus, he was budgeting for that infrequent date. I was sure I wasn't the only filly in his stable, so I filled my time with studying, casual dates and my African liberation work, and thought he was doing something similar.

This day he was dressed in a seersucker suit, blue with a white shirt and dark blue tie; my mother would approve. He picked me up; we drove down and parked at the hotel, and planned to walk with them down to the restaurant. I went to the house phone to call my mother, who said they were waiting for my call and would be down promptly. I knew each of these women; they had known me since my childhood. They were wearing their hats and gloves, their shirtwaist dresses of dimity or linen, their sensible shoes, and were overwhelmed with happiness at the prospect of going out to lunch with my boyfriend and me.

I hugged and kissed my mom and each of them and then introduced them to my boyfriend. He shook hands with each and asked if they would like to walk down to Radio City, less than two blocks, where the restaurant was. "If you don't feel like the walk, we can take a cab," he said. They wanted to walk; we had plenty of time and made our way slowly, and they had questions about everything along the way. The doorman greeted us; my boyfriend gave him the reservation information, and we were whisked up to the 44th floor. The women were breathless, unbelieving at the respect that he was shown by the doorman, the elevator operator, the greeter once inside.

Our table was not quite ready, so he asked, "Would you like to sit (in those lovely Art Deco chairs) and look down at the city?" Mother's friends had not experienced anything like this before. Mother had been to Radio City when it was first built, when we came to the World's Fair in 1939, and had to wait while white people were seated; but we were seated in very comfortable chairs, and not in a segregated balcony either. She hadn't experienced this kind of luxury in Philadelphia, and hardly knew what to do when a turbaned Black serving boy appeared with a tray of hors d'oeuvres followed by a waitress with soft drinks, which my boyfriend had ordered. They stuck out their pinkies and selected a few pieces, and with their napkins spread carefully on their laps, sipped at the drinks and beheld New York City below.

It seemed that Boyfriend was in seventh heaven helping those women, telling them what the fillings were in the selections, saying how they probably have some made of cornbread because the scallops were wrapped in Macon bacon, so we can get a taste of real food. He told them he was from Georgia, and as it turns out, so was one of the women's family, so they were comparing notes and recipes for a particularly Macon way of using bacon. We received huge menus that we could preview, and they each asked him what they should order, as if I wasn't even there. He put them all at ease, so when the waiter announced that our seats were ready, they had just about made their selections, and so had my mother, who whispered to me, "He certainly is a nice young man."

As we sat down, he asked if anyone would like some wine or a cocktail, and with a flutter, two of the women said they would like whiskey sours, wow! My mother, a confirmed tee-totaler, had a Shirley Temple; both my friend and I had a glass of Pouilly Fuisse, which we had learned to drink together at various clubs. There was some confusion about who ate from which bread plate, or who drank from which glass of water, all graciously solved by Boyfriend.

Then into the deep discussion about what was going on at the NAACP event; how they had seen Thurgood Marshall and listened to Leon Higginbotham, his protégé whom Mom had met when he and some friends from Trenton had come to visit me.

They seemed satisfied by what the NAACP was doing nationally and in the Pennsylvania Levittown housing discrimination case. They were pleased with the way they were assisting them on the local level, too. Mom talked about the problems with the school system; that we had gotten a few more Negro teachers, that Park School (the segregated Black school) was more run down than ever, and that they were building a new one on Hamilton Avenue, which she was opposing because it would be segregated, too.

My boyfriend said he was astonished that this would be a problem in Pennsylvania, especially around Philadelphia, which had been so active in abolition and in establishing educational facilities for Negro students. "You should know better, I told you I went to a segregated elementary school, that was Park School, and Mom and these ladies had to fight tooth and nail to make it possible for us to go to the state-of-the-art junior high school in 1938. The superintendent had said it was not appropriate for us, since we would fail academically and bring down the standards." Actually, I don't think I had ever gone into this with such detail, but he shrugged and said, "You ladies are to be congratulated for your hard work."

And then one of the women, who had had the whiskey sour and requested another one, said she would like to be excused to go to the ladies' room. The waiter pointed the way and she sauntered toward three stairs to the upper level. Just as she put her foot on the first riser, and reached for the railing, she missed and flopped, sprawling over the two other stairs. Quick to the rescue was Boyfriend, plus the waiters, and all eyes focused to the scene. Had she been white, she would have been crimson. He got her up, helped straighten her dress and escorted her, arm in arm, to the rest room. He waited there for her and escorted her back to the table, shushing all her apologies for having embarrassed the group. With an exaggerated salute he asked her to accept a toast from all of us for being the first woman from Crestmont to have made a grand exit from the Rainbow Room. Everyone was laughing. There was such delight in those women's eyes; I was near tears as I watched how much they enjoyed themselves. They wanted to share the bill, but he said absolutely not, it was his treat for all the fine work they do and what it means to guys like him who only read about it. "You are on the frontlines," he said. "I respect and admire that."

After taking them back to the hotel, we spent a warm August night on the Palisades; I did let him hug me a little tighter and kiss me very close to forbidden territory, and I sniffled as I thanked him for being so kind to my mother and her friends. My mother and her friends asked me for his address to send him thank you cards, which I did not give them; I told them I had thanked him, and that he truly did feel that it was a pittance compared with their sacrifice. More and more after that, every time I would see him, I would feel a yearning to be closer, that there were attitudes and attributes about this man that seemed to awaken desire in me; he was getting under my skin, and soon, and soon perhaps, under my clothes.

Pittsburgh to Memphis

It was determined that I should be the navigator, as I was able to identify information on signs pretty far ahead of the rest of them. Six and a half hours later we were in Pittsburgh, wending our way to the Black neighborhood, asking directions of the Negroes we would see on the way. Lou had been there before to visit her aunt, but she didn't remember much about the place. She knew their house was not far from Wylie Avenue where all the happenings were – that was the heartbeat of the Hill District. They even had a Savoy Ballroom where Duke Ellington, Stanley Turrentine and Art Blakey had played. She said there was a barber shop called Woogies where her brother used to go and come back full of talk about the Homestead Grays, the Pittsburgh Crawfords, and other Black baseball teams. They idolized players like Satchel Paige, an outstanding pitcher who couldn't play in the white major leagues. She said the Hill District really was a swinging place where Billy Strayhorn and Earl Garner lived, just a short walk from downtown. Officially, white people avoided it, designating it as dangerous. They braved the hazards and came to the "happening joints" to listen to the music, however.

We finally arrived on Webster Avenue, a group of row houses precariously set on the side of a hill overlooking the

Alleghany River. It was great to get out and stretch our legs and be greeted by Lou's Aunt Mattie and her Uncle Pete. They were a childless couple who kept the pots boiling on the stove. They both were too heavy by half, but ready to have us sit down, eat, spend the night and prepare for the next leg of our journey. Uncle Pete was dead set against our going any further, Supreme Court decision or not. "Why just this week in Pittsburgh – and this is not Mississippi – two kids was beat up for going into the white neighborhood after dark. You may have them maps, but they don't tell you what part of the city Black folks is welcomed in," he offered. Eve said we had 2,500 miles to travel to the border, and we have to do at least 700 miles a day if we were going to have any time to stop at the places we want to. "Why in the world do you want to go? We just left Alabama to get to Pennsylvania where we can go to half-way decent schools and get decent jobs, though they are drying up now that the war is over."

Mattie was not siding with her husband, but was all about making us at home, shushing Pete, and telling him to help us with our suitcases and show us to our rooms. We drew straws to decide where we would sleep; Lou and I drew the screened porch, which seemed snug enough though a little scary. Even with the blinds drawn, you could hear people talking as they passed along the sidewalk. Aunt Mattie had made our separate beds on the wicker couches, with lots of pillows and blankets, but it was a trip inside and upstairs to the only bathroom. Theta and Eve got the guest room. We washed up and were called into the dining room to a dinner I was not too fond of, but which was known to be Lou's favorite: liver and onions. She must have told her aunt about liking this dish without consulting anyone else. However, we cheerfully dove in and were satisfied with the meal. The bread pudding was delicious.

Pete was very proud of his neighborhood: "We got the only baseball stadium owned and operated by a Black man, Greenlee Field, where the Pittsburgh Crawfords play. This is prime territory, situated where we have a beautiful view of the river, but now folks is moving out. They're talkin' about demolishin' the whole Hill District, or at least most of it, to build a new arena. You can turn on WHOD any day and that's the main topic. Here we had a man we supported on the state legislature for eight terms, president of the NAACP. We thought Homer Brown was in our corner. No, he ain't; he sold us out to the big boys downtown. Talkin' about urban renewal, telling us how wonderful it will be to upgrade this section which we been in since the Civil War. They're fixin' to have Negro removal, that's what this is. They striking at the heart of Hill, destroying the businesses and nice homes. It's gonna be a slum 'cause most of the hard-workin' people will have to move out to an ugly section the poor whites abandoned, you watch." He got up from the table, visibly distressed about how Negro people were being treated in housing, and segued right into how we would be treated on the road as we navigated south.

Pete dialed long distance to talk to Lou's mother. He found that she knew next to nothing about the trip. He repeated his dire predictions as he told her of our adventure. Lou's mother started crying as he turned the phone over to Lou. It took some comforting from Lou's father for her mother to regain her composure. He was Jamaican, believed in bold ideas and taking risks, nothing ventured, nothing gained. Even though Lou hadn't discussed the trip with him, he said she should go for it, after all this was our country, and we had a right to see it. Not that Lou, as headstrong as she was, was considering turning back. We all had taken the pledge to be intrepid, and none of us was ready to be dubbed the quitter.

It was Sunday night, so the street was relatively quiet, the mosquitoes were screened out, so Lou and I were sound asleep in no time and awakened refreshed to begin the next leg of our journey. After a hearty breakfast, it was nearly 7 o'clock when we left Pittsburgh, getting some last-minute tips from Uncle Pete about detours on the roads south, gassing up and being slowed down by the morning rush hour.

We could make it to Cincinnati along Route 70W in about four hours, where accommodations were not segregated. We had some friends there whom we had telephoned and who planned to meet us. Using our maps, we found that the designated restaurant was not far from the highway. Barbara and Francine, two former schoolmates, met us at the inn for lunch. They were very excited by our bold plans and amazed that Eve had been doing all the driving. Somehow, they didn't even question Lou, who had talked me into the drive-sharing idea. Why, they asked, was I hesitant to take the wheel? I explained that I had never driven a car this large, and hadn't driven anything for the past two months. They thought that was a lame excuse, and said they would take us to a place where I could try out this sedan before I took it on the highway. I agreed.

Francine's father was a driving instructor on the side. He gallantly said he would come over and check me out. He knew just the training spot: an empty parking lot and a surrounding quiet neighborhood with curves and hills. My friends sat in the park chatting and drinking Cokes. From outside the car, my companions would determine my competence before they would entrust their lives to me.

After some questioning about where everything was, I slid right into manipulating the Buick, even parked it easily, and after about two hours including some busy street traffic, I won the approval of my instructor and fellow travelers. However, not being overconfident, I said I would only drive in the daytime, and not during any kind of inclement weather. On this bright sunny day, at about 2 p.m. on I-65S, I took the wheel for the first time and started the seven-hour drive to Memphis, Tennessee.

But dusk was falling when we got near Nashville, Tennessee, and Eve said I should stop because four hours were enough for my virgin flight. We knew folks in Nashville, too, and decided to call them to ask where we might get some refreshment. We stopped at a roadside telephone and dialed Melinda, one of my sorority sisters who knew me well, but it took several minutes before I could make her believe that I was indeed calling her. She wanted to come to meet us, but she lived miles away, and I explained that time was of the essence. She gave us the name of a restaurant and gas station. We refreshed without incident and were on our way in less than an hour. With Eve at the wheel we drove along I-40W to Memphis

There was no way at 10 o'clock at night that we were going to find our way to the Black neighborhood and Theta's uncle's house. Theta called her Uncle Willie to tell him where we were and he came to meet us. He assured her that she would recognize his car: a 1944 black Packard sedan which he used to chauffeur neighbors around, driving maids to their jobs in the white sections and sometimes families on excursions. He came up to the car and Theta got out; he was surprised at how much she had grown, and after some chatter, she was hugging a fun uncle she hadn't seen in years. It was quite a distance, somewhat on the outskirts of town to Willie's house, but Eve maneuvered skillfully down narrow but paved streets behind him until we were in the Black neighborhood. Dusty were the streets; the pavement stopped just where the less affluent looking houses began; all the Black people lived in this segregated section, whatever their accomplishment – the teachers, the doctors, the postal workers, the laborers – it didn't matter.

We were anxious to get a good night's sleep, but for Uncle Willie, food came first, and lots of questions from him and from us concerning *Brown vs Board of Ed*. We were too tired to go out on the town, so Willy urged us to stay another night. He wanted us to go to the famous Beale Street on Tuesday when there would be entertainment. We thought we would content ourselves with a daytime tour so we could maintain our time schedule, but after listening to Willie and Mattie, and understanding how steeped in our history this town was, we decided that more than a cursory look was warranted.

Even though this was a place where jazz had set the tone for all American popular music, everything was strictly segregated – just as in Harlem. Blacks couldn't go to their clubs, but whites frequented the Black neighborhood clubs to learn the latest songs. There was a Black deejay whom everyone listened to, and from whom whites sucked out the songs that made them famous. Elvis was the rage, and would later sing "Hound Dog" and get the copyright for a song that Black prisoners and sharecroppers had been singing for years.

Memphis had its painful episodes; Memphis had been a center for the domestic slave trade, where unfortunate Virginia or Maryland slaves, torn from their families in an estate sale or punished for an infraction, were sold down the river. There was conflict between the Blacks and Irish immigrants who, though indentured servants, because of their skin color soon became the overseers and planters and gained political power repressing the sizeable Negro population. Willie said that Negroes were still stepping off the sidewalk downtown when white ladies were passing by. So he didn't see one bit of difference since *Brown*. He said that he was listening to all that was happening in Little Rock – we ought to go there, he said. That is where the action is. Their NAACP is already taking kids to integrate the schools. He read about it, but didn't see the point of putting our children at such risk.

His wife, Edith, felt he was wrong, "We've got our own civil rights leaders right here; brave men and women like Maxine Smith." Edith had gone to several rallies with the NAACP where the Atkins family, Maxine's parents, had filed lawsuits against the universities because they wouldn't take Negro students. The state paid Maxine's tuition to Middlebury College for her master's degree rather than let her go to the white university. "Things just gotta change," she said. "I falls on my knees every night praying for a change but it's not going to come unless we stop cowering. These people risk everything and I am standing with them."

Willie was adamant. "These women just stirrin' up trouble," he said. "I am not gonna lose my job because my boss seen me picketing against the schools. I think we can make the Black schools better. We already got the best teachers – we have more teachers with master's and Ph.D. degrees than any of the white high schools."

Edith just sighed: "He talks like that – why are all those educated Black folks in dilapidated school buildings with used books that was discarded by the white high school? Our good teachers can't get a decent promotion to the ranks that they deserve, make less money than the white teachers, and work as maids to supplement their salary. We pay the same taxes, more for these shabby shacks than they do on the other side of the railroad tracks. Our children still only get 11 years of schoolin', you know, they start at seven, not six. I support the NAACP. I give money, I go to the meetings, we're talking about making Vasco Smith a county commissioner; we want to do more than protest. We want elected officials. I'm gonna be out there fightin'."

We slept two abed that night, and were mighty glad to get under the sheets and stretch out. We arose to a country style breakfast, complete with biscuits, sausage and eggs, and a more animated Edith. She wanted to let us know some of the history of Memphis, and to make clear that Ida B. Welles had lived here, was one of their heroes, and spurred a spirit of militancy in the people. In 1892, Ida B. Welles had written about three Black grocers who were lynched and about the frequent Ku Klux Klan rampages that put fear and trembling in the hearts of Black people. In 1884, she refused to leave the first-class section on the Chesapeake and Ohio railroad and was dragged from the train and arrested. Did we know that there had been a Civil Rights act in 1875 banning discrimination on the basis of race, creed or color on public transportation? We didn't know, that was the reason Homer Adolph Plessy was within his rights to sit in the white section on the train in New Orleans. This was the background for the lawsuit, Plessy vs Ferguson in 1896 which established the phony doctrine of "separate but equal" and initiated Jim Crow. Edith said that Ida's heroism did not belong solely to Chicago, that it had begun in Memphis where as a very young woman, she established her newspaper, "Free Speech," and continued her crusade against lynching. She was barred from returning to Memphis after a speaking tour, and that's how she got to Chicago.

Willie was more interested in the jazz scene, that is what made Memphis famous. He said he would drive us around Memphis in his car. All the white folks knew him and "there wouldn't be no trouble." After breakfast, we piled into his Packard, luxurious still though ancient. We saw groups of Negro men gathered on the corners; they were waiting for trucks to come by and take them to the farms to pick vegetables or cut lumber. "Too damp around here for much cotton," Willie said. "Most of them work like they was sharecroppers; some had property but had lost it through swindles, hard times and drink."

On Beale Street, we saw a pool hall displaying a sign showing that it was "for colored." He showed us sights like Church Park where Booker T. Washington had spoken and W.C. Handy's home. There was Forrest Park still displaying Confederate plaques with General Nathan Bedford Forrest gallantly on horseback as if the South had won the war. We learned that General Forrest slaughtered scores of Negro soldiers in 1864 at Fort Pillow in a bloody massacre after they surrendered. Whites portrayed him as a hero as they championed "The Lost Cause," but Negro scholars are researching the facts handed down through oral history by their grandfathers who survived the carnage by hiding under corpses. We got out of the car and walked in the fields at Fort Pillow; it was now a picnic ground, a park designated by white historians as a significant battleground where the Union enemy was defeated. Truth be told, Black soldiers were for the first time here in uniform with their white officers; their troops were given guns in 1863. They laid them down before overwhelming

Confederate forces in surrender in 1864. Despite their white flags, General Forrest gave the order to kill each one of them. It was a horrid massacre. We didn't know anything about this history and were deeply saddened by it.

We were chastened by the Fort Pillow episode; I badgered Edith for more information but she knew mainly the "white folk's version." None of us were in the mood to celebrate that evening when Willie and Edith would take us on the town. But Edith said that the music was a response to the horror of the massacre, that the blues was born of the sadness; it is the moans of the pain of enslavement, where the enslaved voiced in song what could not be said under fear of the lash. She was remarkable; one of the most beautiful people we would meet on this trip.

That night on Beale Street, we stopped by W.C. Handy's Blues Hall where B.B. King had sung and Leadbelly and Muddy Waters had played. Most of the famous acts were there on the weekend, but even on a Tuesday night, we could hear good musicians playing the innovative electric guitar. The interior was dark and there were posters on the wall. We sat on the chrome stools at the bar and got a whiff of the smell of bourbon and cigarettes. When the band assembled, we moved to the back and sat at a small table. A Black man in suspenders of Fats Waller's proportions, wailed, "The Thrill is Gone," and Philadelphia, Pennsylvania's Cab Calloway's, "Beale Street Mama," which I requested. We spent a pleasant evening soaking in the sounds that would undergird our mission.

It would take us about two hours to get to Little Rock and see Central High School and hopefully the office of the *Arkansas State Press* where Daisy Bates and her husband were publishing articles about the slow and unsatisfactory progress toward integrating schools. Ms. Bates had been lionized at the last NAACP conference for her activism. Her mother had been killed by the Ku Klux Klan and she had been urged by her dying father to channel her hatred of her mother's killers to the task of finding solutions to end segregation. We were hoping to talk to her and some of the Negroes who lived there. Edith didn't know anyone personally whom we might meet, but Willy told us where the school was and where the Black neighborhood was and advised us to lay low.

It was a day clear and bright and the road, I-40W, was straight, so I took the wheel again to drive the 140 miles. I must say I drove skillfully, never tailgating, as Boyfriend had taught, using my side view and rearview mirrors to gauge the traffic around me and confidently making the two- and a half hour-long jaunt.

We had to go to Little Rock. This was the first place to hit the *New York Times* about compliance with the Supreme Court decision. The Little Rock School Board voted to comply and was adopting a *gradual* plan. In protest, white citizen councils were forming and Governor Orval Faubus had threatened to call out the National Guard to prevent integration. Daisy Bates, the intrepid president of the Arkansas Conference of NAACP Branches, was publishing articles about violations of the court's desegregation ruling, convening her committees and preparing students to integrate Central High. We walked the steps of the high school where Eisenhower would send the troops in 1957; we stood at the door that Negro students were forbidden to enter and hypothesized about the jeers and contorted faces of their enemies. We left with a strange sense of empowerment because Black people were mobilizing; we would demand equal protection as promised to all citizens of the United States. And while we were aware that the decision did not cover public accommodations or transportation, so that *Plessey vs Ferguson* was not completely overruled, we would assert our right as full citizens on this trip. We pondered this on the steps of Little Rock High. We spent nearly an hour there taking photographs and acknowledging the historical significance of what Mrs. Bates had accomplished; there wouldn't be time to visit the paper or listen to the experience of people in the community. We knew we'd better be on our way.

I got back in the driver's seat; we figured we would drive all night to San Antonio, sleeping by the roadside. We could get to Mexico quickly down I-30W. It was still daylight and I could certainly drive two hours more. Eve could stay at the steering wheel longer, but for these initial tests at the controls, four hours were enough for me. After about two hours, Eve said gas was low so we would have to make a stop in a town called Texarkana. I had never heard of the place, but it was to be our first encounter with the separate but most unequal rest room accommodations. We had driven almost 400 miles with only some snacks. and we had hoped to arrive in San Antonio the next morning and stay for a couple of days. Fatigue was setting in, we needed to get something to eat and stretch our legs. We found a gas station with an outhouse for "coloreds," no distinction between the sexes. We had to use it; we had brought rolls of tissue; to cover the seats, we folded newspaper, tore out a hole in the middle, held our noses and entered.

I went to the roadhouse door and was met by a thin white woman with piercing gray eyes and a white apron. She stood back and looked at me as if to say, "How dare you come to this door?" She spoke with a hillbilly twang, hands on hips, spewing out her words that said in no uncertain terms that we could not eat inside the establishment. "Bu-ut, (we still want your money). Y'all can git some sandwiches at that door in the rear." In complete submission, we got the gas, ordered our sandwiches, used the "facility," washed our hands at the absolutely slimy "colored" water fountain, sat in our car at the end of the lot and begrudgingly ate our surprisingly delicious ham sandwiches. We walked around a bit, opened the car doors, stuck our legs out and reviewed our adventure so far.

We pondered our experience in Memphis, and concluded that we would go to New Orleans first, before heading to San Antonio. There the Spanish influence would dilute the impact of Black culture which had been transformative in Memphis. We wanted to have more of the jazz experience, and delve deeper into the history of the music and what it meant for Black people and our development. The heroism of our folks in Little Rock and the information about Fort Pillow was fresh in our minds. I had read about the slave revolts and

massacres in New Orleans and scholarly men who earned renown during Reconstruction. I talked about this with my companions. In preparation for this trip and from my study with
Dr. Hansberry, I had learned that the largest slave revolt in the
United States happened near New Orleans around 1811. More
enslaved people died than with Nat Turner, John Brown or
Denmark Veasy. Moreover, New Orleans, unlike other States,
had a large number of creoles, mulattos and quadroons who
had been sent by their planter fathers to study in France, so
they provided scholarly men who could govern and became
part of the Reconstruction Senate. My friends knew next to
nothing about this history; we were ignorant because we were
easterners who had attended white schools where we got the
"Gone With the Wind" or "Birth of a Nation" versions of the
Civil War and its aftermath.

Eve looked pensively around the shabby yard surrounding
the gas station and said, "Look at these people; ignorant rednecks, who feel superior to us. They believe in Dred Scott, the
decision that said Blacks could never be citizens of the United
States and that the constitution never intended that Blacks
should be citizens in any state, whether slave or free. Whites
want us to be outliers, offering a steady supply of unskilled
labor they could use to pick their cotton and cut their cane."
"Or push their garment trucks down 34th Street," I added.

We began to feel that jazz was the soundtrack for the
"movie" we were making; the appropriate accompaniment
for a people emerging from enslavement to full citizenship in America. So, with my urging mind you, we turned

southeast, down I-49S to the Mississippi Delta. I was buoyed by my emerging status with the group, and took the wheel, fully intending to drive some of the 400 miles and six hours to New Orleans. I had reached a plateau; my melancholia was lifting. My suggestions were beginning to influence the others, my driving was showing confidence and skill, my conversation was lively and often amusing. I was being asked questions about the history of which I actually had more knowledge than they. Even Theta was warming to me a little, not treating me like the boring square she looked down on initially.

It was swelteringly hot and in the darkness, the mosquitos were up and at us. We could not roll down the windows, only slightly crack them when the car was moving so that a breeze crept in and the mosquitos couldn't keep up with us. I continued to drive but when we got as far as Shreveport, I was perfectly comfortable in admitting to my companions that I felt the need for relief. Eve and Theta congratulated me for having done so well as the driver. Not to be outdone, Lou said it would be her turn at the wheel. She had welcome my growing acceptance by Eve and Theta, but would not be outshone by me. Cheerful and alert, she assured us that she enjoyed driving on empty nighttime roads and that driving on this good highway would be no problem.

Eve settled next to me in the back seat. I could see she was a little apprehensive about having Lou at the wheel and so was I, although Lou had been driving longer than I and had driven this car. Lou seemed relaxed and self-assured as she signaled her entry on the highway and smoothly got in the line of right-lane drivers.

She had driven from Pleasantville, New Jersey to visit my family and me in Pennsylvania, so she wasn't a novice at the wheel. For this trip, she had positioned herself as the backup driver, but so far had left the driving to Eve and me as if to give me an opportunity to prove myself as a hip and vital member of the team. She had dated my brother, and I hers. I knew her to be the high-strung sort; a little imperious at times, but my family had welcomed her when she visited. She liked our neighborhood and was pleasant with the characters I introduced her to. Crestmont was a Black town, strictly segregated, with its own leaders and stratified society. It was lodged in the valley between affluent Abington residents who lived across the railroad tracks on the hill, and the Heights near Willow Grove Park. Here white Philadelphians summered in the late 20th and early 21st centuries, when John Phillip Souza captivated audiences with his patriotic marches. We had little interaction with our white neighbors, except as employers and overlords.

I wished Boyfriend had gotten to know my family and community; those women whom he took to lunch never stopped asking about him and hoping he would come to town so they could fix him a decent home-cooked meal. I began to reminisce about him as I napped. Yes, there was good reason why I could not have invited him home that Christmas:

♦　♦　♦

Christmas in Crestmont

It concerned Boyfriend greatly that I had not let him go home with me for Christmas; we had Thanksgiving with his mother and several relatives, but my family was going through turmoil, and I didn't want him to be a witness to that. There had been a fight, and this time, Mom had struck my father with a heavy cast-iron pan, knocking him cold. My older brother, who had lived at home since the war, and was suffering from tuberculosis and psychological illness as a result of exposure and combat in New Guinea, was witness to the event. He tried to intervene. The excitement caused a breakdown which made him spend weeks in the hospital. This time police were prepared to arrest my father, but Mother once again rescued him. She made him swear to never strike her again. At the police station, she filed an order of protection, although I don't know how that could be with her living in the same house with him. He was chastened and swore to honor his pledge under threat of imprisonment.

This would have been the Christmas my boyfriend would have seen. My mother putting on a brave face, my little nephew relishing his presents, but all the rest of us apprehensive about how things could be patched up and my brother brought home again. He did not come home, but went to live with my older sister in Philadelphia; we had Christmas dinner for him at her home. It was so sad to see him depressed and to watch him look at my father like a forlorn child, seething in hatred.

I told my boyfriend that there was illness and turmoil at my home at that time, telling him some of the story about my brother, but leaving out the reason for it all. "I just didn't want to bring you into that scene, although my mother asked about you numerous times." He was skeptical, and obviously not fully satisfied by my answer.

There were days when I didn't see him after that, but he would call regularly from someplace where he was doing a deal for his company. He had managed to get into this trucking business because he was in a quartermaster unit in Italy, where he was a tech sergeant, the highest rank that a Black soldier could reach. His boss was a 1st lieutenant and Italian; he could speak the language fluently. He genuinely seemed to have less prejudice than the usual Italian servicemen. He said his father had sought to get Negro workers in the union in the steel plants in upstate Pennsylvania where he lived. His father was from an Italian Protestant group known as the Waldensians who migrated from Northern Italy. They were persecuted by the Catholics for their beliefs in social justice, for helping the downtrodden and for condoning religious diversity.

He and Paul, the 1st lieutenant, worked together exceptionally well on the battlefield. My boyfriend showed his prowess in mapping out routes, in assigning cover for the convoys and in getting the right Black corporals and sergeants to muster their privates to drive the dangerous cargo over treacherous terrain. He was greatly admired by the lieutenant who did indeed put him out there to do risky missions and won commendations for himself for the gallantry of his unit.

Why Boyfriend did it I have never been able to phantom, but I believe that was his mother's teaching that guided him then as now: If you have a job to do, give it your best. Near the end of the war, he won a medal for pulling Paul, by then a captain, from a Jeep that had been hit by shrapnel as bombs fell all about the convoy. The captain's back was injured, and for the rest of that operation, it was my boyfriend who managed the cargo. Another white captain was rushed to the front; he was nominally in charge, but he didn't know the men, nor did he understand much about getting trucks through the muck and daily assaults of a German blitz. I would never have known about this had a veteran from his unit not told the whole story one day at the Savoy, where we had gone for a Sunday afternoon dance as we often did when we started dating. He said, grasping Boyfriend's shoulder, "This guy put his life on the line for us." To which Boyfriend responded modestly, "Just trying to stay alive, man and not endanger my troops."

The New Year's Eve Party

Every now and then in our conversations, explanations notwithstanding, my boyfriend would express his annoyance about that non-invitation home with me for Christmas. I would reiterate that I could not because my brother was suffering from a breakdown, a recurrence of the mental state caused by a death-defying stay for months in the swamps of New Guinea. I wouldn't mention that my family was recovering from a bitter fight, the real reason why I could not take him there. To make it up to him, I promised him a lovely New Year's Eve. With two friends, we planned the party at a brownstone on Convent Avenue in Manhattan that belonged to a newspaper editor friend of mine.

Lou, Kit and I spent the day decorating the ground floor and cooking chitterlings, rice, collard greens and black-eyed peas, which are a must-have for Negroes' New Years. However, we would do the glamorous thing: have champagne with them, not the beer or corn liquor that used to complete the menu. We had other food too, as some Black people think it is far beneath them to eat hog innards, which was standard fare for their slave ancestors and not only to bring in the New Year. Ten couples had been invited and hopefully no one would crash because this detritus, which the high-class butchers used to throw out, was now expensive.

I was wearing a black velvet, long-sleeved dress; low back, form-fitting but flared with a mermaid hemline. Quite a number I found in a Third Avenue thrift shop. I was there early to meet the guests; my boyfriend would be driving over from Brooklyn and he would be late. When I spoke with him around noon, he didn't sound too happy about the party; he said he wasn't feeling well. I knew he was having a hard time on that job, but I thought this party would cheer him up.

The first to arrive was Naomi, a nurse who was just back from Puerto Rico where she was making arrangements to set up the clinics for testing the birth control pill with Planned Parenthood. She came with Stanley, who was a tennis player most of the time, usually seen in whites, but in the winter, he was delightfully tweedy, in suits bought perhaps by his gaggle of girlfriends. He was the life of the party, with an absolutely divine sense of humor; he knew everybody and was really in-telligent and well-informed. We were great friends; he knew a lot about classical music and would ask about the concerts I had been to.

As others gathered they began bombarding Naomi with questions about the pill. Stanley had all sorts of ideas about how women could begin to live a little not having to worry about pregnancy so much. "It won't be so easy for you gals to trap us guys," he joked. Sensible Naomi said, "Hold ev-erything, there were still a lot of problems around its use;

estrogen levels and other chemical imbalances which we don't know the long-range effects of have to be tested. You guys think you can just give the women something to protect against pregnancy while you experience no ill effects. We have a long way to go with this."

"Absolutely," Cynthia a usually quiet and conservative mother of four, bristled at Stan's remark and blurted out loudly, "Why don't you cats have a vasectomy and take on some of the burden of guiltless sex?" A chorus of "Amen" from the women followed that remark. Carla, a pediatric nurse and one of Lou's friends, before removing her coat, squealed, "Stanley you clown, this is serious. You men have no idea what anguish is because you can never suffer the morning after, which morphs into weeks of anxiety, wondering if, pondering how, questioning who can you turn to."

Lou left her kitchen duties to affirm Carla's remarks and to add, "Imagine you're a sophomore madly in love for the first time, and one spring night under the spell and the smell of apple blossoms IT happens. The young woman carries all of the burdens of that glorious encounter; the results of the heavenly moment begin to grow. Discovery means expulsion from school, shame, facing enraged parents, a mighty bleak future as an unwed mother of an illegitimate child. Women of every stripe, married or single, would die, and are indeed dying for THE PILL."

Everyone wanted to be in on the conversation. Birth control was a huge concern for single and married women alike. Until recently, they relied on sponges, linen and uncomfortable condoms for blockage; now some were using the diaphragm. It was cumbersome and sloppy, requiring a germicide gel application and the necessity to wear it for a proscribed number of hours after use to be sure the germicide had worked. Mighty inconvenient and not 100% certain as a preventive. Some frightened women gave themselves douches of vinegar or Lysol or drank poisonous concoctions to prevent or discontinue a pregnancy. More than one woman we knew suffered sterility because of a botched abortion by friends in dormitories inserting coat hangers or knitting needles into their vaginas. Even so-called midwives didn't use sterile equipment or weren't knowledgeable enough to prevent hemorrhaging because they failed to remove all of the placenta during an abortion.

Steve, a physician from Teaneck, was pumped up about this issue: "Margaret Sanger tried out her family planning ideas on Black women, you know. They wanted to prevent Negroes from having so many babies. I question their motives in this movement. White men are going to stop this so-called "*planned parenthood*;" they are going to fight it without ceasing. They don't want their women to control their bodies; they want them to have plenty of white babies; too many Black and immigrant kids being born in the USA. Darkies will outnumber them."

Naomi glared at him, "You, of all people, who see undernourished women dying in childbirth, who watch poor women having one baby after another that they can't afford, who see rape victims, young girls molested and impregnated by older male predators, should be praying for improved birth control. What chauvinists you men are!" Maryanne, Steve's wife shook her head and smiled at him. "Oh, Steve is just playing devil's advocate. He is far from Mr. Hardhearted. Sometimes he is on the verge of tears lamenting his inability to save butchered young women after failed abortions or, because abortion is illegal, he's unable to help a teen raped by a stranger and destined to carry and rear her rapist's baby."

Steve was not to be silenced. "I want to know why you went to Puerto Rico; why not Denmark or Sweden, to test your pill? They always pick Black people to do the tests on." "That's an absolute fact, I just read about a Negro nurse who helped a doctor test the effects of syphilis on Black homeless men, letting them die without treatment?" offered Eve, a social worker who had ambled over with glass and cigarette in hand. Her fiancé, Ben, was animated. "And worse, that celebrated surgeon in Philadelphia who did all the tests for caesarian operations on poor Black women without anesthesia. We are the disposable people to them."

Steve continued, "So they chose you, a Black nurse with a master's in public health to do their dirty work, eh?" Naomi walked away. "I will not be the scapegoat for all your anger about race. I have an interesting and important job to do and I am doing it competently and responsibly, so there!" "Well, the Puerto Ricans who come here are all white. They can be blacker than me, but they sign themselves in as white, so the disposability imprimatur doesn't apply to them," Stan said with a smile. "I'll bet the women they'll choose will be from

Fajardo. That's where the poorest and blackest Puerto Ricans are," Steve added.

"Yeah," agreed Ben, a real estate man. "But they are certainly breaking down some housing barriers. They are almost down to 96th Street now, moving all around Park Avenue, pushing out the Italians, Poles and Irish. They send their whitest spouses to apply for an apartment; when the rest of the family comes -- Mamma as black as me, and all the aunts and uncles of various shades— it's too late. The lease had been signed, and possession is not rescindable." With that the persecution of Naomi shifted to other forms of racism:

"That's blockbusting of another order," Don, Cynthia's husband, said. "When we moved to Teaneck the whites fled further out, leaving the fire department, the schools, and the police departments staffed with their white employees, so we had to fight mightily to get some Negro teachers and still haven't moved the police and fire departments much."

"They do their experimenting there on us too. Always some new educational program, "sight reading," "the new math," anything they want to test, they throw it in on our kids, and send some "experts" from an out-of-state firm, highly paid with our tax dollars, to instruct and evaluate us," interjected Bev, an elementary school teacher. "And decide that our children are inferior and just can't learn to read and calculate, and the parents, the parents, they declare are hopeless at learning the new systems," offered Maryanne, a psychologist.

"So, you can understand why they consider us the disposable people: We are powerless to stand up for our rights as first-class citizens; they bring that junk to us, and there is always some 'handkerchief head' who is willing to carry water for them, selling it to the community for a meager cut of the big pie," Larry, the politician who had been standing listening, filling his glass several times, said with authority.

By this time the booze was flowing, as each guest had brought something, very often a bottle of wine or spirits, as well as food. The room was filling up with people and smoke. Folks were definitely in the groove. We had a deejay spinning the records and there was room enough to dance. Larry was twirling about the floor alone, then cutting in to do his fancy steps with his friends' partners. I had done some political things with him, but had declined his advances. He was the pawing type, and seemed to have one thing on his mind, although he was a skilled politician, a lawyer, and thought to be a young man on the move. He immediately latched on to me, thinking I was single, and he would have free range tonight. I greeted him, told him I was a hostess, and would be getting food and making sure everyone had a superb time, so I could not dance with him. Undeterred, he was shadowing me. I wondered who invited him, and how he got here without a date.

It was almost midnight, and the spirits were having their effect; folks were thoroughly enjoying the low-class fare and the various combinations of spiked punch, liquor, beer and wine. We brought out the champagne and a cake decorated in black and silver which would be cut and served as the midnight hour chimed. Larry was putting his arm around me as I went about filling glasses. I asked him to please back off, but he was pretty high by now, and was becoming more aggressive.

I didn't see him come in, but my boyfriend arrived just as Larry was attempting to stand behind me in a really inappropriate manner and put both arms around me as I held the bottle to fill a glass. Boyfriend walked over to Larry, and not so gently removed his arms from around my waist, and pushed him aside, possessively giving me a kiss on the cheek. He then turned to Larry and said, "Lay off man, get your own brown bag." Larry staggered back and said, "Hey wait, who do you think you are, manhandling me," and swung his arm, almost striking my boyfriend in the stomach. I put the bottle down, stood in front of my boyfriend, and said as softly as I could, "Please Larry, this is my boyfriend, he's not feeling well, so please don't upset him."

Now all eyes were on the scene, and talking stopped; I beaconed to Stanley, who came over. He took Larry by the arm and said, "Come on, man, you've been acting pretty obnoxious ever since you got here, let's go outside and have a talk." Larry was having none of it: "I came to celebrate the New Year, and it's almost here, I won't be going outside for no talk. This woman here is a friend of mine, and I don't know why I can't be friendly. Does this cat think he owns her?" Then Boyfriend, who wasn't in a very friendly mood, said, "Why don't you and I go outside and have a talk. I think that would settle things." "I don't go out in the moonlight with no hard-ass suckers like you; I think I'll stand right here and we can settle up." Larry was shouting, "Come on," bringing his arms up to a boxing stance. Two other men joined Stanley in removing Larry from the room, as he shouted curses at my boyfriend, mentioning color and references to status, and what he would do to him on the witness stand.

Lou asked the deejay to play "*Take the A-Train*," and folks started snaking around the room like a subway train, saying "choo-choo" as if it were a locomotive, and singing lyrics about the "shortest way to get to Harlem."

Lou took over the oenologist duties as I escorted Boyfriend into the outer room to calm him down. I kissed him as he said, "Who is that guy?" I said, "You have probably seen him in Brooklyn, he works with those West Indian politicians out there, and is going to try to run for a seat on the state legislature." He said, "My question is: Who is that guy to you?" I smiled. "Jealous, are you? He is someone with whom I have worked on several congressional campaigns, is on the Democratic State Committee and close to DA William Fitts Ryan in Manhattan. Beyond that, I know little about him. Come on, be an angel, let's not welcome in the New Year with anger and jealously clouding our evening. Let's go back in smiling." "I can't, in the first place, I shouldn't even be here, I feel lousy, and then this goon had to make things worse." "Honey love, it's almost 12 o'clock, come with me, please," I begged. We walked in hugging, and singing "Ole Lang Syne" with the crowd. But we didn't stay long after that. My friends told me they would clean up, and I was free to go with Boyfriend.

At about 12:50, he was taking me home. But he wasn't ready to take me home; his partner, Paul, had a cousin who had a restaurant near Columbia University; he had asked Boyfriend to spend New Year's Eve there, he would have a table for him. It was late, but we went to Morningside Avenue. He got out of the car and called upstairs on a street level phone; he was invited up. We parked around the corner and took the elevator to an elegant restaurant, inhabited entirely by white people. We were given a lovely seat by the window, so we could look out at the snowy street, sparkling with a full moon and Christmas lights. His cousin and his wife came over to welcome us, and said that Paul had been there, but left right after midnight because he was not feeling well. He took us over to introduce us to the family and neighbors gathered; an elegant Italian assemblage complete with sleepy children and grandmothers. Some were warm and smiling; some showed surprise and perplexity; all were cordial.

Neither Boyfriend nor I had eaten a thing at the party, so we were ravenously hungry; we ate a pleasant meal and drank a glass of champagne with Paul's cousin and his wife to celebrate the New Year.

Then Boyfriend started to unwind: he was downhearted about the events at his business, Paul is not able to come to work, and his uncle is filling in. This uncle loaned them some money to buy into what will be called containerized intermodal shipping; a whole new way of transporting goods. You pack bicycles or grain in boxcars, and the entire boxcar is moved from warehouse to truck, to train, to ship. "We wanted to be in on the ground floor of this innovation. The guy who invented the process is an old friend of Paul's. We are in just the right place for when this takes off in a couple of years with the interstate highway system becoming a reality. We could transport goods from inland to coast, from train to warehouses." He was almost starry-eyed as he talked about it; his whole being perked up. "So, is your partner out of the business?" "No, on paper he is still there, he was the inside man. I did the strategic mapping out of routes, developed contacts and met with the CEOs, but he's not able to manage the office and the finances as he had done so capably. He is in a great deal of pain; it is heartbreaking to go to see him. He can barely turn his head to look at you.

"Uncle CN is not at this party, thank goodness. He is from Paul's mother's Sicilian side; extremely racist, almost as brown as I am, with a heavy black mustache, hairy arms and a filthy mouth. He hates that I am there, has slipped up a couple of times, saying 'Nigger' when he was talking about Black men whom he feels cannot and should not drive trucks. He revels in telling how untrustworthy they are; how cargo would be stolen, how there would be 'an underground railroad of pilfered goods if we let these darkies on the road,' he jokes. Just when we were getting the big break, just when all I have worked for these seven years was coming to fruition...." He blew out his breath from puffed cheeks, shook his bowed head, and seemed unable to say more. I took his hands in mine and kissed them. I put them on my face, and let him feel my tears, so unhappy was I for his distress.

He moved around the table to the bench that I was sitting on and held me in his arms, "What would I do if I didn't have you," he said. "I couldn't bear all the hate spewing from that bastard's mouth; I couldn't think straight about what to do next. I have got to hire an expensive lawyer, because Uncle Cosa Nostra is stripping my authority away from me now, so it's only a matter of time before he will be turning me into the streets without a cent."

"How could he do that? You and Paul are the registered legal owners," I said. "Yep, but he has the note for that loan which he can call in at any time. It will devastate us to have to pay it. I don't have an ally in the plant; I can't call on anyone in the bookkeeping department to give me the unadulterated truth about the finances. He has fired just about all the staff we had there initially and filled the office with relatives who are his accomplices."

"God, what a predicament. It would break your heart to lose this business; what can you do to salvage at least part of it?" I said, shaking my head. "I don't know anybody in the corporate world, no legal or entrepreneur expert who could advise me," he said. "I know some Black guys who purport to be masters of business administration, but they have never dealt with anything larger than a candy store. Uncle Costa Nostra has experienced empire builders and the Mafia to protect his interest." "What about your friends in the corporate world?" "Oh, I've talked with them several times. Their stuff is all theoretical, bookish ideas that I know myself, stuff that won't fly in the real world of corporate manipulation." "You know what, I could ask Golda about Jewish lawyers experienced in finance who are sympathetic to the Negro cause, and maybe they could suggest someone or advise you on what steps to take," I offered. "Now that would cause a bigger ruckus than the situation in *On the Waterfront*. Can you imagine a left-wing Jewish lawyer going toe-to-toe with the Mafiosi?" "Look, I just want you to emerge from this still breathing; they are such a vicious bunch," I said.

"I'll be OK so long as Paul is alive, making them pray for me at church, all of them including Uncle CN. But Paul grows weaker every day; his wife and mother are the only ones sticking up for me. Maybe I told you, his father died soon after the war ended. He gave me every support and prayed for us on his death bed, holding my hand and telling me to stay strong, and that he would be watching over us. Paul's mother often comes to the office when I'm away to prevent Uncle CN from locking me out."

"Baby, I need you so much," he was whispering in my ear as he tenderly kissed me. He was becoming passionate, squeezing my buttocks, slipping his hand down the low-cut back of my dress, and generally forgetting where we were. He was perspiring and when I leaned on him, I could feel his erection. He said, "Baby, come home with me tonight, please?" "You know all the reasons why I cannot..." I said as I started to shiver, as if overcome by the cold. He wrapped me in his arms, beseeching me, "Are you OK?" I buried my head in his jacket, and sobbed, "I think we'd better be going." My teeth were actually chattering and I was feeling nauseous and terrified. He said, "I can't just now. Sit with me until I calm down. I don't know how long I can take this overstimulation without satisfaction, you know that! I want you, I need you. You are the only woman who could satisfy me, and yet you deny me. Why, honey, tell me why?"

We walked in silence through the snow, he held my arm tightly so I wouldn't slip on the ice, and helped me into the car. Once inside, I clenched my teeth to steady myself against what I realized was a passionate aching for him, but Mamma intervened: "Chastity until marriage, the only path for decent Negro girls!" I turned to him and said softly, "You don't want to be intimate with me, I would be a lodestone around your neck, expecting you to be with me, always being dependent, insistent, persistent. You have too much you want to do; you are under so much stress now, with goals you want to meet, you don't need worrisome me in addition to all that." "Persistent, insistent, I long for that kind of passion from you," he said as he started the car. He took me home, walked me to my door and kissed me goodnight; a very sterile kiss, one I hadn't experienced in months.

I called in the morning as he was arising from sleep. He was groggy as he told me he would be out of town for a few days; he would call me from wherever he was, and not to worry about the situation at his job. I wanted to talk more about his ordeal or about us, but he was terse, rather sad. I was asking myself, what am I protecting and for what? We have been going out for almost a year; he's been the only man I've been out with for months, except my African friends, whom I consider not dates but colleagues in the fight for Black liberation in Africa. Some of them would like to be a little amorous, but I can fend them off, lying that I am actually engaged.

I sat at my dressing table and beheld a face in the mirror that said in no uncertain terms that I am becoming dependent on my boyfriend, that he wants intimacy and … so do I. He has been faithful, I think, and certainly attentive. Last night that shivering was spontaneous; I was experiencing a physical reaction to the sexual stimulation of his presence, his caressing me. My body is telling me that I am falling for him and want him. He has shown that he cares deeply for me. I felt his jealousy for the first time at the party last night. Look at me: tears are streaming down my face—involuntary tears, and not of sadness either but of passion and desire. I don't think I could bear to see him with another woman.

His visits were irregular after that, usually with groups, at civic events or where teaching me to drive was the main event. I asked if he was losing interest in me, and he answered, "Never." He was investing in another business that takes some of his time, and he would be mustering out of this trucking caper eventually. I didn't like the way he looked when he said that. "How can you just discard a dream you have had for almost a decade, into which you have invested so much time and treasure? What are you talking about?" He said, "I am making my peace with that hairy situation; Paul won't be around much longer, so I'm looking at next steps. Don't think I'm giving it away."

He changed the subject: "I want to do something pleasant now, like teach you how to drive. You seem so happy to please me with what you have learned, I'm hopeful it will carry over into the rest of our relationship." So, we went out many afternoons to deserted spots where I could practice, and ended at dusk with praise for becoming more adept at parallel parking or braking distances or whatever he felt I should learn that day. And then the petting, the petting was becoming less satisfying for me too, vows of chastity notwithstanding.

Fear of not being chaste was the demon here, and plain old fear: a student of my mother's religious teaching; wrestling with the archaic warnings of "Silas X. Floyd, still trying to be one of his "flowers." Floyd was one of the authors of books that were required reading for my mother and her friends at 2nd Baptist. She believed their strictures were still appropriate for 1950 women. Combined with the ethics, I must confess, I have a latent fear of men. Heretofore their deep voices would rattle me, but with Boyfriend, I find his voice soothing. On a subconscious level, men's bass voices have made me feel that they were scolding me for my actions or non-action. Like my father, making me feel guilty for not doing what he ordered promptly enough. But this voice was comforting, I could envision him as my …lover. But what would my lover think of me in the morning? Just another conquest? Now I had him on the ropes, wondering what it would be like to bed me, anxious to please me in whatever I want in anticipation of the surrender. How stupid of me, I am suffering too; for how much longer; I was wavering.

Would I be like my mother tied eternally to one man, unable to leave even though she was mistreated since she had given herself to him? Yes, I was asking him to marry me first, and was he stubbornly saying he didn't buy a pig in a poke. Anyway, I told myself I didn't want to get married too young as my mother did at18. I want to live a little before I'm a housewife, a mother, dependent on a husband to support me, and therefore his subject.

On several Sundays, we went to visit his mother for dinner. Sometimes I would go to a Baptist church in Queens with them, and his mother would ask why I was not taking communion. I told her I had been baptized at the First Baptist Church of Crestmont, but didn't feel that I was prayerful and sanctified enough to take communion. I enjoyed the service, and was inspired by it, and the music was affecting, but I didn't feel ready to become a devout Christian at this time. That was the one thing I knew she didn't like about me; her son should be with a God-fearing woman.

Sometimes, after an early dinner, we would go to the Village Gate and listen to Harry Belafonte, or to Birdland or the Royal Roost. As the weather broke we would drive to restaurants in West Chester. When I went home for a February birthday celebration for my brother, my father expressed his approval of my driving; I took him for a spin down to my sister's house without a hitch, and he was delighted. I was an accomplished driver. I showed I had mastered the skills as Boyfriend let me drive his car around parking lots and for short jaunts on deserted side streets. I got my license on the

first try.   On our next date, he insisted that I take the wheel
and drive down the winding Bronx River Parkway after a dinner before a blazing fire in a 1780 house. I cannot deny that I
was reaching a point where I wanted this man; our nights on
the Palisades or in the parking areas off the parkways were
becoming steam baths; our petting was becoming deeper,
longer and more persistent. I found myself just as deeply engaged in the fondling as he.

◆　◆　◆

In the Deep South

I looked over at Eve, fretfully snoozing in the back; a little apprehensive, as was I, about Lou's jerky driving. Eve asked if she should take over, as four hours was a long stretch, but Lou assured us that she was wide awake, and would take a break at Baton Rouge. Eve and I continued to chat amiably evaluating our experience so far. We were anticipating all that we might find; the five days we had spent getting thus far had been rewarding. Lou and Eve had Brownie cameras and had taken some photos that we could not wait to see; Lou had used a whole roll of film and had promised to make copies for each of us.

We were beginning to feel that New Orleans would be the icing on the cake, and we were pleased with our decision to go east to New Orleans before entering Mexico. Lou didn't stop, but drove down Route 49S through Baton Rouge, that romantic place we would like to have visited. But, as time was of the essence, we could only glance at it quickly as dawn broke, blue and orange and dappled with fluffy white clouds. In less than an hour we would be in New Orleans.

The entry into the city was beautiful. Over the swamps onto the esplanade along a sparkling Lake Pontchartrain; live oaks standing tall with Spanish moss swaying on their branches – it was a sight to behold. Unfortunately, Lou was enjoying the view too instead of watching the road. She wouldn't admit it, but I'm sure she was tiring; four and a half hours was a lot for her first spin. All of a sudden, there was a screech. Theta yelled for Lou to put her foot on the brake; Lou lifted both feet up, leaving the gas and brake pedals on their own as she careened toward the curb. Theta pulled on the emergency brake bringing the car to a sudden startling stop. Luckily, we narrowly missed grazing a parked car. Eve and I hit the front seat as the force of the near crash pulled us forward, throwing pillows and blankets to the floor. We were not injured and quickly regained our composure. We sat for a minute in silence, and then having observed tailgating and other faults with Lou's driving, Eve said calmly, "That's it." We got out, walked around the car to survey the damage; seeing none, and with a sigh of relief, Eve took the wheel. That was the end of Lou's driving. For the rest of the trip, she sat in the back, her previous confident assurances to the contrary; she seemed delighted to be relieved of the driving duty.

We had to do some searching to find the Black community, but we took our clue from the usual lay of the land – where were the railroad tracks, where was the industrial section, where did the paved roads stop? I had read about the famed 7th Ward, and we all agreed that was where we would go. This was a section where some middle-class Blacks lived in a section called Gentilly. The lowest section was the 9th Ward where the poorest of the poor Blacks lived. The ritziest section was the segregated Garden District; near the French quarter but separated from it by levees. This was the English district, populated after the Louisiana Purchase by British and Yankees with gardens in the front yard, unlike the grilled porches with columned Creole-style mansions along the broad avenues where the French and Spanish earlier settlers lived.

We passed the Corpus Christi Roman Catholic Church where children were playing in the schoolyard. I wanted to take a closer look. I knew that most of the schools were Catholic; Loyola University was here, and, Xavier, that supposedly trained more Black doctors than Howard and had an all-white faculty of sisters and priests. At Corpus Christi, sisters in their habits stood watch over the children, two of them were Black. The kids were beautiful to see with their mulattoed faces; some were darkly African, but retained the hazel eyes and the curly red or sandy hair of their French or Spanish fathers. There were no white children in the mix. I thought of my teenage hunger for books then considered salacious, about New Orleans, extolling the exotic beauty of the hot-blooded quadroons - *The Foxes of Harrow*. The women were concubines to the wealthy white French and Spanish planters. These mixed-race women had to tie up their hair, and wear a head scarf so their luxurious tresses would not be seen by white men who would be driven to act upon their sexual fantasies by these sorcerers.

I got out of the car and went inside the fence to speak with a pleasant Black sister overseeing the children at recess, who greeted me with outstretched arms. I asked her if this school would be integrated following the *Brown* ruling. She laughingly said there was no sign of desegregation here. Some of the kids are only in the school a few hours each day, she said, and not every day at that. They work on the plantations. But she told us that this was the most interesting parish in New Orleans. Dillard University was here. She suggested that there was a well-kept Negro motel nearby where we might find a room. She sketched the route on the map.

Off we went and met a man named Pinky who was the proprietor of the Flamingo Motel. It had pink metal awnings and air conditioners in the windows! We planned to stay three days, but stayed four, and Pinky rolled out the red carpet for us. Immediately upon getting us settled in our rooms, he told us there was a swinging club nearby where we could hear some real New Orleans jazz and that he would take us there that evening after dinner. We all took naps in our small but comfortable rooms, listening to the loud hum of air conditioners that did indeed cool the space. I took the opportunity to wash clothes in the sink and hang them on a line I had bought. I took a long shower and readied myself for the evening. We had no fear of going on this outing with Pinky. He wanted us to tell everyone about his establishment, gave us post cards to send, and seemed delighted to have us.

The dinner was exactly what I had asked for – gumbo with plenty of oysters, absolutely delicious. When we told Pinky about our mission to observe attitudes among citizens concerning the *Brown vs Board of Education* decision, he laughed heartily. He said New Orleans has experienced several decisions that at first seemed to advance freedom and equality for Black people, but were reversed by the persistent white supremacists. He began to rattle off historical events we knew nothing about: The Black codes of 1615 which sought to make everyone, slaves as well as Jews Catholic, giving status to the enslaved who were baptized. I told him I had recently read about the Slave Revolt of 1811: he was pleased, and said that Charles Deslonde should be celebrated by Blacks as a national hero; thousands of Blacks were killed in that revolt that put fear in the hearts of plantation owners. Black men and women fought with the Union Army for their own liberation in 1863, were prominent in Reconstruction, gaining the right to vote, to attend school, to hold public office, to be armed and serve as soldiers. It was all over in 1877 when the Hayes-Tilden Compromise reversed it and blood ran in the streets. Pinky became so animated that he was perspiring, shaking his fists as he said, "People come to New Orleans and enjoy the clubs, and think all is fun and good times here. They don't see the poor Black people struggling to make a living in near-slavery conditions on sugar plantations right outside the city, today! I want you girls to see some of the places where Blacks fought for equality, and have had to fight the same battles over and over again. That's why we can't get excited about *Brown.*" We told Pinky that we would love to go to see the sites he mentioned and read more about the history. Truly, we had not read much about New Orleans Black heroes in the north. He simmered down as everyone concurred that they wanted to become more knowledgeable. He relaxed,

smiled and said that the jazz event would be the proper intro-
duction for our first night.

We piled into Pinky's car and he drove us to the club. I
never knew the name of it or its address, but it was storybook
perfect – a wooden structure on a slight rise, with a large live
oak tree in the front yard and space to park on the sides; a real
honky-tonk of a place. Pinky assured us it was not a "sport-
ing house." The maître d' greeted us warmly and wanted us
to know that the night was young: The real music didn't start
until the clubs closed downtown, and the top musicians came
for a set out here. This was a facsimile of Storyville, the fa-
bled, red-light district and disreputable home of jazz. There in
the 1920's Black and white musicians entertained the prosti-
tutes and their clients together, and segregation barriers fell
under the novel harmonies. The musicians could be innovative, blending cultures and styles, combining blues songs of
unremitting sorrow with French can-can beats and German
waltzes. A housing project now stood where the madams had
proffered their white, mulatto or Black girls to their affluent
clientele in separate houses.

The music that was playing when we arrived was what we
knew as "gut-bucket" music, with a bluesy combination of a
stride piano, bass, trumpet, guitar and the steady, loud beat of
the drums. We got right into it, talking to everyone who asked
where we were from and were struck by their kindly inquisi-
tiveness. My companions contented themselves with one
rum-and-Coke with lemon and I had a gin and tonic. We were
careful not to be too friendly with any of the men; there were

several attractive ones there, but who knew who their woman was and what their game was? Some of them seemed very hip; maybe they were pimps. Others spoke as though they were well educated and enjoyed the authenticity of a place like this, the sincerity of the sound. It was a mixed audience, white couples scattered among the Blacks, the kind of thing you would see often in cities, even though Negroes lived in strictly segregated neighborhoods.

Pinky was thoroughly enjoying himself, dancing with each of us and introducing us to his friends. We danced only with the men he introduced us to; one single man and a couple joined us. The very pleasant twosome suggested things that we must see like Congo Square and the French Quarter, but they talked little about desegregation. Most shrugged when we mentioned *Brown vs Board of Education* as if it made very little difference to them. They intimated that the people here seemed to be satisfied with their relationship to the white people even though whites controlled just about everything. They believed they lived in a fairly egalitarian society, as there were some pretty wealthy Negro "Nawaulineans," and they felt they had a culture of their own that included folks of all shades. But how black or near white you were made the difference. I sensed a weariness, a shrug signaling, what's the use, let's enjoy the status quo. They seemed to ignore the segregation; even among the people of color that hierarchy of color determined power and influence. It was the mulattoes, octoroons and quadroons, products of miscegenation, the illegitimate descendants of African women and white planters and shipping magnates, who got their educations in France and returned to be the professionals or business owners. And then there was a whole segment that excluded themselves from the Negro population: The Jelly-Roll Mortons, early ad-mixtures of Spanish, French and Africans designated Creoles who would have no part of the "Indians" or formerly enslaved descendants of Africans who paraded at Mardi Gras.

Pinky looked askance at the compromisers, those who thought everything was ok. "Some people don't want to ac-knowledge that there is a race problem in New Orleans," he lamented. "They don't want any more trouble; but me, I can't stand being blocked from the goodies white folks enjoy."

The next morning, we gathered around the table in the dining room and spread a large map of New Orleans. Unfortunately, Pinky could not go with us to give us a sense of the city, but he had listed some points of interest, and marked the significance of the sites with a red pen: "This was the banking center of the US before the war, and slaves were the liquid asset that property was leveraged against," he began. He circled several sites where slaves were sold; at its height, there were 57 depots in New Orleans. The evidence has been and is being destroyed, and Blacks need to put up markers so people will never forget whose sweat and tears was the source of wealth in this town. Go to the corner of St. Louis and Chartres Street, the St. Louis Exchange Hotel. Let peo-ple see you staring at the place where thousands of slaves were bought and sold. 750,000 people were shipped down the Mississippi from the upper slave states to the deep south.

"New Orleans was the biggest city in the south; they sent thousands of soldiers to Virginia when the war started, leaving New Orleans unprotected. Go to New Orleans City Park and see the statue of General P.G. Beauregard, sitting up there with his coat drawn back heroically. They say he started the war, firing the first shot at Fort Sumter. We have got these expensive statues of Robert E. Lee, Jefferson Davis, and other confederate slave owning generals, built to honor their "lost cause." Our kids should be honoring a statue of Dr. Louis Charles Roudanez who published the first Black newspaper in the United States which gave voice to the enslaved's yearning for freedom, supporting the constitution of 1868 which granted social equality. He marked the place where *The New Orleans Tribune's* office was. Go there to recognize this hallowed ground.

"Nine years after the war in 1874, when the Reconstruction government was turning racism on its head by eliminating property requirements for voting, and legislating that all children should get schooling, the former Confederates knew that their wealth was the bodies of enslaved men, women and children. They couldn't bear to see their butler or stable boy now in control of government, while white people scrambled to stay alive. They formed the White League which arose from the chaos between the political parties and the incompetent Grant administration. In New Orleans and nationwide, white groups were forming to reinstate white supremacy. In New Orleans, the White League overthrew the elected government; President Grant stepped in and recognized the elected government, but didn't disarm the White League. The racists united: The White League now had the support of the US soldiers. The Freedmen were livid as they saw the federal government deserting them, and they threw their forces into battle at the foot of Canal Street. It is the bloody end of the Reconstruction government: The Battle of Liberty Place, a battle for equality in 1877 between Freedmen and white supremacists. I marked that spot with an X, you must go there and read the plaque which *praises the duly elected white government for overthrowing the carpetbaggers and ousting the usurpers; the election of 1876 recognized white supremacy in the south and gave them back their state."*

We were like children on a treasure hunt trying to find the sites that Pinky said we must see. We found Canal Street, the divide between the English and French sections with which the important streets merged and drove down it and found most of the historical sites. We parked our car and walked the blocks to Jackson Square where public whippings and even hangings had taken place. There was the infamous St. Louis Cathedral with its combination of Spanish and French architecture that had issued the Black Codes which declared that everyone even Jews must become Catholic. The Catholics were significant in regulating enslavement. We decided against taking a horse drawn carriage. We knew needed to stretch our legs to prepare for the long drives ahead and save money.

We came upon a market where I got to buy some pralines, all brown sugar and pecans, delicious and fragrant. The store had a painting of a stout Black woman making the candy, but the ownership was obviously white. Everyone could come into the store, have coffee, sit down to eat, and purchase the merchandise. We put a nickel in the juke box and played Fats Domino's famous song, "Walking to New Orleans," making us one with the people who visibly approved of our choice. I bought several boxes of pralines that I would take to my mother and others and munched on a few myself. My formerly disparaging companions liked them too, but seemed to prefer the sugary doughnuts, beignets. I understood that it was not so everywhere, but in most places all shades of people could sit together. This social inclusion hid a multitude of sins like the segregated schools, the blighted neighborhoods, and the injustice that the music they created was making millions for others, but a mere pittance for most of the Negro composers.

We went to Congo Square which, we were told after much prodding, had been a slave market, and became the place where Black musicians like Louis Armstrong gathered to play music on their day off. The custom continues every Sunday, and we would come back for the music.

The Metairie Cemetery was the next attraction with its graves built above ground. We were retracing our steps, not following a contiguous route, but getting lost and serendipitlistly finding the places of interest. We finally found the cemetery and lingered among some famous tombstones, hoping to see a jazz funeral playing dirges as they entered and swinging jubilant music as they left. But no, we weren't that lucky. We marveled at the fact that here we were in a city built on drained Cypress swamps where escaped Maroons used to hide from the slavecatchers; where huge plantations once held captive armies of enslaved men and women to tend their crops, build their colonial houses, tree-lined streets and levees, and lade the ships which moved the harvests to ports around the nation. We immersed ourselves in that history.

We walked at dusk along the river and saw that Mark Twain's paddleboats still plied it. We climbed up on the levees holding back the muddy waters of the Mississippi, snaking through the city with the Gulf coming up to meet it at lakes, inlets and peninsulas. We strolled along Bourbon Street, enjoying the sight of some of the beautiful historic houses with their iron railings, quaint balconies and half-hidden gardens as darkness fell. We found our car and drove back to the motel to a welcoming Pinky, anxious to hear our opinion of what we had seen.

Saturday night was the hottest time in the French Quarter. Pinky told us about a club downtown where Fats Domino would be singing and he could get us in. Weary as we were from our tour, we decided to splurge and go.

Fats was born and bred in New Orleans, and the people loved him, but he seldom appeared in the clubs. This night the place was packed, and Fats didn't disappoint. He and his co-writer, Dave Bartholomew, were trying out a new song, "Ain't It a Shame," and the audience went wild. After a few boogie-woogie chords on the piano, with the bass, guitar and cornet chiming in, the audience was singing along with the catchy tune. The back-up band was excellent, playing standards and

Fats' first big hit, "The Fat Man." It was after midnight when we left, but the streets were still alive with musicians, even kids' spasm bands playing ragtime, entertaining for dollars and coins thrown in their hats or instrument cases.

Sunday morning in New Orleans was vibrant with a clamor of church bells, summoning the faithful to worship. In our Black community, Negroes were rising too and donning their best clothing to go to the Catholic, but also the Methodist and Baptist churches in the neighborhood. I arose early and watched the procession while the others were sleeping. I was amused at the many dark-complexioned women with parasols, the favorite accessory of the white fair-skinned woman seeking to avoid the darkening effects of the sun. The women looked elegant, bedecked in their print garments with matching headdress, like their Senegalese ancestors where the French had gotten most of their slaves. Some walked with a proud swagger; these were strong women, in the tradition of their Creole concubine ancestors who had sued their former masters for support of their mixed-race families.

This was the day we would go to Congo Square to hear new musicians and jazz innovation where it all began. We decided against church, lounging around after breakfast until Pinky was ready to drive us down Rampart Street to the Square. Our Buick was at a garage owned by a friend of his, getting a check-up before we took to the road again.

When we arrived at Congo Square the crowd had gathered around a woman who was belting out risqué blues in the style of Bessie Smith. There were deep moans of approval to her words about the man who left her and how she was sorrowing at her loss. Then she segued into another song about how she got the better of her man, and there was loud applause and clapping of hands from the women gathered. A not too shapely, rather stout woman stepped out and swayed her body to the music, making suggestive gyrations that elicited laughter from the crowd that was now moving with her as heartbreak and triumph emanated from the vocalist.

Whole families of musicians had come to play. Fathers with their small children, who were precocious to say the least, had their own band. The enthusiasts loved the kids, tossing coins into their horn cases, swaying and snapping their fingers to their music. I love jazz concerts but wished the audience would wait until the entire selection was played before they applaud and audibly interrupt the sounds with their "yeahs" and other grunts of approval. Loud clapping followed each horn player so you couldn't hear the next artist as he started his solo.

We moved around the Square, listening to one group then another, chatting with whomever was amenable, learning about the ordinary people and their lives in New Orleans. We thought there was not much interest in *Brown vs Board of Ed*. Most of the folks didn't even know about it and didn't think it would change their lives. I spoke with a saxophone player as he was finishing his gig. He had recently come from Chicago on the train, where he was a Pullman Porter. He said he was reading about it in the newspapers but "sorta felt that we been livin' our separate lives for so long and developin' our own ways of doin' things that I sorta like things this way; don't have too much to do with white people. We been makin' our own music, cookin' our own food, socializin' with our own friends, and marryin' our own women." He didn't see why "some of the guys had to run after those white women hangin' around the jazz clubs in Chicago, just waitin' to make trouble."

A short balding man with horn-rimmed glasses was listening to our conversation. He said the NAACP, of which he was a member, was working frantically trying to stop police brutality against Negro youth, and to desegregate schools and buses. "How can folks say this ruling don't matter when they spend less than a third on Negro kids' schooling than they do on the whites? That is just not right; we have been pressing Mayor de Lesseps for change. This Supreme Court ruling will help. We can have separate social clubs, even churches, but the economy-- how we work, where we live and where our kids go to school-- is public and should be equal. We pay the same taxes and should have the same rights as everybody else."

I was glad to hear him speak up, and a small crowd was gathering with some folks nodding approval of his words. Eve told him about our trip and about the negative opinions we were hearing about the ruling. He shook his head. "Our folks don't know the history of this town. We are still reeling from the swindle after Reconstruction that deprived emancipated Negroes as well as the Creoles (who thought they were better) of equal rights. They put us all together in a racially segregated bag once the Dred Scott decision said none of us with a drop of African blood had any rights a white man had to respect. Why there were riots here in 1900 where masses of Negroes were slaughtered and they imported European immigrants to whiten this town. We got a lot to do to bring equality and justice to New Orleans."

Monday morning, we would go to the universities. We started with Dillard, a historically Black college founded in 1869. Paul Robeson had recently spoken at this lovely campus after refusing to sing to segregated audiences and being barred from singing in Chicago by the House Un-American Activities Committee smear. He had retired from the stage in 1947; his passport was revoked in 1950 and now he was a full-time activist against Jim Crow, headlining left-sponsored rallies for Black voting rights and peace. Posters of that event were still on display in the handsome white colonial columned buildings built by the American Missionary Society, whose abolitionists also established Fisk and other centers to educate emancipated slaves. We walked down a lane with gnarled overarching cottonwood trees to a lovely view of the river; we chatted with some of the students hastening to class across the carefully tended lawn. They didn't have time to talk with us, and faculty members were cordial, but didn't invite us to talk more because we had not made an appointment to speak with anyone.

Dillard was named for a Tulane professor who had dedicated his life to providing libraries and schools for Negroes. Tulane and Loyola were segregated. In Dillard's library were logs and ship documents on the Atlantic slave trade which catalogued its horror, and implicated the North as well as the

South in the carnage. The few examples I had seen at the Seifert library paled beside this assemblage. We learned that until 1654, Blacks were treated much like any indentured servant, able to serve seven years and be free. Chattel slavery, declaring Blacks less than human and making them and their offspring ineligible for release from servitude, was made legal that year. We also read about Black bravery and participation in the Civil War. Over 24,000 Black troops comprised the *Corps Afrique,* playing a crucial role in defeating confederate forces at Fort Jackson, Fort St. Philip and Port Hudson in 1862. We only knew of a small regiment from Boston that was massacred, and soldiers at LaMott, Pennsylvania who were armed near the end of the war.

Reluctantly I tore myself away and we took the short jaunt down Broad Street to Xavier, the Catholic college for Blacks. I had heard about it in Philadelphia because Katherine Drexel, a founder, was heir to a large fortune from a prominent family there. She, and the Sisters of the Blessed Sacrament, had built these attractive green-roofed additions and subsumed some lesser schools to form Xavier in 1925. Xavier offered outstanding science programs producing pharmacists and physicians. The sisters welcomed us and wanted to talk to us about the Supreme Court decision. They didn't feel that it would make much difference to their operation. Possibly there would be some grants to help them extend their work; they were looking forward to that. They let us visit one of the chemistry labs, which was well-equipped and able to offer students hands-on experiments under the supervision of watchful teaching assistants. We spoke with a young pre-med student from Ardmore, Pennsylvania, who had come here because she was Catholic and was very pleased with the education she was getting. She enjoyed being able to do everything, and not feel restricted or be denied entry into certain student activities because of her color as she had experienced in that Philadelphia main line suburb.

We strolled down Magazine Street and had a light lunch at the Café du Monde. There were buskers on every corner, but the attraction here was the artwork leaning against the buildings. Eve had her portrait done by a skilled charcoal artist, while the rest of us bought some postcards and admired the clothing, baskets, pottery, posters and statuary in the street stalls along the way. I wanted to go to the mysterious bayous, see some of the eerie-named islands: Cat, Bull's or Devil's, but that would require waterway travel constrained by time and money.

We were pretty tired when we got back, so Lou and I decided that we weren't going to the clubs that night. We wanted to get one more good night's sleep in a real bed before the next leg of our journey, when I was to drive. Eve and Theta said, "No way, we didn't come to New Orleans to miss the music on Basin Street." So, they rested for a few hours and after a dinner of pecan-battered catfish, took off to the famous street and partied until the wee hours.

Now on to Texas; we were eight hours away from San Antonio, and it was my turn to drive in daylight, but it was raining and I chickened out. I didn't trust myself behind the wheel on a strange road that might be slippery. So, a tired Eve got in the driver's seat and we made our way on Route I-10W. The windows were foggy, but I could make out the towns and calculate with our maps how far we had to go. After about two hours, to my surprise, I saw a sign way down the road that said Austin. Maybe she was bleary-eyed from fatigue, but Eve had entered the wrong lane at the Houston juncture, where there was a lot of road construction, and instead of continuing on Route I-10W, we were sidetracked to Tx-71W, which landed us in Austin, two and a half hours off our route. Austin is the home of the University of Texas and was known to be slightly more egalitarian than elsewhere. It was afternoon, still raining, but Eve could drive no further, so she pulled over in what seemed like a safe neighborhood. She would sleep in the car on the side of the road. Theta would join her, as she hadn't slept either.

Lou and I got out in the slackening rain and walked around a bit; there were department stores nearby with names with which we weren't familiar. We decided to take a peek in Robertson's, a store we didn't see up North; what restrictions would prevail as we looked over the merchandise?

There was a uniformed Black attendant waiting to open the doors of cars that drove up and to offer umbrellas to the white ladies so not a drop of rain would hit them as they alighted from their limousines. He didn't open the store door for us, but we stepped inside what looked like Lit's or Snellenburg's in Pennsylvania, not Gimbel's or Macy's in New York. There were some small racks of clothing overseen by salesgirls and a manager in a boutonniere standing by the door to guide us as soon as we entered. The manager approached quickly, rather apologetically saying that there was another entrance for pedestrians, this one was for automobiles, but it was OK that we came, and asked what items we were seeking. I spoke up immediately, saying, "We were hoping to see the latest hats, what women are wearing in Austin." Hats were displayed just across the floor, and we could tell immediately whether this college town was liberated, since it was only recently in Philadelphia that Negroes could try on hats. The manager said politely, "Right over there, ladies, have a look."

Two salesgirls were talking when we arrived, and I picked up a flowery number on a flexible band. One of the women rushed over, gently removing the hat from my hand and holding the hat up high, saying, "This is the latest thing from New York, flowers on flexible bands with short veils. We can make them up, using just the flowers you like, with shorter or longer veils. Just as you please." Seeing she was tactfully preventing us from trying on the hat, Lou went into her most supercilious putdown: "Ah, we don't want the latest thing from New York, we've got plenty of those, that's where we are from. We want to see what they're wearing in Texas." The other salesgirl joined us. "Then this is not your department; you should go to the Stetson shop where they have the 10-gallon hats that are typical for this area," she laughed. "Aren't they just for men, or do they make them for women too?" Lou asked. "Oh, yes, they are made to order, they measure you individually so you get a perfect fit." "Do they let you try the hats on there," I asked, "or will we be prohibited from trying them on as we are here?" The salesgirl reddened and put the hat she was waving in the air back on the counter-head mannequin. "We do have some restrictions as to who can try on the hats. Our regular customers whose hair is not greasy would have free range, but you can understand that your hair is oily and might soil the merchandise." "We understand that this college town that we thought was enlightened is still suffering from Jim Crow ignorance," Lou said, as we turned to walk out.

We would not go to look at authentic Texas Stetsons. First, we had made our point, and secondly, we knew our budgets and the need to have money for accommodations when we got to San Antonio.

It was starting to rain again; we rushed back to the car, and let the windows down ever so slightly as the rain was now coming down in buckets. I didn't sleep, but kept an eye out for anybody coming near the car. Surprisingly no one did. Cars whizzed by, splashing water on our doors; a police car obviously on a mission flew by with siren and flashing lights, but no one stopped during the two hours or so that we were parked there to even ask if we were having trouble. The rain stopped, and since Eve was still drowsy, I drove the 80 miles down Route I-35 to San Antonio.

We found a place to stay in San Antonio with a Spanish tile roof that was run by Mexicans and cheap. They were light-complexioned, spoke fluent English, and welcomed us with hospitality and no sign of racism. These "motels" were springing up where you could drive your car and park it at the door in front of your room. We got one room with two beds and the four of us slept two to a bed there. The proximity affected us: we were beginning to get on each other's nerves. Lou was a neat freak; she brought a bottle of Lysol with her, and wiped down the toilet before she would use it. She checked the bed for bedbugs and the whole place for roaches and set standards for eating and leaving food around that annoyed Theta, especially.

Moreover, it was becoming obvious that Lou and I were not as "hip" as Eve and Theta thought they were. Theta talked like a real swinging gal, declaiming her experience with men, her depth at knowledge gained as she made her way around Manhattan and Brooklyn, citing the clubs she had visited and the company she had kept. Her appearance belied this glamour; she was tall and gawky, not the least bit shapely, and her wardrobe was not the kind you would expect to see on the sophisticated lady she claimed herself to be. Citing their "fabulous" night on Basin Street, she made it known that we were not going to cramp her style, that she was going to party every place we went, if she got the opportunity, and squares who didn't want to could stay behind and be drags. I said I expect to thoroughly enjoy myself too, but we wouldn't have to go in lock-step everyplace, because it was obvious that our tastes were not identical, and what I enjoy, she might find abhorrent. So, we agreed that we could go our separate ways, but settle on a time and place to meet every day.

How different the country was – the soil was yellow and dusty especially where they were developing a park and restoring a monument, the Alamo, one of seven missions that Father Antonio Oliveras build in the early 18th century. It was to become a National Heritage site. Texans wanted the symbol of their hero Davy Crockett's bravery against the Mexican Santa Anna to have a more attractive setting and moved it near the river. We learned that Davy Crockett, a frontiersman and politician from Tennessee, was in Texas as a volunteer, and had been promised a large tract of land if he would fight against Santa Anna. He arrived in 1835 and was killed March 6, 1836 by Santa Anna's troops. His body was burned and buried in an unmarked grave. There are several versions of how he died, myths and exaggerations of his bravery, but the slogan, "Remember the Alamo" was a rallying cry for Sam Houston and the troops that defeated Santa Anna at Fort Jacinto when Texas became a part of the United States. The docent at the temporary museum beamed with pride as she told this story, and we tried to be enthusiastic, but it reflected none of our history, and had been so distorted in film that we wondered about its authenticity.

The San Antonio River, called Yanaguana by the native Americans and Spanish, meant beautiful waters and was being turned into The Riverwalk, as a site for recreation. It was bordered by lovely cypress trees. We walked along its banks and rested on the benches. Even while it was being redesigned there were row boats navigating the wooded stream and food vendors offering corn tortillas filled with meat, cheese and lettuce. We leisurely enjoyed the scenery and even Lou ate the street food.

We hadn't planned to but we would spend two days here, as we were having engine trouble. The garage mechanic said he would have to order the part, the alternator, which would arrive overnight from Houston. We decided we would visit several Missions, built like fortresses of heavy stone with latticed walkways and rough-hewn log cabinetry. The guide told stories steeped in cowboy lore about the Chisolm Trail that wound through San Antonio as men made their way herding cattle from the Gulf of Mexico to Kansas. We found that many of the "cow boys" had been Black; a fact that you would never get from the Saturday matinees we watched as children. We relaxed, sitting by the river, listening to mariachi bands, watching flamenco dancers and eating inexpensive Tex/Mex food. I practiced my Spanish on children or their mothers, if I could strike up a conversation with them.

We spent a day trying to learn about life in the City and its small population of Black people: about seven percent. We asked the hotel manager if there was a Negro community in the area, since we hadn't seen any of our people so far. We had seen some pretty dark-complexioned Mexicans, however. He was reluctant to talk about it, as living conditions for both groups were not great in San Antonio, but he pointed out on the map where a sizeable group of Negroes lived. To fulfill our purpose, we had to find those Negroes and inquire about their experience of the Supreme Court decision. With care, we could drive our car in its impaired condition, so off we went, map in hand, and found that the area complied with our usual formula: near the tracks, an undesirable lowland location, close to the industrial section. However, locating Blacks was not going to be easy, because poor children of Mexican descent played in the dust around the slum-area shacks too. What we finally discovered was pretty well integrated in its deprived state.

We found a Baptist church, and from a congenial man tidying up the grounds, we learned that most impoverished Blacks and "wetbacks" picked vegetables on large farms together. There was definite class distinction, as Mexicans used to own this place, and the upper class maintained their property and ran the businesses. This group had pretty much crossed over into the "white" community. One or two mestizo or mulatto families had slipped through the cracks and their descendants were the professionals among the Blacks. He didn't know of any activity around integrating schools, but the NAACP had been trying to get use of public accommodations like municipal parks. As a matter of fact, they just closed the swimming pools supposedly for cleaning because a couple of Negro kids went swimming in the pool restricted for whites. Schools around here are strictly segregated, and, he jokingly guffawed, "Just like Emancipation that happened in January, but it was Juneteenth before Texans found out about it."

Our Mexican hosts gave us some advice about crossing the border; it wasn't necessary to have passports, though each of us had one; there weren't many restrictions about what you could take across the border, but you couldn't bring much back. We could cross at Nuevo Laredo, about two hours straight down Route I-35. He suggested that we stay in Monterrey, a small town where his brother had a hotel, to prepare ourselves for the mountainous trip to Mexico City. That jaunt, while picturesque, wasn't going to be easy. Eve said that part of the excitement of coming down here would be the thrill of driving through the Sierra Madres. I was wary of high places, would not even consider driving around mountain curves, but I had signed on to the adventure and that meant both pleasure and peril. I practiced my Spanish on the proprietor, who was very pleasant and helpful; he said I had a pretty good accent, and that it would improve when I had to use it regularly.

We spent as little time as possible in our crowded room with two women per bed. We were looking forward to Friday when the mechanic said the car would be ready, and had our clothes, some food and water ready for our departure. He delivered the car around noon, washed, gassed up and purring. I took the wheel. I would drive the last 155 miles on I-35S in the U.S. and let Eve take over in Mexico. I wouldn't trust myself there. The hotel manager assured us that the road down to Nuevo Laredo was in good condition. Once on the highway, I saw only two-lanes and dirt shoulders. I was always being honked at since I was not a fast driver and Texans didn't like to waste time on the highway. For miles there was barbed wire fencing to restrict animals and keep interlopers from the crops, not much more in the way of scenery. You hardly saw a house, but intermittently there would be a shack that sold tobacco, groceries and gas.

As we neared the border, traffic slowed down; we were near the checkpoint. We drove in and uniformed U.S. agents approached us, asking for credentials. We went into the building, got visas for two weeks in Mexico, filled the gas tank, purchased some food and used the facilities, which were clean and not segregated. The Rio Grande was not as grand as I thought it would be – a narrow stream, gray and sluggish, suffering from irrigation activity upriver. Within an hour, we were across. We were just waived on at the Mexican side, they didn't ask our business, check our visas or ask how long we planned to stay. With Eve at the wheel we rolled down the 195 miles on a road marked US-83S to Nuevo Ciudad Guerrero. There it turned slightly west to become Mexico 54 on the three and a half-hour drive to Monterrey. We passed two lakes and attractive villages on this leg of the journey.

I assessed my driving so far. I did very well on the road from San Antonio. I had lost my fear of strange roads; could gauge my speed depending on the condition of the macadam, was careful to note the width of the road and whether there was a shoulder. I snoozed and began to reminisce about another day when I felt competent about my driving for the very first time:

◆ ◆ ◆

The Surrender

I was feeling jubilant about my driving. I had taken lessons with my father in his green '50 Plymouth with a stick shift. He always bought a used car – "It takes me and brings me," he would say, "and there is no need to pay a premium just for having something brand new." We had practiced in Crestmont, beyond the Mason Dixon line – a row of pine trees designed to grow tall and bushy to make sure that the new residents in cottages built after World War II for white veterans – like a mini Levittown – would not have to see the section beyond the paved roads where the Black people lived. Our house was on one of the dirt roads, bought by my grandmother in 1908; bottom land, near the brick mill, where the mini Levittown now was full of white recipients of the GI Bill. My brother-in-law, a decorated veteran of D-Day, had sought a house as soon as he learned of their construction, but was denied, because "all houses were spoken for." The roads were paved, with gentle hills and curves on streets named after famous generals and there were sidewalks, but few cars, so it was an ideal practice space.

At first, I was reluctant to take lessons with my father – he had never instructed me in anything that required me to sit next to him and take his advice. He sat in his bay window study area learning his schemes to throw mail at the Post Office, as we marched up to his room one by one to show our report cards. He was interested in results; if your grades were low, he would growl "stupid" at you, with no offer of assistance, or acknowledgement of the anxiety-filled atmosphere in which we were required to do our homework. But this was a retired man, more relaxed, I thought, and maybe just a little remorseful that he had never spent much time doing pleasant projects like teaching his daughter to drive. He seemed to relish the opportunity, was extremely patient, spoke softly at mistakes, when I had only known his wrath at the slightest error. I had gotten my learner's permit in New York, because my boyfriend felt that the modern woman should know how to drive. I was shocked at that too. He liked so much being in control of everything, having me wait until he came to pick me up, depending on him to take me places like shopping or on a drive to some lovely section in the suburbs that he wanted me to see.

This day, all the tender thoughts came back to me – my father's unexpected kindness, and now that I was a licensed driver, my boyfriend's trusting me enough to lend me his car for the day. The feeling of competence that comes with driving in city and suburb, parking, being able to navigate the highways and the narrow lanes without a scratch. I remembered the first Black woman I had ever seen own her own car. She was my second-grade teacher. It was a beige Chevrolet with a tire in its own steel case on the back. I would stand in the schoolyard just to watch her alight from that car, impeccably dressed, with gloves yet, and a fashionable cloche revealing just a tad of her Marcelled hairdo. She would stride past us as we said in unison, "Good morning, Miss Johnson," and she'd say her "Hellos" in her cultured English, reinforcing my resolve to be like that.

I had driven to Westchester to shop. Up the Bronx River Parkway to White Plains, taking the curves easily, parking between two cars to watch the swans, admiring the flowering tree branches hanging over the water and revealing, as if from behind a curtain, the elegant homes beyond.

The plan was that I should pick Boyfriend up from the small hotel in which he had bought an interest. He used to work there as a clerk when he first came to New York, and this day he had to go over some accounts with his partner. He would be finished by 6 o'clock. I would wait up on the overhang across the street from the hotel and we would go out for dinner. I arrived at dusk, when the lights were just twinkling on in the apartment houses below. The air was crisp with the scent of spring as the pear and cherry blossoms were just bursting into bloom and tiny, lime-green leaves were budding. I parked in a slightly secluded spot (where we had smooched before) underneath a particularly beautiful cherry, old and gnarled, its branches soon to be heavy with pink clusters; surely too soon they would prune it. I got out of the car and walked to the wall to look down at the scene below.

The sky was darkening; there was laughter floating on the air, and people seemed to reflect my happiness as they passed. He was late, but for some reason I didn't mind it at all, so full was I of the warmth and well-being I had experienced that day.

He walked up behind me as I was bending over the wall, rubbing his genitalia slightly against my derriere. It was electrifying! I suppose I reddened under my brown complexion as blood rushed to my face. I turned and he kissed me squarely on the mouth. I fell into his arms with such passionate surrender that he and I were amazed and both of us laughed. What had we discovered in that moment? I who had protected my virginity so steadfastly, so afraid was I of getting pregnant; since we started dating, I had hardly allowed anything but the most restricted petting, although lately I had been dying for more. This day I seemed to be throwing caution to the wind, allowing him to run his hands around my waist and drop them to grasp the cheeks of my bottom. He continued to kiss my neck and eyes, as I leaned against the stones; I felt the pressure of his body, the perspiration from his cheeks, and the urgency of his touch. He put his hands under my blouse, and gently squeezed each breast, pinching the nipples. He said, "Let's sit in the back of the car for a while," as we were both out of breath, and I don't think he could have driven anywhere, so large had he grown in those few minutes.

I acquiesced, fairly falling on the seat, not saying a word of reprimand, returning every caress, stroking his head, loosening his tie, unbuttoning his collar and kissing his throat. The world faded away; where were we? Neither of us seemed to care. Deftly he lifted my skirt and did away with the underwear somehow. In a flash he was inside me, but just barely, as the hymen barred his entry. I felt the probing for the slight opening, then the tear, and so did he, as it took a powerful thrust to dislodge. I was in the most exquisite pain, moaning as he muffled my voice with his lips. Instinctively I rose my hips to meet his, for several minutes, I rolled from side to side in ecstasy, then rested. I felt I would burst as every nerve seemed to be ready to explode. He continued his gentle probing, as my face was buried in his shoulder. I was holding onto him for dear life when a warm wonderful stream soothed and seemed to run through me. I uttered a deep breathy anguished cry, and heard a loud knocking. It was, I imagined, the pounding as my brain sought equilibrium. My boyfriend was in a daze too, but he gained his composure before I did. There was a man at the window; his voice finally becoming audible, saying something like he was a plainclothes policeman. I remained in the back of the car, while my boyfriend rearranged himself, got out and paid off the badge-less intruder.

I opened my eyes wide as if to ask, what in the world just happened? Suddenly, I was silently crying, my shoulders shaking, as I tried to gather my lingerie and cleanse my sticky dress. He was driving and turning to ask, "Are you OK?" and praising me with words like, "You were wonderful, I believe I have known a woman in love," and "Do you know I love you?" I wasn't responding, still rather euphoric, but conflicted as the fear of pregnancy returned.

When we reached my apartment house, he got out, pushed his seat forward and got in the back, moving onto the seat beside me. "Baby, I'm so sorry it had to happen this way;

will you forgive me? I guess I was just afraid that if not now, when?" he said, lifting my chin and rubbing a slight stubble against my face. I sighed, "Please, no more, I am a mess, and you need to get home to change." He said, "I have to have one more kiss. I can't believe I was the first guy, all those cats you used to hang with; I remember that swimming instructor who was crazy about you, and you saved it for me." He was smothering me with kisses again, and this time, I was pushing him away. I tried to reach across the front seat to the passenger side door, ready to bolt to the apartment entry, forgetting my packages in the trunk. It was dark, but I pleaded with him to open the door and gather my purchases for me so I could place them in front of me to hide my sloppy, soiled clothing from my neighbors'gaze as they exited the building.

♦ ♦ ♦

Monterrey and the Metropolis

We got lost following our San Antonio maître d's directions, once we got into the city, so it was early evening when we reached the Monterrey Royale Hotel. We wanted to be in our rooms before dark. The hotel was a quaint white Spanish style building; pillars and balconies were on the façade. It faced a lovely square with a fountain and garden and we learned that we were in walking distance from the National Park of Monterrey. The area looked upscale, clean tree lined streets and mansions; but they had high walls around them, with gates and ornate iron bars to prevent intruders. It seemed that this must be a dangerous place. Even on Fifth Avenue, shops had no bars, and there were few gated communities in the States. We discussed the propriety of our stopping at such a town, but were won over by the simple people hurrying home along the *avenidos* – colorfully dirndl-skirted women in straw hats carrying baskets, closely followed by little children who gamboled along unafraid.

We entered the hotel and the proprietor came forward; he knew about us and was prepared to make sure we enjoyed our stay in Monterrey. He showed us to lovely front

rooms with high wrought-iron beds, facing that pleasant plaza. Each of us would have her own room! It was charming,
and we decided to stay at least two days while we prepared
for our Sierra Madre crossing. Tension seemed to leave us as
we were being accepted in a way that we would not generally
experience at hotels in the States. We were the paying guests
whose money was worthy of the finest accommodations and
the graciousness of our hosts. The proprietor told us that the
area was perfectly safe, that we could walk around without
fear; they hadn't had a robbery or murder here in his memory,
and he was born here. So, we could relax. He showed us
a map of the city, where we could find the post office, the
Catholic Church and the city offices. We washed up and
came down for a delightful meal in a dining room with hammered metal light fixtures, colorful tablecloths and ceramic
dishes. The meal was family-style; we ate what was prepared
from heaping bowls or platters of beans and rice, tortillas,
grilled chicken, salad and a local beer; all very delicious. We
marveled at the cost for each of us: five U.S. dollars per day
included everything.

The proprietor sat down next to our table to talk with us.
He told us we should get some money changed at the bank
on Monday. We would need pesos in Mexico City. He also
said that we should leave our car in Monterrey and take the
train to Mexico City; he did not advise four women driving
through the Sierras at night; it's 562 miles, an 11-hour drive,
the road was not well-marked, and the curves treacherous.
Eve was not convinced, but I agreed with him. I shelved my

concern, practiced my Spanish with him and studied phras-
es and vocabulary. He helped us with the pronunciation of
places on the map, suggested some foods we might like, and
circled places that we must see.

Tomorrow was Sunday; he suggested we go out to the
Plaza after dinner, to see the handsome young men and
pretty girls as they did their promenade around it. After a
good night's sleep and a relaxing day, we ventured out to
meet the populace at the square. We found it delightful: The
older men, arguing animatedly off to the side, paused to greet
us with a courteous nod as we found a bench. Musicians in
black trousers and white ruffled shirts played mariachi tunes;
the matrons sat fanning and chatting as they watched their
daughters smiling modestly as they walked around the square
holding hands with suitors. It was right out of a picture book
and not staged for tourists, as we were the only ones there;
they completely accepted us as part of the crowd.

Monday morning, I rose early when the roosters crowed;
the group would find our way to the "business section," go the
bank to get some pesos and I would practice my Spanish everywhere. I ate quickly and walked outside. I was attracted to
a high wall with an opened wooden gate and decided to walk
through it.   It seemed that the wall separated the peons from
the elites. There were bare-bottomed children, scruffy dogs
running about, women washing clothes or tending chickens
and small animals and men in huaraches hoeing in the gardens. It was as if I had stepped into another world. The adults
looked up; then went about their work ignoring me. I tried to

speak to the children, but they scurried off, my Spanish probably unintelligible to them. It was then that I saw the flowers. I had seen zinnias before in the states but they were small and usually a dull purple color, and my mother didn't grow them. These were huge, standing boldly in masses of gold, crimson, fuchsia, and white against the house and in rows in the garden. I went up to a woman and in my halting Spanish said, "*Buenos dias.*" She nodded and smiled, so I asked, "*Cuanto estas las flores?*" She shrugged and said, "*Dos pesos.*" I didn't have any pesos, so I gave her two U.S. quarters. She overwhelmed me preparing to cut a heaping bouquet which, I protested by shaking my head was "*Muchos grande.*"

Feeling confident now that I had actually talked with ordinary Mexicans, I decided to take another route; I strolled through a different gate that brought me to a street with adobe walled houses. I prided myself on my navigation skills as I found my way back to the hotel. The minute they saw me, I was nagged by my friends about the flowers: what did I need them for, since we would be leaving today. I would take them with me and put them in our hotel in Mexico City. My companions were annoyed that I had wandered off, admonishing me to stay with the group; I complied as we made our way with the map to town to get money changed and, I was relieved to learn, buy our train tickets. The proprietor had persuaded Eve that she should not drive to Mexico City.

We had to rearrange our suitcases, leaving behind the blankets and pillows, but taking some sweaters, since the proprietor said it got quite chilly at night in the high city and its environs. He told us to be sure to visit the pyramids, and go to a charming town called Cuernavaca so we could see old Mexican haciendas and the silver mines. He helped us store the car, suggested some hotels where he knew the managers, and in late afternoon, went with us to the Ferrocarriles Nacionales de Mexico train station to see us off. I was toting my flowers, wrapped in cellophane and wet towels, along with my suitcases.

Immediately upon boarding we met three young American college boys on their way to study for a second year at the University of Mexico. At first, we merely smiled and told them our destination, but within a short time they were back, immersing us in conversation. They were from Colorado and wanted to know more about these sophisticated women from New York. They were amusing, telling us about their exploits, how they did a lot of skiing at home and had to adapt to this warmer climate. Their parents wanted them to be fluent in Spanish, as businesses all over the Southwest and thereabouts were becoming bilingual; they were studying anthropology as well as engineering and the arts. Their knowledge of jazz was limited, but they were anxious to learn more – were wild about Duke Ellington, had we ever seen him, did we ever go to the Savoy, had we been to the Cotton Club? Of course, we hadn't been to the Cotton Club; that was before our time, and furthermore if you were Negro you couldn't go there as a patron and only "high yellow" gals were able to dance in the chorus line, and even they had to come in the back door.

We didn't say all that, as these guys seemed not to have noticed that we were Negro. We were just young women, older than they, but fascinating. We had seen and heard Duke Ellington and Count Basie. I sang Sarah Vaughn songs like *I'm Walking by the River* in my sultriest, deepest voice, and I must say not doing too badly at reaching her highest highs. They were fascinated to know that we had been to 52nd Street, making the scene to hear Charlie Parker and Miles Davis. We hummed instrumental music like Dave Brubeck's *Early Autumn*, and philosophized about its importance. They made the ride down such fun. They brought us food and pointed out picturesque towns when the train stopped at the mile-high city, Saltillo, or we passed San Luis Potosi and Santiago de Queretaro, until darkness blotted out the mountains and valleys. They told us to steady ourselves as we walked the aisles and the altitude rose to more than 5,000 feet above sea level. They showed us maps of Mexico City and offered to squire us around to all the best places as soon as they got settled at school. I said that I wanted to go to El Salon Mexico, the place where Aaron Copland had composed the music that I adored, and to see the Diego Rivera murals. My companions shrugged, what did I know about that? It sounded so pretentious to them. But the guys accepted the charge: Sure, they would take us, we would enjoy it, and the Diego murals were a "must see." They said that the hotel where we planned to stay was pleasant and reasonable. We could eat their food, but maybe we should avoid Mexican street food initially until our stomachs got used to the water and we learned our way around. There was a place called Sanborn's where we could eat American style with a bit of Mexican thrown in.

The hotel was a collection of small, fine old houses that looked authentically colonial; it was family-owned, and the owner, like our Monterrey host, was welcoming, calling the bellboys to carry our suitcases and helping us settle in. Breakfast was on the house, but you were charged extra for the modest, but delicious, dinners. Our room had twin beds with chenille bedspreads, and windows covered with lace curtains.

My flowers were a welcomed addition. We were pleased that we were in the heart of town, within walking distance of a town center, and surrounded by pleasant houses where seemingly nice people lived. We were not near the railroad tracks, the slums, or the dangerous section. It was apparent that our hosts regarded us as intelligent young women on an adventure, and treated us with respect. It was Tuesday afternoon, so we would get a good night's sleep tonight and begin our tours on Wednesday. Immediately we began to plan what we would see and how we would spend our money. Me especially, as there were 17 days to go, and I was figuring how much I could spend each day before we got home or to Washington, D.C. If I set aside $50 for gifts and $25 for emergencies, it would be about $10 a day. I squirmed as I would certainly want to buy some souvenirs for my mother. I remembered the embroidered sheer blouses and obsidian and jade jewelry my brother had sent us when he was stationed at Fort Huachuca during the war. I had worn mine until the blouse was in tatters. I still had the silver bracelets and a dogwood-shaped ring. This budget would take judicious management.

One thing was certain: I would have to depend on Eve, who had the car and the cash. She didn't ask the rest of us for anything as she paid for storing the car and the room down payments at the hotels; she seemed to understand that we were traveling on a shoestring to say the least, and considered this her adventure, for which she appreciated having us along. I gingerly mentioned going to Morelia to see the artist EL was sponsoring. Eve had no interest in that and when we looked at the map and considered our other activities, the consensus was that seeing the sights around Mexico City and going to Cuernavaca would be all we could do.

I telephoned EF who immediately knew who I was as EL had written him about our coming. He and his wife, who was Mexican, were looking forward to it. We would get a taste of how rural Mexicans lived if we came. He was ebullient describing the country: "This is near where the monarch butterflies come," he said. "The mountains are lovely; I thoroughly enjoy living here." There was no feeling of difference; he said he experienced complete acceptance, and felt free to paint and express himself artistically. He had come to study under the great Diego, and had found happiness too. He asked if we had seen any of the murals or visited the museums. He emphasized that we should be sure to, however, the community was still in mourning over the recent death of Diego's wife, Frida Kahlo. As women, we would want to see her work.

I knew very little of Frida, but promised I would search her out. I thanked him for the kind invitation and advice, and apologized profusely because time would not permit a visit.

We began our walking tour using the book I had brought and the maps marked by the hotel manager. We headed for the National Palace to see the Diego murals. It was to be quite a walk from our hotel, but eventful. We came upon the Zocalo, or town square, especially large and treeless, circled by a road, making crossing dangerous. There were people gathered around a massive flag pole, shouting in Spanish, heckling a speaker. I wanted to stop for a while and try to understand the Spanish and get an inkling of what politics were the topic of street oration. Lou and the others emphatically said, "No."

Dominating the square was the Catedral Metropolitana. We learned it took 240 years to construct and was now sinking into the spongy soil on which Mexico City was built. Everything would be a little off balance here. We decided not to stay long, but we covered our heads and entered the sacred place, lit only by slivers of sunlight and candles burning at the crypt dedicated to the Virgin Mary. Devout women in headscarves knelt and prayed, mumbling in Spanish as they fingered their rosaries. We moved about silently around the pews admiring the folk-art statuary, the gilded altar and the Christ, not in the image of the Medici patrons of Leonardo da Vinci, but a shade or so darker, with black hair and Aztec noses. We walked out of the Zocalo and passed the ruins of the Templo Mayor where we paused briefly and posed for photos.

Then we went down the Pino Suarez to the National Palace built by Cortes on the site of Moctezuma's palace, which he destroyed. After Diego returned from studying in Italy, he spent 20 years painting 1,200 feet of murals on the second floor, channeling Michelangelo. I held my breath as I beheld them: the heavily mustachioed peasants in white baggy trousers with Viva Zapata signs, the women with large dark eyes, the fact that there were so many people whose skin was dark chocolate; the vegetation and exotic fruits and flowers, dark-skinned, lighter-skinned and white men clasping hands in solidarity. Our guide said the painting, entitled "Epic of the Mexican People in Their Struggle for Freedom and Independence," idealized the peasant. Prehistoric times were portrayed as innocent, except the selling of an arm alluding to the Aztecs' gruesome practice of human sacrifice and cult of death. But the savagery of the conquistadores was depicted in detail. Karl Marx was there as the working class struggled against the bourgeois. I could have spent the day studying the implications of Diego's vision, what it meant, and why each figure was placed where. But my companions soon had enough; I reluctantly followed them to the exit, bought some post cards and departed.

We decided to have some lunch at Sanborn's, the safe eating place. I feared it would be as bland as Horn and Hardart's without the nickel slots. We took a taxi there, since it was in the oldest part of town in a refurbished mansion called the House of Tiles. The door was adorned with ornate carvings and the facade covered in blue and white tiles. Sunlight was streaming through the glass patio, illuminating a mural by Orozco on the wall beside the staircase. I walked to it immediately and studied it, writing its location down in my notebook. The food was decidedly Mexican. The menu was in English and Spanish, so I didn't have to use my dictionary. I ordered tortillas filled with a pork mixture which came steaming hot, soft and fresh, along with salsa and cheese. We all drank the signature of the place, strong coffee, and washed it down with the certified pure water.

Outside Sanborn's were small shops filled with tourist fodder. I was interested in the statuary: replicas of sundials with images that looked like horoscopes, plump animals, gods of terra cotta, and female dolls in brightly colored flowered dresses. There was also jewelry in silver with semiprecious stones, or heavy ceramic or glass beads. We tried on some dirndl skirts and considered a striking white embroidered and intricately pleated Mexican wedding dress. But in the end, I settled for two papier-mache bracelets in hot pinks and yellows, saving my money for Taxco silver and waiting until I had seen more Mexican crafts.

We were a pretty weary troupe when we got back to the hotel, but there would be no rest. There was a message for us that our college boys would be by for us at 7 p.m. to go on the town, so please be ready. I took a long bath, washing up as I had done the morning after that night on Sugar Hill, but not feeling the ecstasy that I felt then. All bathed and spruced up, we would iron our meager but prettiest dressy clothes. I had made my own clothing so the material was of good quality that I knew would stand up: a black cotton sheath, with a yellow, white and black bolero; my legs would be bare, and I would wear my Capezio pumps, ancient, but low-heeled and easily packed. I had bought some of the new wrinkle-resistant cotton for these clothes, which was a godsend in the humidity. We made futile attempts to fix our hair, which was "going back," suffering the heat and constant activity. Eve to the rescue again: She knew how to do hair, had brought some instruments – the straightening comb and curlers. She would touch up our edges and make us presentable for our night out.

I stood at the long mirror and beheld myself, and went right back to thinking about that night in Harlem, and the morning after my deflowering:

The Morning After

I suppose there will be no steaming up the windows on the Palisades anymore, now that the seal has been broken. With nostalgia, I thought of all of those nights looking over the Hudson and upper Manhattan, watching the leaves sprout, bloom, turn to gold and fall, and the branches hang heavy with snow. We had a favorite spot, and maybe for old times' sake, he would take me there again.

I am reclining late today; it's Sunday, I'm thinking, and I know he will want to visit his mother and probably he has ideas for another evening like our Friday night event. It seemed I couldn't wash myself enough, everything was so sticky; a hot shower alone couldn't do it. So, I sat for a while in the tub. I knew even the most careful douching would not remove those little tadpoles that were well on their way to ground zero, if the time was right to make contact. I know how to count on my fingers: When was the last ovulation period, how many days from my very regular period? It was a safe time, according to my calculations.

I must say, I felt like I was on cloud nine, stretchy and yawning a lot. I don't know when I've had such a restful sleep, once he got off the phone -- all the questions, such concerns that he was too rushed, all the apologies for where it happened, for being too rough and the pleas for another chance to make it all up to me.

I had practiced the previous day, Saturday, how I would forestall him, since I had many chores to do. But luckily, he had to go to Baltimore to prepare for a shipment on Monday. There's the phone: It is he. "Did you sleep well, darling?" he asked. "I haven't slept for two days thinking of you, thinking that I was the first guy, I still can't believe it. Why, I remember you and your friends going on a weekend in the mountains with some of the horniest guys on the campus, and you're telling me you survived that?" "Please, I'm not telling you anything, or asking you anything about your previous seductions," I said. "I know the girl you were with for several years, and I'm not inquiring, but just kinda curious, was she the one who taught you to be so deft with lingerie removal?" "I'm not claiming to be a virgin, but I am delighted that you saved it for me, or did you, tell me that you were overcome by something special Friday night? You were so warm, surrendering so beautifully, I can't wait to see you today. We do have a date, don't we?" he asked. "Yes, I suppose your mother will be expecting us, about two this afternoon?" "I could come early and come up to your room, and we could...." "No, we couldn't, I don't entertain here. It's only a room and bath, in a large apartment, and my landlady would be full of questions about you that I don't feel up to answering," I countered.

"You've got to understand that I am crazy about you, got it? I don't think you believe it, but I am aching to see you and hold you again," he said. "Tomorrow is a work day, when you have some important decisions to make," I said, "and I have some books to proofread, and I need to be alert; evenings with you lately are not conducive to work preparation." "We'll just have to cut the time with Mom short. I want to see her, and want her to see you as a full-blown woman who has experienced a full-blooded man, not as a shrinking violet virgin." "You are amazing. I don't think you can call me a shrinking violet, and I checked the mirror, I don't look any different." "Oh, but you are different, and as if you didn't have enough, I am ready to make a genuinely beautiful woman out of you. Tell me, what was it like for you to open yourself and accept a living being inside you?" "Oh, please, it's 10:30 already. What time will you be here?" "I'd say 12 o'clock, I'm dressed already," he said. "Would you consider stopping by to see my apartment after we leave Queens? It's really not far, and I could get you home no later than 10 tonight." "You've got it all figured out; this is the first time I will have visited your abode, is there something special happening there tonight?" "It's not because you haven't been invited many times before, but I think it's about time you saw how I live, and we get a deeper understanding of each other," he responded.

It is absolutely crazy how aroused I am by this conversation. I can feel him inside me, I am almost pulsating at the thought of another encounter. "I won't be ready until one, and I will meet you at the front entrance." "Oh, come on, what have you got to do that's going to take you that long, you're cutting our time together short. You know how my mother is; she has no conception of time, especially when it's the one day I spend a few hours with her. I'm going to be positively jumpy, you know I am, thinking about us." "My final time … I have things to do, and you have to drive sensibly here from Brooklyn." "OK, it will give me time to spruce up the place for you … you are coming, aren't you?" "I'll be waiting outside your apartment at 1 o'clock." Without answering that query, I said in my sexiest voice, "And don't be late."

He wasn't, he was waiting when I emerged from the apartment building, smiling, opening the door, kissing me before he let me slide in. "You look divine," he said. "Is this one of your creations?" "Yep, my landlady helps, she was a Ladies' Garment Union Worker and knows all the tricks of the trade." "Gorgeous, darling, sexy, beautiful, intelligent and talented too, what a prize I've got." "Oh man, you are just extravagant with your praise these days, do ya mean it?" "How can you doubt it, you know the song, '*There's nothing in this world I wouldn't do, for you, for you-ooo,*" he crooned as he started the car. "Thank you for the music, but could we have the radio?" One thing he certainly wasn't was a singer; I had only heard him once before that evening at the Savoy. He always complained about my taste in music, especially my love for Harry Belafonte. "That bare-chested crooner, sitting on that stool, and I pay while you swoon over him," he would grumble at our Sundays at the Village Gate. I don't think he has any interest in going to the Village Gate or anywhere else to entertain me today; he thinks he's got all I need.

It was pleasant chatter all the way, with lots of innuendo and allusions to all manner of sexual behavior, even some corny jokes; lots of testimony about how he felt about me and for how long, and the other guys he saw me with before I finally went out with him. He was feeling pretty confident that we had sealed our relationship with the kisses and more on that backseat Friday night, and he was not wasting any time to bring our relationship to the new stage.

It is not how I thought the man who deflowered me would behave. In fact, I was wondering if he would be interested in me the morning after, so imbued had I been with the idea of chastity until marriage, ingrained into my skull by my mother from day one, and reinforced by my fear of retribution on her from an enraged father once he learned that I had broken the rules. Indeed, I can say I felt liberated, my banter with him was casual and lighthearted, he was laughing at my chatter, and I at his. Anything he said was worth a giggle. We had so many evenings before when we said nothing to each other, when I would shrink from his touch. But ever since last summer, and all through our tumultuous winter, even before the Friday night encounter, I had begun to appreciate him. He had shown me qualities that I wanted to be surrounded by like his sincerity and generosity. I had been allowing and responding to his intimate touches as a kind of prelude. I'd say ever since last summer, I had been softening toward him. I wish it had happened sooner; what a waste of time when all winter, I could have been enjoying this wonderful warmth in the arms of a loving man.

◆ ◆ ◆

El Salon Mexico

The college students came on time, handsome and talkative, full of questions about how we had spent our day. I was gushing about the original Diegos I had seen and Orozco, in the most unlikely places such as restaurant entries, as though these muralists would paint anywhere there was a wall for a canvas. The seven of us piled into a taxi, which fortunately had jump seats, to go to El Salon Mexico. No question, it was not in the exclusive part of town; we passed through narrow streets, down what looked like back alleys, passed vegetable stalls, littered avenues of cobblestone and over rough roads; we passed our first burros and arrived at a building that had seen better days: El Salon Mexico. I could see that my companions were horrified, especially Lou who was practically sitting on one guy's lap in the cab and was glad to emerge. Even the devil-may-care Eve eyed the men in black, silver-adorned suits and sombreros loitering around the entrance with suspicion. Our spritely escorts told us not to worry, that we would savor the real thing here.

We entered to a flutter of Spanish only, spoken fast and loud. The mariachis were playing and women were dancing in their colorful skirts. Immediately the waiter appeared, seated us graciously and took our order for soft drinks – Cokes if they had them or orange juice. We felt we needed our wits about us on this jaunt, and didn't want to be the least bit high.

The guys continued in their chatty mood, asking us about our first day, what we had eaten, what people had we met. We talked with them about their registration and were invited to come to the college the next day. They asked if we had listened to much Mexican music? I said, well, I know a couple of songs in Spanish like *Celito Lindo* and *El Rancho Grande*. In a flash, one of the students asked the band to play the songs, and with him, in my halting Spanish, I began to sing. I was really getting into the spirit of the place, as the crowd joined in. There was so much laughter that we hardly noticed when two of the very tall men in black suits with silver embroidery down the legs, on the sleeves and breast pockets, sent us over a bottle of tequila to drink. We had never heard of the stuff, and would certainly not drink it. Our college boys said it was the national drink of Mexico, and they were sure that this was of good quality, because this brand had a caterpillar in the bottle. We were aghast, especially Lou, who practically threw up at the thought.

He repeated his comment in Spanish to the mariachi standing near, and the joke went around the entire bar, where everyone erupted in laughter. The mariachi told us he was from Guadalajara, where our escorts explained they were probably cowboys or *charros*. He said he would show us how to drink the tequila as a *Marguerita*. He took the glass in hand, put salt on his wrist, took a piece of lime between his thumb and forefinger, licked the salt from his wrist, and in one gulp drank the tequila and squeezed the lime into his mouth. I had to try that, and found it delightful, amid lots of laughter from the group. Soon everyone was drinking *Margueritas*, laughing a little more loudly, singing or humming the Spanish songs. And then, the mariachi threw his sombrero on the floor, lifted me up from my chair, to the shouts of our escorts – "Oh, he's going to teach you the Mexican Hat Dance." I was flabbergasted, but got in the spirit of the thing. I glanced at a couple nearby, and found myself holding my sheath, which was too tight to flounce, but I stamped my feet as I had seen the flamenco do, and did the turns, and touched the hat, humming the tune, with which I was familiar, until I was transported, aglow with the spirit of the place.

Sitting nearby was a tall, slim young man who was observing all this, and I thought he was making sketches. When I finally sat down, all flushed and animated, and Theta, Eve and Lou took their turns with the hat, I noticed that the young man was smiling at me. In my giddiness, I smiled back, and he walked over and asked for a dance. We just two-stepped, without the hat; he immediately began to ask questions about where we were from and what we had seen in Mexico City. I said how much I had enjoyed the Diego murals, and wanted to see more and understand them better. He was delighted, told me he had studied with Diego, that he was still alive, that maybe if we were around for a few days, he could arrange for us to meet him. That would be divine, I said. He escorted me back to our table, and asked our escorts if he could join us.

He said that he was PR, whom the college guys knew about as a local artist. I asked him if he knew EF, whom I falsely intimated was a friend from New York whom we planned to visit. Yes, yes, he knew him as a student and accomplished artist who was doing important illustration. He passed around the sketches, which were of us, but he wouldn't give them to us, as he said they were too rough, and when he had developed them he just might let us have them. He asked us to take a walk down the road to his studio and he would show us some finished stuff. There was not much interest from the rest of the table, as they were awaiting the food they had ordered, but I was intrigued. What does it mean when a guy invites you to his atelier to see his etchings? I knew I was taking a precarious adventure, but the college students assured me that they knew him, and knew that he was an honorable man. PR gave our escorts his address, said he would bring me back in less than an hour, and I walked out of the café with him. After all, EF knew him, too, and he wouldn't harm a friend of a friend!

As we left, he asked if I knew who my hat dancers were. I said the students told us they were from Guadalajara, and were the Mexican cowboys. PR said there are a lot of descendants of African slaves in Guadalajara, who unfortunately don't seem to want to acknowledge their ancestry. But it is obvious, many like those dancers are dark-complexioned and some have tightly curled hair. They recently renamed the city for a hero of the revolution, Yanga, who was a Nigerian prince who fought against the conquistadors and finally won freedom for his people. Diego painted these dark-complexioned

Mexicans, despite the anger of his critics. He was enthralled by Diego and talked about him all the way to his studio, asking if I had I seen any of his work in New York. He talked of the Rockefeller debacle, when they had refused to pay him his full fee for the mural in Rockefeller Center because he had put Lenin in the painting; that there were other Diego murals in the U.S., in Detroit for example, and that worldwide artists were copying the Diego style. I had seen the place where the mural once was, read about the reasons for its destruction, and seen some Diego paintings in the new Museum of Modern Art, but I had no idea that some of the peasants depicted were of African descent. He excitedly explained that many of the people in the mural were descendants of Africans, for which Diego had been much maligned. He was appalled at my ignorance of the fact that there had been African slaves in Mexico, and went to great length to let me know that there were more enslaved Africans brought to South and Meso-America than to North America.

We walked up an outside side staircase to the studio. It was in an old building with bare inlaid hardwood floors and large windows without curtains or shades. There were easels, paint pots and canvases everywhere. It was larger, but a reasonable facsimile of the studio in the film "An American in Paris." He went into the miniscule kitchen and made coffee, brought out some tortillas and began bringing out his paintings for me to see. These paintings, too, prominently displayed dark-complexioned women; their eyes were exaggerated, seemingly staring directly at you. His brush strokes were bold, and obvious, not blended as Diego's, but requiring that you stand back and let your eyes make the colors blend as with Van Gogh and the Impressionists. I could see that he was indeed a talented artist who was working hard at his craft.

He said there was a place in Mexico where the people were very dark, that there were large sculptures of men with large lips and flat noses, with definitely Negroid features that predated the conquistadores and slave trade. He suggested that if I were to stay in Mexico City for a few more days I should travel to Olmec country in the Oaxaca province. I was absolutely entranced by all that I was learning. Clearly, I was swooning over this young attractive man with so much respect for my people that he would make them the central theme of his paintings. He was a fair-complexioned Mexican, the *casta divina*, a descendant of the conquistadores, showing no sign of the Mayan or Aztec nose or heavy jet-black hair. However, he was the kind of guy my father had admonished me to be aware of – the ones who just wanted to experience sex with what they considered easy immoral Negro women. He sat down across from me, took my hands in his and asked me to go to Olmec country with him. He got a map – it was in the South, in the state of Chiapas pretty far away; the heads were there. "If I would see them, it would change my life," he said.

He abhorred the subjugation of the Aztec and Mayan culture, was involved with the communists who wanted to have self-determination for the darker Mexicans, the disenfranchised peons who did the back-breaking work on land that actually belonged to them. He told me to look for Diego's mural at the museum and search for the woman in the red blouse. He brought out a postcard to show me. That was Frida Kahlo, distributing arms. "Oh yes," I said. "EF said I should visit her house; and even though they were still mourning her death, he would write to get me permission to visit." "Excellent, I will do the same, just to be sure, you must go there; she was Diego's wife and a fighter for women's rights and recognition." He talked animatedly about Frida Kahlo, how he had studied under her for a short time, and how her illnesses had made it necessary for her pupils to come to her house for lessons. "She fought for constitutional changes, giving women the right to vote, and next year, women will finally have suffrage; although it won't mean much in the way of who controls things, it is a step forward," he said.

He knew about the Supreme Court decision in the States – he had been to New York, Texas, California and Washington, D.C. "It's a very segregated place," he said, and it was about time that the Negro people began to demand equality. I gasped and stood up: We had certainly been here more than an hour; I had better be getting back. I was fairly reeling at my ignorance, and I thought I was a student of Negro history. He was clearly in the mood for more, suggesting that I come back tomorrow, that he meet me for breakfast or lunch, anything to continue the conversation and connection. He moved toward me to dance and held me close to him, humming one of the café tunes, moving about in a slow two-step, mentioning that he would like to paint my attractive body. He found especially alluring the slim waist and curvaceous bottom. He maneuvered me over to the table where he had dropped a sketch he had made at the café but not shown us. It was of me with one curvaceous line from the head to the feet, over-emphasizing a large derriere. I was not flattered, and recoiled as I felt his admiration was moving from the artistic to the salacious.

I stood aside and crossed my arms and said that we really must be going. He smiled, and said he had something he wanted to give me. It was a painting of one of his large-eyed, dark- complexioned girls with bangs made with the wide brush strokes, probably an early work. I said I would treasure the painting, which embodied so much that I had learned of him this evening. I knew, however, I had better start moving as I was beginning to feel more than enlightenment; I had not felt the touch of an interested male in whom I felt interest in many months, and my loins welcomed the attention. We walked hand in hand to the café, and I wondered aloud where the women were whom I'm sure he attracted?

He said he would call about the lunch date and that he knew my hotel and would try to get by there some time the next day. We entered the café to the stares of our companions. Our escorts blurted out, "We were just about to come and get you!" Lou especially was giving me the once-over, smugly trying to guess just what had gone on. It was past 11, and we had to get home and get up early to go to the pyramids. I whispered to PR that I wished he could go with us, but he demurred, saying that he had so much to do that he could not arrange it. The luncheon invitation still stood, and he would call me. Our taxi returned and we took off for the hotel.

Mexico City

Eve had made the arrangements – the hotel manager had found us a car and guide who would take us to the pyramids. One quick look at my finances told me that I would have to choose; the Pyramids of the Sun and Moon, Teotihuacan, which I had read about and longed to see, were about 30 miles away, and it would be an all-day trip costing each of us around $15. Lou and I decided to spend the day in and around Mexico City; there was still much to see, and we would not take Eve's offer to loan us the money for the pyramids. I was heartbroken to see them go. Eve and Theta would return that evening bursting with excitement at having seen a wonder of the world, as interesting as the pyramids of Egypt and practically unknown to us. They were fatigued from having walked the Avenue of the Dead to both the Pyramids of the Sun and Moon. They had seen Quetzalcoatl with the carved heads, and the Mural of the Great Goddess that was recreated in a Diego painting – remarking about how much I would have loved that. There was a bit of gloating, especially since I had rhapsodized about the archeological significance of the site. Eve was so impressed that she decided she and her husband would go on a cruise to Cancun, where they were building a resort around the Mayan pyramids.

However, Lou and I did not waste the day. I received a call from PR just as we were finishing breakfast; I had said that I could not take him up on the luncheon invitation because of the all-day trip to Teotihuacan. Now I would not be going, but he had made other plans. I asked him to tell me more about what I should see. He was unhappy about the fact that I was not going to the pyramids, but said that I could learn much about Teotihuacan without making the trip if I would go to the National Museum of Anthropology where they had many artifacts from the ruins. We should also see the Frida Kahlo paintings, which are of special interest to women, showing her anguish, the pain of miscarriage and separation from Diego. He also said I should visit her home and studio and that he would arrange for that singularly important visit. I said I would certainly try to heed his suggestions, and expressed my apologies for abrupt changes in my schedule.

I decided that PR's suggestions were exactly what Lou and I would do with our day. PR said he had started painting early, as he usually does to get the morning light; that he had to do some teaching and would fulfill appointments pertaining to his next exhibition in the late afternoon and evening, meaning that a dinner date was out of the question. I said that I would be back at the hotel about 6, and we could talk about it then if he would call. I had a sinking feeling that I would not hear from him again, but cheered up at the realization that it was not a wise idea to become enamored of a Mexican guy, 5,000 miles away from home who was probably just interested in a dalliance.

Lou and I mapped out the route; we would take a taxi because it was a considerable distance to the museum, but for her sake, we would have lunch at Sanborn's. Lou was afraid she might catch something eating in the Mexican restaurants. Someone had told her that they use human feces on their vegetables – well, the vegetables looked perfect, and I'm sure Sanborn's was not importing theirs from the U.S. We would find the Kahlo paintings and end our day looking at shops and other points of interest around the city. We tried to call our college boys to say we would like to visit the university, but they were not to be found; we should have made the arrangements the previous night. We got their address and would send a note thanking them for being such great hosts. We talked about the way they had been so protective of us, so courteous and helpful; they paid for everything, and didn't once make any allusions to our being Negro, except to ask about the jazz scene in Harlem; they behaved as if they were showing off their *savoir faire* for their older sisters. What a really fun bunch.

Our maître d' told us to get to the Museo Antropologia early, as we could easily spend the day there, and he was correct. It was on an expansive plaza too, with several smaller museums around it. We were certain we could not visit them all, and decided to get a guide and tour the one that was supposed to have a world renown archeological collection. Our guide was an older woman who spoke very good English. She had visited the United States, and wanted to know what we were most interested in seeing. I wanted to see as much of the artifacts and lifestyle of the pre-Columbian people as was possible. I mentioned the Olmec; she was a bit surprised, but said they had some artifacts from that period. She said they were in the process of doing some renovations, but the plan on the first floor was to show the cultures by region 3,000 years before the coming of the conquistadores. We walked into each of the rooms and tried to pronounce the names of the various peoples – the Zapotec, Mixtec, Sala Teotihuacan -- and listened intently to her descriptions of the objects they used. There was a magnificent headdress that was a replica of the one worn by Moctezuma, and various reconstructions of Mayan murals from the temples Eve and Theta were visiting. We were able go down into a reproduction of a tomb of a Mayan ruler which contained a well-preserved skeleton.

Upstairs were photographs and domestic objects, clothing, and religious artifacts of present-day Mexicans. How different were the faces of the people! Some looked strangely Asian, as if people from India or China had indeed been in the mix; others were as dark as the Senegalese or as white as their Spanish forefathers. Some had the magnificent Inca nose, Egyptian with a hump. There were some Casta paintings showing the admixture, and the societal ranking of each person, whose status rose higher as he moved toward the ultimate pure Spanish blood. We knew of societal ranking in the United States, but never had we known it was codified in such detail as Ferdinand and Isabella required of their colonies.

We were absolutely dizzy as we left, having seen and tried to synthesize so much. We crossed the square to Zona Rosa, where there were shops, and thought we'd have a respite in one of the restaurants. The guide had suggested one on Avenida Chapultepec, where there was lots of street food in a little park. We found the restaurant among a group with food from France, Switzerland and Italy as well as the one offering Mexican specialties. Lou relented and decided that this restaurant looked clean enough to try. We had freshly made lemonade, enchiladas and a salad. We sat in the open air for a long time and talked about all we had seen. We strolled along the avenue, looking in the shops, trying on Mexican clothes, and getting a little adventurous as we sampled some *antojitos* at a street stall with a long line around it. That was an indication that the food was delicious, and indeed it was exceptional. In one of the shops, I bought a white embroidered blouse, which I would give as a gift. It reminded me of the one my brother had sent me when he was in the army at Fort Huachuca.

We took a taxi back to the hotel since we were pretty tired. We were resting when the very animated Eve and Theta arrived and talked excessively about all they had seen. They said that the pyramids were not far from Cuernavaca, but we would be going in another direction on Monday. We had a pleasant dinner at the hotel and tumbled into bed early, preparing for our next and last day in Mexico City.

I wanted to see some Frida Kahlo paintings, and maybe go to the house where she lived. All agreed with that, and then we would go to Xochimilco, the floating gardens, as our final stop in Mexico. Lou was feeling religious, so she insisted that we all go to church with her and give thanks for our good fortune so far, and ask for traveling mercies for the rest of our trip. During breakfast, we plotted out our tour, looking at the map to see what church we would pass on our way to the floating gardens.

People were making a pilgrimage to the Casa Azul where Frida had lived and recently died. The plan was to make it into a museum, but our maître d' said there were crowds around it, bringing flowers, and it was not open to the public. We decided to take public transportation; we went to the Metro station and headed off to La Norio. When we debarked, we saw the beautiful San Bernardino church, which we entered and stood in the back, as Mass was being chanted, and some penitents were receiving communion. None of us was Catholic so we did not go up to kneel at the altar, but my companions said their prayers at one of the smaller niches.

There were some stalls and shops nearby, so Eve and Theta said they were going to do some shopping and would catch up with us later. Lou reluctantly agreed to visit Casa Azul with me. The map showed it wasn't far from the gardens, but that was as the crow flies. We began a long walk across the intersection to Casa Azul, but the distance was much longer than we thought and had inaccessible dead ends, so we gave up on going to the house. We had to get to the gardens nearby but they were inaccessible by foot. From where we had wound up, it would require a Metro ride to get to Embarcadero and a change of trains that was complicated and made more so by having directions entirely in Spanish. It was the scariest adventure we undertook, with dark tunnels and staircases that connected one route with another. Moreover, we had to ask directions, as routes were not well marked. The people did not seem friendly or helpful, and we survived an actual attack by a pickpocket, who tugged at Lou's purse, which she was holding in her hand. We shouted at him and he released his grip, but no native passenger came to our rescue. They merely stared at him as he leapt from the train at the next station. Lou was disgusted with me for having suggested this hazardous side trip, and was very annoyed when we finally reached Xochimilco.

We waited at the gate for Eve and Theta, who were to meet us there about 3 p.m. They arrived by taxi, full of tales of their adventures, the discussion of which we tabled as we surveyed the bustling, charming scene. These were the remnants of the gardens and canals that were built by the Mexa people who first settled in this swampy territory. Ingenuously they moved the produce and flowers that they grew in the raised beds down these canals. The sky was beginning to darken and we feared rain, since this was the rainy season; we had been so lucky to have had sunny weather every day in Mexico City and hoped rain wouldn't spoil this trip.

Flat-bottomed boats painted in the whole bright spectrum of colors, decorated with arches of blossoms and the name for each, abounded, and one came up to meet us at the dock. We negotiated a price for two hours, and two dark-haired boys began to paddle us gondola-style around the canals. We were very hungry, but I did not feel like eating the food being passed around from hand to hand by the boatmen, so I decided I would starve myself until we could go to a proper restaurant. I was surprised that Lou was the first to take one of the platters. It was a tortilla with a meat and vegetable filling; it smelled delicious and she and the others were really enjoying their treats. I was a little unnerved by that ride on the light rail, and maybe other thoughts were bothering me, but I didn't want any of the food. Boats drove up with small porous clay cups into which a not-too-clean woman poured a white liquid. My companions each ordered the drink, and said it was delightful. I was amazed that they were thus imbibing, especially Lou, but I figured it was her way of being one with Eve and Theta, and leaving me alone to brood about whatever was making me melancholy and whatever made me insist on going to Casa Azul. I was enjoying the mariachi who drove by in their boats; I bought some flowers and snuggled down in the seat and watched the families and scenery. "Get a hold of yourself," I said to myself, "You are becoming a bore with your idiosyncrasies; try to be a little more in sync with the rest, OK."

We took a taxi back to the hotel, an expensive ride from the suburbs of Mexico City, but we didn't want to take another chance on the Metro. The maître d' had a light dinner for us, which I greatly appreciated. We were quite ready to turn in and prepare for our trip to Cuernavaca. We were all packed in the morning, but we didn't venture out in the rain. Instead we listened to the radio, had lunch and chatted civilly to be ready to leave before noon when the rain was supposed to stop. I sat by the window and of course thought of him and a Sunday afternoon dinner with his Mom:

Queens with His Mom

Mamma greeted her pride and joy warmly and took me by both hands. She knew he liked me; anyway, she behaved as if I was the only girl he brought to see her. I sat on the wicker furniture in the covered front porch where she had been waiting, and spoke about the pleasant day and lovely ride we had out to Queens. Her angel was especially effusive, asking if I wanted something to drink, and offering to do the honors himself, telling Mom that he knew where everything was. She asked that we go into the parlor, which featured overstuffed upholstered chairs and a sofa, all properly doilied in white starched crochet. He returned with iced tea, with lemon, and she admonished him, "You should have brought sodas, the iced tea was for dinner." A perfect segue to, "Well, let's have dinner then and not let the tea get hot," he said.

She didn't take him up on it at first; she wanted to talk a little before dinner, and we did. She asked me about the dress I was wearing; I told her that I had made it mostly myself, but it had some difficult touches that my landlady had helped me with. For example, because the fabric was sheer, for the gathers and the easing of the sleeves, we used tissue paper to give it more body when we sewed it. She came over to inspect, and we got into quite a spirited conversation about sewing, she was admiring my handiwork, asking for more details about the stitching. Boyfriend was grinning from ear to ear.

She ushered me into the dining room and as she stepped into the kitchen, Boyfriend nuzzled me, biting me on the cheek, and running his hand over my bottom when mother wasn't looking. Boy, he was getting possessive. Well, he couldn't feel much, since this dress had a bouffant coarse tulle slip, that "won't be that easy to get into, Casanova," I thought. I suppose that little sampling cautioned him, and he was now figuring out what his disrobing strategy should be. He sat across from me at the small table, gazing and rubbing his chin; he did make me feel self-conscious, and a little embarrassed as he seemed to be looking right through me. I wanted to yell, "Will you please stop it; you are making me feel as horny as you are; stop or your mother will see what a hound you are."

Boyfriend got up to help her with the food, returning with a plate of green salad for each of us. His mother followed with a tray of fried chicken, then potato salad, string beans, and corn on the cob. She blessed the food, asking us to hold hands, and then said the *piece de resistance,* her homemade hot rolls, would be ready in a minute. When she bought in the fragrant basket, Boyfriend spoke: "Now I'm not expecting you to make a dinner like this, Love, just fresh food, not scorched, and ready on time." Whatever was he talking about? I blushed. "Silly, you know I can cook, and I don't burn things." I said. "What kind of food do you cook, dear?"

his mother asked. "Well, mostly sandwiches, I usually try to make something different for him that he can't get at the deli, or those greasy spoons where he eats, like cream cheese and olives on some decent whole wheat bread." He was ready to burst out laughing, and his mother grinned like the Cheshire cat; something was amiss: She knew he didn't like olives. I had never made so much as a sandwich for him.

There was dessert: apple pie, perfect, and coffee; profuse praise for a lovely dinner, and then a heartfelt "So sorry, Mom, but we're going to have to leave a little early today. That big shipment from Baltimore is due in at 7 a.m. tomorrow, and I have to be bright-eyed and bushy-tailed when it gets there. I'm going to have to go to Manhattan and then back to Brooklyn, and I need to get a decent night's sleep." "Oh," she said, "this is indeed an eat-and-run visit; we haven't finished our conversation about the sewing. I was going to show you this dress I'm fixing; you can probably give me some pointers." "No Mom, I really am serious, your dressmaking will have to wait; tomorrow is an important day for me, and I just can't blow it." He walked over and hugged her. "Can you forgive me, this time?"

What was she going to say? Despairingly she said, "Would you like to take some food? Both of you take some food." She ran to the kitchen to get paper plates and filled them with potato salad and chicken and covered them with cellophane. I didn't want it at all, I ate practically no fried food, but accepted it and graciously thanked her again for a splendid dinner and promised to come again when there would be time to talk about dressmaking. "I'm really no expert," I said, "but I am getting better."

Boyfriend ushered me out the door with a "Whew, I thought she'd never let us go. Can I kiss you right here? I don't think I can drive all the way to Brooklyn with this ache in my heart to hold you, Honey Love, you got my nose wide open as the old folks used to say." And then there were kisses that seemed interminable, which Mom was probably observing from the window, and probably thinking, "I don't think my son will be taking that young lady directly home."

I loved his neighborhood in Brooklyn. I had been near there many times, as white friends lived in the next block and the Africa House owned by a white philanthropist was nearby. He said he got the apartment through his Italian partner whose father was the landlord. There were rumbles about it as Brooklyn Heights was strictly segregated. But the neighbors finally accepted him. He had a floor through second-level flat that overlooked a well-kept garden below. The hardwood floors were golden and artistically parqueted, the woodwork oak and the mantel marble. There was a powder room near the front door, with a full bathroom right next to it for the only bedroom. There was a small parlor across the hall that he used as an office, which had papers stacked up that seemed to have been hastily gathered into a pile. He had green plants growing in several pots, one of them brass, on the floor in the room at the far end of the hall. This was a sunlit kitchen with room enough to eat in. How lovely this place was! I would die for an apartment like this, and had looked so hard and been turned down so often in the Village, in upper Manhattan, in lower Manhattan, and everywhere else I had ventured to think this might be the one that would accept a Negro applicant.

He had fresh flowers in the kitchen, and when I entered, he handed the bouquet to me. "How thoughtful of you," I said. "In those few minutes between 11 and 12 did you arrange all this and run to the florist?" He started singing, *"For you my love, I'd do most anything...."* He then put his mother's food in the refrigerator and asked if I'd like something to drink, like a glass of wine. The Pouilly Fuisse was cold and delicious; we talked, we kissed, we toasted the newfound happiness we were experiencing, and drank from each other's glass, and then he said, "You will not get me drunk, I am going to savor every moment we spend together, and I will savor it soberly."

I had already kicked off my shoes when we walked in so as not to scar the floors. He fell on his knees with the idea that he would pull off my stockings. But these were panty hose, and he was exasperated. With an "ugh," he said, "What is this new foil you are wearing?" "I see," I said, standing. "The master disrober has met his match, panty hose." "OK, OK, you did not wear the proper clothing for a quickie this evening, so be an angel, and let me take it all off, without tearing a thing, without snaring the panty hose, because you will show me how to remove them. I want to see you nude, tonight; in all these years, I never have." "Well, you've come close," I said leaning on him as he escorted me to his bedroom, "I was always at the pool, and I think I do remember you looking." "You with that tiny waist, and curvy bottom, I'm going to see it tonight." I turned my back to him so he could unbutton my dress, four little pearl buttons; he was laughing at the tediousness of it all: I stood so he could untie the sash, unzip the zipper, and lift the full gathered skirt over my head. He unbuttoned the underskirt of stiff tulle and let it fall to the floor, then off came the full slip, and not without kisses to the arms and neck, almost forgetting the lips as he started to remove the bra. "Oh, no, you must remove the pantyhose," I teased. He let out a deep breath, and then decided to continue to play the game, reaching around my waist, figuring out how to remove one leg at a time of the sheer fabric without a snare, fondling my thighs as he progressed. When he was done, he held the garment up in the air as if to say, "I gotcha," then gathered it and the slips into a pile and threw them on the chair. There was still a bra and panties between us; I fell upon the bed and slipped under the covers. He dove in after me.

I don't remember much of what happened after that; I know that I was profoundly moved by him; that he was gentle, that he was masterful, that he was strong, and hard and soft, and caressing with words and sighs that matched mine; with questions about the depth of my love and confessions of the sincerity and interminable quality that had become his. I know that we had forgotten time, and that it was past midnight when I left his house, and 1:30 a.m. before I finally was at home in bed. I knew that I had experienced a sensation that I had longed for all my life; that I had sung about with Frank Sinatra and Billy Eckstine. That every fiber of my being seemed to be alive: the air smelled fresher, people seemed friendlier, next day my job seemed easier; that I was happy and at peace with myself.

◆ ◆ ◆

Arrival at the Hacienda

It was early afternoon before we took off for Cuernavaca, Eve in the front with the driver, Lou, Theta and I in the back. Ramon, our driver, asked us what we had been doing in Mexico City; we talked about the museums, the churches and the *chinapas* or floating gardens. My three companions were suffering from "Montezuma's revenge." They had all drunk that milky beverage which I think was *pulque* in porous cups at Xochimilco, so I did most of the talking. When I said, we had been to a café called El Salon Mexico, Ramon gasped and put on the brakes: "*Cuesta, mea Madre*, that's one of the roughest places in the city, I can't believe you went there. What did you do there?" I said we had a wonderful time, learned to do the Mexican hat dance and met a well-known artist. He gave a sigh of relief, and said that with him we wouldn't be going to dives like that. "That's one of the most notorious places in Mexico City."

Ramon came highly recommended by the hotel manager, but he was a jerky driver. He took the hills fast, and screeched around the turns as we climbed the mountains and plunged into the valleys on the 55 or so miles to the Hacienda de la San Domingo Cuadra. We were soon on the cobblestone road, *El Camino Real*, the highway built by Aztec and

Mayan slaves to connect the cities of the Spanish colonies through the Sierras. About six o'clock, we descended into an exquisite valley with a large Spanish colonial mansion, flanked by smaller out-buildings, all white adobe with arches and arbors, surrounded by lush fields and woods, and in the distance, fenced enclosures housing various farm animals. We stepped from the car as the hotelier clapped his hands and two small boys appeared; they threw the luggage on their broad backs, their bodies misshapen as if dwarfed but muscular; I wondered if the mercury used in silver mining was the cause. They were cheerful about their task as though hard labor was all they had known. I blurted out, "Oh, no," because they seemed too young and small to be lifting all those bags. But Ramon admonished me, "They're well off," he said. "At least they're in the fresh air. You should see their brothers who work all day in the silver mines."

White-aproned young girls with dark braids down their backs showed us to our rooms. They were small too, but moved about quickly, smiling and speaking in halting English, as I tried my best to respond in fragmented Spanish. The room was a masterpiece – white adobe walls with hammered silver ornaments and candle-shaped lights in extruded fixtures. Small vases of zinnias sat on the wide hardwood window sills. The curtains of heavy, intricately tatted lace barely moved in the breeze. Two of the windows opened onto a small wrought iron balcony. I could not see it well, but I could hear water running just about two stories below. I determined that tomorrow I would rise early and go down to sit quietly beside it and see what birds would be nesting there. The double bed was very tall with dark wood legs that extended high enough for a canopy, but there was none. The coverlet was thick quilted cotton with organza ruffles in two layers forming the skirt. The furnishings included a wardrobe, a dresser with a leaf-patterned, tin-framed mirror and a large basin with pitcher on top; an easy chair, covered in heavy white cotton; the two side chairs had seats of white cotton tarpunto pillows with their duplicate tied to the chair back. A small throw rug partially covered the wide-planked dark waxed boards of the floor. I imagined that everything had been handmade on the premises by family craftsmen who were apprenticed early to perfect the skill. The shower was in a white tiled room, with hand-painted blue flowered pieces symmetrically placed as accents. There was a flush toilet too. The bathroom would be shared by the four of us. A maid was on call nearby if we needed her. She would wash and iron our clothes, bring hot water for the basin, and fetch coffee or tea or whatever else we wanted. I felt she was too young to stay by the door all night waiting on us, but I squelched my egalitarian impulses and decided to enjoy the luxuriousness of it all.

I was hanging up my clothing when our attendant told me that I had a phone call. I went down to the lobby to the house phone and was pleased to hear it was PR. He had gone by the hotel, and the hotelier told him the name of the hacienda where we were staying. He wanted to call to say goodbye to me; he would be leaving town tomorrow, as he had a commission to work on a fresco being done in one of the swank new hotels being built in Acapulco. He wanted me to know how much he enjoyed meeting me, and how sorry he was that we could not have had our luncheon date, or that he could not show me the artistic sights of Mexico City. He was pleased at my choices, when I told him what I had seen; he once again told me that I must visit the Kahlo house. I gave him my address in New York, and said that he might write or call if ever he was in town. I once again told him how much I would treasure the painting; I knew it would be worth a fortune someday when he was famous, but I would never sell it. He laughed and said this was truly goodbye, and he wanted to level with me. He told me he was married with children, so I could understand why he had not been more aggressive in pursuit of ardent kisses and late-night dates. I told him that his suave manners and controlled responses gave me an inkling that there was a woman in his life, someone close who had schooled and shaped him in the finer ways of wooing. I thanked him profusely for his honesty and for all that I had learned from him about the African diaspora, Diego and the creativity of the Mexican people; my trip had indeed been enhanced by knowing him.

I was impressed by his respectful demeanor; he had behaved adversely to my father's prediction. I was moved as I had met other foreign guys, like one Chinese student at NYU who said he came early to watch me take my coat off, and was so bold as to offer me money for a date. I stood in the hall a few minutes to regain my composure; my friends had gone down to dinner, and I knew when I entered questions would

be fast and furious. Inquisitive eyes turned toward me immediately. I simply said it was PR and he called to say goodbye;
he was leaving town early the next day and I would not see
him again. But he would call if he ever came to New York.

The two middle-aged senores of the hacienda, we learned
from Ramon, were bachelors, but they had children with some
of the servant women. They sat down to dinner with us to a
meal served family style. Large platters of food appeared
on the sideboards, and two waiters walked around the table
offering each to us. There was salad with tomatillos and avocado, fragrant yellow rice with peppers, steaming spicy beef
wrapped in corn husks, tortillas, corn with lima beans in a colorful succotash, a lovely red wine with chocolates and coffee
for desert. Everything was delicious and delightfully served.

They talked about what we would do tomorrow; we could
go hiking around the farm, which was over 100 acres. Yes,
there was a stream that ran into a larger lake. There were no
dangerous animals like jaguars roaming around; anyway a servant who could talk to the animals would go walk with us, so we
needn't be afraid. There was boating and swimming on the lake
if we wanted to do that. He asked if any of us had ridden horseback. I had, and so had Lou and the others; everyone was
game for it, but none of us was an expert. One of the senores
said that we should spend time the next day practicing, and
the following day we could ride the horses down the mountain
to the center of town. That way we could see the countryside
and see how the people lived. We sat out on the veranda after dinner, relaxing in the hammocks, listening to the crickets,

marveling at the millions of stars in the jet-black sky. There were no skyscrapers or floodlights to obliterate the Milky Way. It was a tranquil and pleasant evening, just what we needed to digest all we had seen and done so far.

I could not wait to wander about the farm, so when the rooster crowed, I came down and walked outside while there was still dew on the ground. I went immediately to the stream and sat on a stone bench watching the birds that seemed indifferent to me. There were plenty of them, colorful and communicative, chirping questions and awaiting answers, which made the forest ring with their melodies. I could not identify any of them; although some resembled sparrows or robins, the coloring and size were different. The countryside was abloom with an abundance of flowering bushes and ground cover, some native and some probably imported pe-rennials growing wild now; I walked passed a kitchen garden where the servants were picking fresh vegetables and fruits for the table. Beyond that, up the hill, were the stables where several horses were being washed down as they munched their hay. I watched them for a few minutes, then asked the stable boy which one was the mildest. He laughed, and in English said most of them are for the guests; they are trained to be gentle and walk slowly. Someone was tugging at the bell cord, which produced a clang that could be heard for miles; the stable boy said it meant that breakfast was about to be served.

I hastened down the hill thinking I would see what lay be-yond later. I passed groups of women, children and men with hoes and rakes ascending the hill; I gasped as I surmised they were walking toward their work in the fields. I thought of the music of Dvorak, who was inspired to write the New World Symphony after seeing the ragged, weary slaves on a plantation he visited in the United States' South. They had staggered home from the fields after dark, and now at dawn they were trudging passed his window down the path again to their endless toil. My ancestors! I hesitantly said, "*Buenos dias*," and the laborers responded with smiles and good wishes. All the way down the hill I was humming the New World Symphony melody we learned in junior high school and remembering the humiliating words someone had attached to it:

> *Massa dear, Massa dear, oh look down a while.*
> *Winds am still, heaven am clear, you can hear*
> *dis chile'. All de home folks is gone, and its*
> *lonesome here, work is o'er day is done, take*
> *me Massa dear. Take me home for de light,*
> *went away wid you. Take me home from de*
> *night, as you used to do.*

Demeaning words for a Negro student, in a class full of sniggling white kids, to sing and internalize declaring that his ancestors, the Negro slaves, were entirely dependent on their masters to manage their lives. The slave was so degraded that toiling for his master provided the greatest happiness his simple mind could envision even in death. Has the system – enslavement and Jim Crow – succeeded in making Negroes love their chains, accept being three-fifths of a person 90 years after Emancipation? Sometimes a sense of powerlessness creeps over my entire psyche in the U.S., watching new arrivals of all shades except black live on Fifth Avenue, open businesses on Wall Street and take full advantage of the American Dream while the Negro is still subjected to ridicule as crows in Dumbo, or as stores persist in selling the distorted images of the grinning pinhead mammy. Here Africans had intermarried with the indigenous population, and the Spanish accepted as lower class the various mutations so long as they became Christian. Still these descendants of the proud Maya and Inca seem bound to toil without adequate compensation too, albeit their plight was better than the U.S. enslaved; their families were intact, they could marry, and they had companionship with people who spoke their language. The servants here often speak in an unintelligible tongue, one of the indigenous languages that has kept their community together.

At the breakfast table, the more talkative of the senores told us some of the history of the farm and the reasons his ancestors built this splendid hacienda beside El Camino Real. It was once more so, and now still was -- though the silver was greatly diminished -- one of the mine haciendas. His ancestors were soldiers of Cortes who were granted property and silver rights. Later it became an inn, a way station on a busy trade route. Travelers stopped for the night after having crossed through the steep and dangerous passes between here and Mexico City. Silver and produce were being transferred and bandits lurked in the caves waiting to waylay the burros as they transported their cargo between Acapulco and Mexico City.

Yes, they had burros on the farm; they were still the beast of burden, smaller than our mules, but strong. I told them of a song we used to sing about the burros going to market; they were delighted as they knew the melody, and we sang some of it in Spanish:

Adios Mama, adios Mama.
We're going to market very soon
And won't be back 'til afternoon,
Just see us, Mama, just see us, Mama,
Our burro's packed higher than the moon.

Ramon, who did not sit down to eat with us, was waiting outside when we finished. He said that we should get started on our horseback riding lessons, since we needed some skill to get those animals over the mountain and back. We put on slacks and tennis shoes, not exactly the right clothing, but all we had. We each approached a horse, and the stable man observed which horse was the right height or which seemed to like our smell or at least was not offended by us, and made a decision as to which would be whose mount. They each had names that we were to remember and say them softly with our best Spanish accent. Never yell at them, stroke the horse's neck; never pull the mane. Don't stand behind them, pat down their sides and see if they respond by nodding their heads. My horse, named Sancho, was dark chestnut with a black mane. He seemed gentle enough, nodding slightly as I took him by his lead and walked him around the corral several times. Using a specially designed chair with a saddle that he measured for each woman, the stable-man instructed us on the way we were to mount, hold the reins, and execute the signals to stop, move more quickly, slow down, or walk at a steady gait. We were trying to take it all in, realizing that it was not easy, but might just be lifesaving. He assured us that he would be with us all the way there and back, and that all the guests who made the journey considered it the highlight of their visit. By lunchtime, we still had not mounted the horses, and there were expressions of apprehension as we discussed the difficulty of mountain horseback riding. These horses were not like the tame old nags that we had ridden on smooth level pathways in Pelham Parkway in the Bronx.

After lunch, we were right back at the stables, preparing for the next phase, which was actually mounting the horse. As soon as I was in the saddle, Sancho took off. I tried pulling up on the reins, but obviously, I was not executing that move correctly. A stable boy was beside me with the lead; he calmed Sancho down and further instructed me in the use of each command as we sauntered, then trotted around the corral. We were some frightened women, but no one exhibited anything but confidence that they were learning the ropes.   Our backs ached a little, and our legs were sore from the physicality of our lessons. No matter, I would go to Cuernavaca via horseback tomorrow, and game gals that they were, so would my companions.

Our little maids awaited us, quickly gathering up our clothes to have them washed and ironed for the morning, since they were our only "habits." We washed and dressed for dinner, gallantly talking with our surprisingly spirited hosts – it was as if they were amused at our travail with the horses. Nonetheless, one of them had maps and illustrations to help us understand all that we would see the next day at and on the way to the city.   It was going to be a perfect day for it. They felt that the loveliest part of the trip would be the road itself. It seemed that each stone had been carefully laid down, making a tile-like pattern; then there was the scenery, the vistas that we could admire, the tile-roofed houses and ornate churches.   There were silver mines, we could not enter them, but we could see where they were, and the *casitas* that belonged to the peasants who worked in the mines. We would see lots of people, but no bandits. We would have lunch in the city. Before we crawled into bed, we each took a bit of Lou's alcohol for a rub on the sorest spots.   I was so pleased that I had seen some of the farm that morning, because I never got to look at a single furrow after that, so preoccupied were we with the riding lessons.

It was indeed a splendid morning when we started out. The stableman with the saddled horses was waiting at the front door, and immediately after breakfast we were identifying our mounts and with as much confidence as we could muster, settling ourselves in the saddles. The stable boys put our few personal items in the saddlebags, making sure that we had our money and anything valuable on our person.

He said the stable boys with the leads would only go with us to the top of the hill, and then he alone would ride with us to town. I was comfortable in the saddle enjoying my birds-eye view of Cuernavaca when I realized that Sancho seemed to be always in the lead, preferring to walk on the very edge of the mountain. When he kicked a stone, it bounded down the cliff, the bottom of which I could not and would not try to see. I knew I was supposed to sit straight in the saddle, but I tended to lean to the left in an effort to avoid the drop. This only seemed to make Sancho walk closer to the edge. I was terri-fied to do anything with the reins but hold them loosely and let Sancho, who knew the road and I would hope wanted to save his own life, do as he chose. I began to feel confident as the scenery was so tranquil, and the horses seemed to be saun-tering along together without a care. It was kind of sexy: the feeling of the Sancho's warm flanks against my inner thighs, and the need to squeeze my vagina as I raised my pelvis to match the horse's rhythm. Every step as we sauntered along, has me aching for Him:

◆ ◆ ◆

Brooklyn and the Lesson

From the moment he and Paul went into the business together, Boyfriend had to be junior partner, playing second fiddle to his white boss. This was the only way to manage the racism that permeated the industry; the rank and file were ready to fight physically for their jobs and the men at the top reluctantly acknowledged a Black corporate head. The very idea of a Black man in corporate ownership and top management was totally new to me too; I knew one other person, who worked for Coca-Cola in an executive position, and a co-ed who worked for IBM as an engineer. There were Black funeral directors and one insurance company that was Black-owned. Attempts to build motion picture studios or operate record companies, even local night clubs generally failed, or required Jewish ownership, with Blacks as managers. Dr. Hansberry had told us of Black Wall Street in Tulsa, Oklahoma, where Negro men had businesses and banks in the 1920s. It was burned to the ground and its owners killed by white vigilantes, with no one ever prosecuted for the crime.

As the company grew, Boyfriend was going by plane to meet with the heads of companies, to arrange for trucks at ports and railroad terminals to carry the goods overland. It was grudgingly accepted that he was Paul's trusted assistant, because of Paul's incapacitation. Paul was now in a wheelchair most of the time, suffering from that wartime injury. He managed the finances, procurement, investments and the office staff. Much of the business was done by telephone, and I wondered why more of it could not be. But Boyfriend said that a face-to-face discussion was often necessary, and he liked to see firsthand what kind of plant these fellows had, and what kind maintenance was being done on the trucks his company owned. He said he often played the messenger or clerk when he went to some of his outlets, not just in the South either, but in Ohio and Pennsylvania. Where there was found to be outright hostility and racism, he would send in his white assistant, who would call regularly to consult, or talk it over in the car before the assistant went to the boardroom to make any deals. They were independent carriers, but wanted to build a fleet to carry more than produce or loose goods. They were negotiating for refrigerated units to transport seafood from Eastern Shore Maryland inland and semis to transport heavy equipment.

Among the CEOs, it was generally known that there was a Black guy in an executive position up there, and strangely the corporate bosses respected the military connection: This Black guy had saved the boss's life. So long as there were not Black drivers taking over the truck routes, Boyfriend was able to get his program through. He tried to get Black men to be drivers, but the racism in the truck stops and on the docks was too much, the nepotism too ingrained, and the unions too protective.

I didn't like his flying everywhere either; there was always a plane crash in the newspaper, and I found myself asking him to please not come or go in inclement weather. I would wait for his phone call, get in the bed and snuggle next to my pillow, and listen for his voice. He talked sex throughout the whole conversation, after the pleasantries of hello and how are you. He would say that he was licking a lollipop, pretending it was me; or ask me to place some whipped cream in inappropriate places and he would slurp it loudly. He said he liked to get it all over his mouth, and let it stay there throughout our conversation, and lick his lips every few minutes to savor the taste. At first it was embarrassing to listen to him, especially the sounds he would make, but after a while I found myself deeply immersed in the conversation, and touching the places on my body where he said the cream was and feeling very sexy.

When he finally was to arrive one Friday evening, I met him at LaGuardia and drove his car and him to his apartment in Brooklyn. I had the key and had arrived earlier that day to tidy up the place and prepare a surprise meal for him. He was absolutely elated that I met him, but I had to tell him to keep his hands off or I would make him sit on the back seat, because I could not drive with his affectionate distractions. He bounded up the stairs when we arrived at his place and opened the door to a very neat and fresh-smelling flat, with flowers, and a savory meal already prepared. He said he was not hungry, for food, but would shower and sit down to dinner with me.

He invited me to help him shower, but I said I still had much to prepare in the kitchen, and slipped from his arms to resume my culinary tasks. He returned in his bathrobe, smelling divine of something lemony and masculine. I had prepared a simple meal: really expensive baby lamb chops, with spinach, rice fixed in a new way called *pilaf*, and glazed carrots. It was colorful and cooked, I must say, to perfection. He was surprised, but sat down nonchalantly and talked about the food, friends, old times and politics throughout the meal, not a word to indicate that he was even thinking of seducing me.

He filled the wine glasses only once, and eschewed the store-bought lemon meringue pie. He had, all of a sudden, become rather quiet and contemplative. And then I said, snapping my fingers, "Maid, Maid, will you please come and clear the table and get these dishes washed up?" That brought him back from his reverie, then he said, "Look, let's just put the food away, and stack the dishes, I wouldn't want you to even think of washing dishes after such a pleasant meal." He got up and walked around the table, kissing me lightly on the forehead. "Sweetie, everything was delicious, I never knew you could cook a meal like that," and began to remove the remaining food to the refrigerator. I helped and soon the dishes were in the sink, and he was standing behind me, kissing my neck and saying, "I have something for you, something for us; we've been careless, and I want to know when your next period is?" I blushed, "Why would you want to know that, I mean, that's personal." "No, baby, it's personal for you and me to know, when's the next one?"

He shepherded me to the bedroom, removing my clothing as we walked, and draped my shoulders with one of his robes. Then he sat beside me on the edge of the bed and brought forth the present. A box of condoms. "Look," he said, "these are for us, and I want you to put it on me, so you will be sure I'm wearing it before I barge in." After a gasp or two, I agreed and said that I should have known better than to have taken chances, but we had, and I'd been worried. "I don't want us to worry about anything, darling, I'm going to show you what to do." He handed me the package, which I unsealed ever so carefully. I took out the plastic sheath; he said I was to put it to my mouth and blow into it, to extend it like a balloon, and to make sure there were no holes. I did as I was told, and then he presented himself to me. I had never actually looked at him before, and I began to feel unsteady and breathless as I watched him grow firm and erect right before my eyes. His penis became a brown pulsating obelisk with a foreskin covering a slippery red tip. "He said, "OK, quick, before all is lost, grasp it firmly in your hand, and place the open end on the tip; it's going to take your two hands to pull it on." I was far from expert, and he said, "Baby, please don't rub it, your task is to cover, and fast." I got the opening over the tip, and began to roll the thin plastic down toward his groin. His penis seemed to have a life of its own, moving like the pendulum of a clock, independent of his control, disdainful of my efforts to sheath it. Finally, the job was done; deftly with one hand he applied a gel, then rolled over me, pushing me to the mattress, removing the bathrobe, kissing me on my breasts; he switched off the lights, and pulled up the covers.

I don't know how long he engaged in foreplay, and I wondered how he managed it, as he was ready for the plunge when I began the condom act. I was aroused too, but by the time he entered, I was begging for it and that is what he wanted. He made me wait until I was fully moistened, as the condom was preventing him from sharing his fluids with mine, and he wanted me to enjoy every moment of this encounter. I felt him inside me, but without the splendid warmth of having my vagina bathed in his semen. We stayed clasped like this for several minutes, until he collapsed, and the pleasure probe shrank. I was asleep in his arms in a few minutes and would spend the night, and experience the dressing of the probe twice more before morning and the trip home.

◆ ◆ ◆

Cuernavaca and Taxco

We stopped to watch people running down the hill. We learned that they were hastening to hear a radio broadcast of President Adolfo Ruiz Cortines' speech. Ramon said a woman named Amalia Castillo Ledon had led the Mexican suffragettes, and had just gotten the right for women to vote the previous year. Even though they still couldn't vote for president, the peons wanted to know what it would mean to them; there was much excitement and anticipation that things would get better, but he wasn't holding out much hope.

We visited the *Jardin Bordo*, once the home of Don Jose de la Borda, a wealthy miner, now open to the public. It was fairly overgrown and it looked unoccupied. However, you could imagine what a striking garden it must have had. There were avenues with blooming plants on each side, and huge ferns and trees covered with vines, shading the duck ponds and pools with fountains that weren't working. We could ride our horses down the paths through archways and in front of what had been an elegant residence, doubtless built originally by slave labor as Borda was here with the French around 1717.

At the Palacio de Cortes just off the main plaza, we were able to see some more Diego murals among the pre-conquistador artifacts. I was beginning to feel that these murals were

stiffening my backbone; I identified with the indigenous upris-
ings. Their complexions were dark chocolate brown, and they
were depicted fighting with the Aztecs against men in armor
in scenes from early colonial history.

The next sight to see was the famous Cathedral of Our
Lady of Guadalupe, the saint of the peasants. We dismounted, covered our heads and went inside to admire the ornate
altar originally built by Cortes. The intricate carving and richly
gold-leafed statuary around the altars seemed such a distor-
tion of the religion of a humble carpenter's son. How disori-
enting it must have been for the devout peasant population
who lived in abject poverty to come to worship in such opu-
lent churches.

We had lunch at La Manetas, a small inn with exotic birds
such as macaws and peacocks in cages or wandering the garden. We ate *mole poblano*, a sauce made of chocolate and hot
chilies; definitely an acquired taste. Although there were ce-
ramics and some silver items for sale, we didn't buy anything,
since we were anticipating our trip the next day to Taxco.

We began the journey back to the Hacienda, stopping to
see a waterfall and a pink house with a high wall around it. I
was anxious to get back to the hotel; it was a steep climb, and
I had had enough of horseback riding. My legs and knees
were sore from grasping Sancho's flanks; my derriere was
hurting from not having moved it up before the horse rose to
meet it; my thighs had been stretched to the limit, not being
prepared for how broad Sancho's back was. I fairly limped as
we dismounted.

I took a long soaking bath before dinner, and borrowed more of Lou's alcohol. Our hosts were lively, telling us about the history of Cuernavaca: that Zapata had been here, that it was the summer home of Carlotta and Maximilian, and that some U.S. gangsters had tried to escape from the law here. I relished the delicious food, but did not linger, as I wanted to get a good night's sleep and rest my weary body.

We were up early for the day-long trip to Taxco de Alarcon, the City of Silver. Ramon would drive us the 30 miles there; it would take about an hour and a half, much shorter as the crow flies, but people had to take the winding trail through the mountains. Our host advised that we were to visit several shops before we bought anything and then go back to purchase just the jewelry or souvenirs we wanted. He suggested one or two of the best, and pointed out some exquisite silver items in the room that had been made in Taxco. One item was made by a famous American architect named William Spratling who came to the town and trained many silversmiths to produce his designs; in fact it was he who transformed the town into a jewelry-making center.

The scenery was once again beguilingly beautiful, winding down the Sierra Madre with a bird's-eye view of the white stucco houses with their red tile roofs, surrounded by tall pines and rimmed by cobblestone streets. Silver was discovered here, and that Frenchman named Jose Borda became a wealthy man. We had visited his mansion in Cuernavaca the previous day. We wanted to visit William Spratling's shop or those run by his apprentices who had become expert silversmiths and made the town world-famous. In one of the photos of Frida Kahlo that the hotel manager had shown us she was wearing his chunky silver jewelry modeled after pre-Columbian designs. But first we would visit some churches, especially the pink colonial San Sebastian y Santa Prisca, which had been built by Jose Borda and dominated the square.

Ramon let us out; we covered our heads and entered. As with the other churches we had visited, women in headscarves, some of lace, some bound in fringe, knelt before the altars lighting candles and fingering their rosaries as they prayed. The style of the church was *Churrigueresque*, a Mexican-Spanish baroque. Its numerous gold-leafed carvings of saints and flora were faded, and a little dusty, as were the paintings by the Mexican artist, Juan Cabrera. We got some postcards on the way out, since you could not take photographs, but Ramon took our photo in front of the ornately carved doors as we left.

In a little museum named Casa Humboldt we were able to see some works of art done as early as the 16th century. How quickly the native Mexicans had accepted the Christian religion and were carving the disciples and Jesus in their own image, painting the saints with heavy black mustaches, and adorning them in bright yellow, avocado, and chili. We wanted to look at some specimen of jewelry in the museum to get an idea of what to buy, but very little of this art was silver, since the conquistadors mined the silver and shipped it back to Spain. We walked down the hill from the church to Avenido los Pajaritos and began to visit the shops. There were so many with dazzling jewelry, some hammered, others using the lost wax process, some specializing in rings, others in expensive sets embossed with carvings and local stones. I tried on many pieces, but I decided I did not want the traditional bracelet of linked silver squares set with large stones of Mexican jade or onyx. My brother had given my sisters and me several of these pieces, which he bought when he was stationed at Fort Huachuca just across the border in Arizona. I bought a jade ring in an art deco setting. It looked old, and the salesman told me that it was a vintage piece. Ramon came up and examined it, assuring me that it was indeed sterling silver; he wanted to make sure it was not silverplate or cheap German silver, an alloy which contained nickel. It was $5; I was confident that it would have cost many times that in the States.

We stopped shopping for a while and had lunch in a small hotel overlooking the square. We could watch the crowds go by, such a mixture of tourists in New York casual, and the indigenous people, wearing colorful dirndl skirts and baggy trousers just as you saw them in National Geographic magazine. Automobiles drove carefully next to burro carts and pedestrians trotted carrying huge bundles and baskets. We compared our selections: Lou had bought carvings of Mexican peasants, some silver rings, and inexpensive bracelets for gifts. Eve was shopping for some masculine jewelry for her husband, but hadn't found the right gift yet. She had some embroidered pillow cases that were charming, very inexpensive and easy to carry. I thought I might buy a few of them. Theta had made the most extensive and expensive purchases; several bracelets containing a variety of semi- and precious stones.

We went to the Galeria de Arte en Plata Andres, where supposedly the finest pieces were to be found. There were families of Hildalgos, Tallers, Martinez, and many others whose designs were dazzling. My friends and I were snapping them up, forgetting our budget and what funds we would require in the days ahead. I came upon a designer named Zaloveta; his pieces reminded me of Danish Modern, which was all the rage in New York. Tiffany was selling this work at fantastic prices. I became immersed in conversation in broken Spanish and English about his art, asking if he was a student of William Spratling. He said that his father before him had studied under the master and followed his designs, but he was now developing some modern pieces.

I wanted to know about the painting of Frida Kahlo draped in black on the wall behind him. She was wearing large stones in a pre-Columbian setting. He became invigorated talking about the painting, how sad he was at her death, that the painting was a study for the finished product which she had given him, and how important she had been to the Revolution and in the fight for women's rights.   Other customers were gathering, and my friends made it obvious to me that I was taking too much of his time. Finally, I bought a tubular piece, molded so that it pivoted on a silver spike, and fastened by pushing the two pieces together under the wrist. I thought it was spectacular, and something that I would never see again on an arm in the States. It was $25, certainly a bargain. Ramon agreed, noting the there was a stamp on the back assuring me that it was made by artisans in Taxco of sterling. I went outside and sat on a bench under the trees to observe the people, and to keep from spending another cent. My purchases had made a big dent in my budget, but I could not think of leaving this place with nothing to remember it by.

We returned with our bundles to the hacienda, heady and delighted about our purchases, not much concerned about our extravagance. As soon as we were settled in our rooms, however, we decided that a powwow was necessary to make a final count as to just how much we had in total to get us back to the States for the 10 days that remained in our trip. We had 3,000 miles to go. We had set aside funds for our one-night stay in Monterrey; our train tickets were round-trip and paid for. We figured that we could not afford to stay a night in Mexico City, so we would stay one more night in Cuernavaca and pray that we get to Mexico City in time to catch the train the next day. Then we figured on the cost of the storage of the car, gas and possible upkeep, and food on the road, to which we added $50 just in case of something unexpected. We discussed the additional night with Ramon and the senores, who said it was OK with them. So, for $5 more each we enjoyed a delicious meal at the Hacienda, our comfy beds, relaxing on the veranda with three local musicians who delighted us with mariachi music, and a sumptuous breakfast before taking off for a wild ride with Ramon up El Camino Real, through the Sierra Madres, back to Mexico City and the railroad terminal.

On that spectacular ride in the daytime when you could see the majestic forests, valleys and streams, I was overcome by how wonderful the natural world was. I was cognizant of the fact that I had experienced one of those wonders, love between a man and woman. I am missing him; I am remembering the day I knew I was madly in love. I can hear his voice, I am remembering how patient and gentle he was with me:

♦ ♦ ♦

At the UN

I did get him to go to the United Nations one time. There was a reception for a Black undersecretary who had just been given a position working with Ralph Bunche after he had won the Nobel Peace prize for his work on the Israeli question. This situation was explosive as far as my African friends were concerned: Why Ralph Bunch to do the dirtiest job, displacing other people of color so that European Jews could have a homeland after the Holocaust? Why could not this Black diplomat work for Black African liberation? I invited some of my African friends to go with me; reluctantly they agreed, especially one of them from Tanzania, who was slated to become prime minister when his nation was liberated; and two from Nigeria, Ibos, whose territory was smack in the middle of the oil fields that Shell was planning to develop.

One of the Ibos, Ndukwe, who was especially close to me, was studying here on corporate money, and managing the Phelps-Stokes Africa house in Brooklyn. Ibos were the first people to embrace Christianity when the British invaded Nigeria; they early on got Western educations and became the civil servants for the British. They were deeply resented by other tribes that had been hunter-gatherers, were more war-like and less eager to submit to foreign rule. My friends adopted British mannerisms and speech but often laughed about how British the returning scholars became, bravely wearing their Saville row wool suits in Port Harcourt's sweltering heat. However, they did not swallow the colonialist divide and conquer, indirect rule theory wholly; they wanted control of their territory. After all, the boundaries delineated by the Europeans were for their own convenience, had nothing to do with the ethnicity of the groups they included or excluded, and did not take into consideration ancient alliances and treaties. Indeed, for the Europeans, nothing the Africans had in the way of governance was worth noting.

Dr. Ralph Bunche would be at this event, and my African friends decided that they would try to speak with him, at least to invite him to their art exhibit, although he had little to do with Black African affairs.

The reception had some important Black politicians and society folks among its numbers. Everyone was dressed to the nines. One of my sorority sisters who had worked with the UN from its inception was there with other upper echelon personnel from several fraternal groups. I was able to invite folks because my boss had provided some of the money for the event. Moreover, my African friends and I, with my connections at the Carnegie Endowment across the street, had on the ground floor the first indigenous African Art Exhibit, which guests were invited to see before or after the reception.

I came with my boyfriend. He was handsome in a dark suit, wearing his white shirt with cuff links—I had given him these as a present and he said he didn't know when he would wear them. This was the first and last time he did, as far as I know. I was wearing a huge silver ring he had bought me in the gift shop, where we stopped as I was giving him a brief tour before the event began. I was pleased to introduce him to my boss, who greeted him warmly, and my African friends; now they knew he existed, and was not some fantasy I concocted to avoid their romantic advances. He was very cordial, but quiet. He said he knew nothing they were talking about and to avoid being designated a complete idiot, would remain silent.

With cocktail in hand, one of the upwardly mobile Black women, after introducing her husband and declaiming all of his degrees and accomplishments, asked my boyfriend if he was in the diplomatic corps. He smiled and said, "No, I am in trucking." Immediately she laughed, and I believe actually raised her nose to sniff, "You mean you actually drive trucks?" He said, "No, I am the co-owner of a long distance trucking business." Her eyes widened, "Uh, I didn't know any Negroes were in that business," she said. "We keep a low profile, Madam," he said. "It's not exactly the kind of business whites are welcoming us to." She seemed flustered, and retreated to a group of people who were obviously her friends, to whom she probably spread the news that there was an actual Black businessman here in a most unlikely business. Her husband stayed to chat awhile about trying to have a business in New York, how difficult that must be, and what obstacles one must face.

We were introduced to Ralph Bunche who had come to present the honoree, but stood aside as the Africans shook hands and made conversation with him. We both knew Bill Ketchum from college, so we quickly moved down the reception line to talk with him, congratulating him on his new position. Bill was handsome, tall, very dark-complexioned, married to a woman older than he, who could easily pass for white. He expressed his pleasure at seeing us and invited us to come to his office when he was in town, because there was much going on that would be of interest. "About Israel?" I questioned, since I knew his field was economics and that he had studied at the University of Pennsylvania's Wharton School, hoping to get into the corporate life. He also spoke German, having been in Germany during the war, knew a lot about the recovery, had written his thesis on the Marshall Plan, and was snatched up by the scouts at the UN for this diplomatic job which he said would probably take him to the Middle East. When Boyfriend said he was "breaking his balls" in the trucking business, the honoree was fascinated, was eager to know more, and thus the invitation to visit his office and an exchange of cards.

A glass was tinkled, and the house quieted as Dr. Bunche took the stage to speak of the work they would now be doing to fulfill the UN Charter pledge to ensure the peace. He talked of why William H. Ketchum was uniquely qualified to take this job, and why especially a Black man, objective and informed, could with patience and deliberation bring disparate factions together. Bill followed the applause, expressing his pleasure for having been selected to work with Ralph Bunche, the distinguished scholar and diplomat, who would roll up his sleeves on the Isle of Rhodes or anywhere to prove his philosophy that human difference could be adjudicated. He was pleased to be a person of African descent at the United Nations in a diplomatic role, hoping to presage an awakening among nations that another barrier had been dislodged, another myth dispelled about what was possible for Negroes in America and Africans around the world. Indeed, after his speech, the air was heady with promise: Black guests and white guests were talking together about how this move might be reflected in some Washington appointments, since there were many men and women like Bill K. waiting in the wings.

After the speeches, my African friends swarmed around Ralph Bunch; Boyfriend and I stood close to listen. Not only my Ibo friends, but students and UN delegates from Senegal, Northern Nigeria, Sierra Leone and Ghana joined the conversation. They expressed their pride in having Dr. Bunche receive the Nobel Peace Prize for his work on the Palestine/Israeli conflict, and asked, "What would be the difficulty in achieving such a détente in a colonial nation like the Congo?" Dr. Bunch said such a question would take more than a few minutes in this setting to answer, but in a few words he would say that the European nations wanted to remain in control of the natural resources in the Congo. Unfortunately, the indigenous people did not speak with one voice, but were affiliated with different European factions, and thus there was infighting. One very articulate young man who was a Philip Jessup scholar at Columbia aggressively asked if Dr. Bunche's work on the Trusteeship Council might now emphasize the dismantling of the colonial systems in Africa. He felt that as a man of African descent, he might have a special affinity for bringing independence to these captive nations. Ola, a Nigerian and well-known drummer who came fully attired in his native dress to play at our Carnegie exhibit, interjected that he had read of Dr. Bunche's work on the Declaration of Human Rights, and was "so proud that he had emphasized human rights for everyone, which certainly must include the peoples of Black Africa."

Dr. Bunche was being nudged to move on to another appointment, but he lingered a minute longer with the students and said that he was trying to devise a system whereby troops of the United Nations composed of neutral soldiers from uninvolved nations would support peacebuilding and not engage in war in these conflict situations. He was hoping to bring these forces to the African colonial debacles. Everything was in its infancy, but he felt this was the direction the UN should go, and was using his influence to bring such a system about. The Africans contemplated this response, and as Dr. Bunche retreated, began to discuss its merits among themselves.

Boyfriend listened intently: Here were Black men discussing the future of nations that they might actually control. Here were scholarly African men, the objects of ridicule in Tarzan and countless movies with exaggerated lips and rings in their noses, depicted as afraid of wild animals with which they had lived all their lives, cowering while a blond, blue-eyed white man subdued the beasts. Boyfriend shook his head thoughtfully and whispered to me: he wondered if just bringing these bright, articulate students to speak with our school kids would give them an incentive to study and take their education more seriously. I said that it would be a step, but more was needed to dispel the mindset borne of unrewarded labor that made them behave as though an education was useless.

I was so pleased that he was enjoying the conversation; my Nigerian friend, Ndukwe, seemed to take a particular liking to Boyfriend. They began to talk about Ndukwe's observations of Negro behavior, a favorite subject for him, as he couldn't abide the casualness with which Negro families seemed to take the educational opportunities afforded them here. I warned Boyfriend that he was especially hard on Negro women; I had argued with him often about his thoughts on their competition with men, and disdain for motherhood and family life. He doesn't appreciate the history of struggle for Negro families in America without men in the home: fathers sold away from mothers and children during enslavement; fathers impressed as convict laborers during Jim Crow; despondent jobless fathers who had no experience of family or home. With this background, women had to assume the breadwinner roles and thus did form a kind of matriarchal society.

This discussion continued. Other African students joined in, and Negro women defended their need to study and become independent as the reception ended. We crossed the street to the African Exhibit on the Carnegie Endowment building's ground floor where authentic objects for Ibo, Hausa, and Yoruba Nigerian societies dominated, and were lauded by representatives of each ethnic group who stood and told the history of the object. Ola and his group entertained with spirited African drumming. Before he began, he wanted to make clear that he was a drummer, but dancing and drumming was not all Africans did. He was a serious student, in liberal arts, but there were others in the sciences, learning at the finest U.S. colleges and excelling in the academic rigor. He, who was engaged to an American Negro woman, cheerfully added his comments concerning the scourge of American women's bossiness.

Boyfriend and Ndukwe were chatting as he took him on a private tour, and I wondered if I was the subject as I observed that they laughed a lot, and sometimes looked my way and smiled. Eventually they sat together, with a lot of nodding, hand gesturing and chin rubbing as the conversation seemed to have taken a deeper turn.

Boyfriend would discuss nothing of their conversation as we prepared to leave. Since this was the last day of the exhibition, Ndukwe had an announcement to make praising me for having made the exhibit possible and presenting me with a very heavy mahogany sculpture of a woman with a baby on her back. I was overwhelmed, and expressed my gratitude. I said that the exercise of preparing and presenting this exhibit had whetted my appetite to know more about my ancestry, to deepen my appreciation of the contributions of Africa to world culture. I now look at Picasso, for example, as not being original, but as having directly borrowed ideas from the indigenous peoples of Africa.

I was on cloud nine as we left, and Boyfriend wanted to sit on the bench in the little park behind the building and show his appreciation for the evening with caresses and kisses. "What a great guy I've got," I thought. He found so much here with people of Africa, of whom he knew little. My brother and an old friend from Philly had visited the Phelps Stokes House with me and couldn't abide all the Africans they met there. The friend was the first boy I had ever felt a surge of passion for, when I was about 8 years old. He had fallen from my great uncle's ice truck, injuring his hand and elbow. His friends remained hanging on the truck cooling themselves with ice slivers, laughingly deserting him. I helped him to my grandmother's porch and rushed to the kitchen, got a basin of water, towels, Mercurochrome and gauze. I washed the wounds, administered the medicine and bandaged them so meticulously and with such skill that he gazed at me tenderly with his blue-gray eyes and I was smitten. We had an attachment forevermore, but I was too dark-complexioned and my hair too kinky for him. He brought each fair-skinned girlfriend to visit me when I lived uptown as if to say, "Before I get serious about her I want you to say she's OK." Given his prejudices I wasn't surprised that he considered my African friends too loud and primitive, but mainly he couldn't bear so many ebony people crowding around him.

He and my brother were annoyed at my expressing a desire to visit the Ibos in their homeland when they returned, my study of their language and my courses at NYU on African civilizations. I thought my boyfriend might take a similar bourgeoisies approach, but no, he was entranced. He felt that these men had a confidence that originated in their having been born in a society that praised their ancestry and treasured each child. He held me close, and whispered hardly audibly about his admiration of their determination to reclaim their own: Colonialism had not made them second-class citizens in their homeland, but had stiffened their resolve to be their own masters. I could see that he was buoyed by having been surrounded by these Black people; this massive continent held his history too and he wanted to find it and add that support to the elements that would make him a complete and competent man.

Misting rain was glistening on his hands as he raised them in a gesture that said, "What was the use of striving?" Then he clasped them before his mouth and closed his eyes. A boy who grew up battered by life's circumstances: having to work from the time he was 9 years old, shining shoes, picking cotton, trying to make a living for himself and his mother might well have struggled with the meaning of his existence. Her love was eternal, but able to supply only the minimum essentials. "When I was drafted," he said, "I thought that at last I could supply her with decent money to live on, and if I were to die in combat, she would have my insurance, which I took out to the max." My eyes widened in horror; he had never talked like this before. I reached under his jacket and wrapped both my arms around him. I snuggled close to him with my head on his chest. He turned and kissed me on the forehead, then continued, looking out at the passing traffic:

"Sometimes I purposely endangered myself; a heroic death was preferable for me, whose life to this point had stood for nothing. Anyway, as a Black man, who might at any time be accosted by a white man and would not dare retaliate, who still faced lynching and street shootings, I didn't plan on living long. My feats looked like bravery: dauntless skillful planning and execution of troop movements. I threw myself into it; never before in my life had what I thought, what I designed, meant so much, and I was good at it. Moreover, I would back up my schemes by putting my own life on the line. The Black troops had experienced the danger of capricious careless maneuvers designed by white officers, disdainful of their well-being. They trusted me never to endanger them unless everything was planned thoroughly, with saving their lives paramount. When orders came down, I, a master sergeant, was called in with the white brass. I studied the maps; I listened to the briefings, I paid attention to the weather reports and Kraut troop movements. Those white officers could barely use a slide rule; they were ignorant of calculus, but I had some terrific Black teachers in high school in Macon who had gone to Howard and the best Ivy League universities. At last I was doing a job where I could use abilities that I subverted on the crappy waiter and busboy jobs available to me. Paul got field promotions, moving up from lieutenant to captain. I knew he depended on my calculations and they had a lot to do with his promotions. He acknowledged me, he respected me, but could do nothing to cross the hard line to give me a field promotion in that segregated army. He also

Marietta J. Tanner

needed me on the front lines to keep up the morale of the Black soldiers who were driving those convoys over the Alps, dodging shrapnel, slogging through the muddy, churned-up streets of devastated towns and confronting the grenades of Nazi troops. The Italians were helping us; Paul had made friends, and was getting good intelligence from them."

"Wow," I said pinching his waist, "and we are getting soaked. Let's go over to the Beekman and warm up." He came back from a far-off place, stretched as I removed my arms from under his jacket, took my hand and stood up, "Phew," he said shaking his head, "I wonder where all that came from? I guess your friend, Ndukwe, made me think about how much we have underestimated ourselves in the USA; how we have accepted the mantle of unworthiness, in-feriority, inequality; he doesn't have any of it." "You two really hit it off," I said. "Yeah, we might be talking business; he's got some good ideas and although it's a long shot, he may have the wherewithal to carry it out...maybe." "Ah, there you go, preparing to push that rock up the hill, trucking in Africa, I suppose?" "No, no, no, I'm not talking, it's premature to even mention it, but I will be looking into some things with him," he confessed with a laugh.

We walked across the street to Beekman Towers and took the elevator to the top. For some bizarre reason, he wanted more time in the misty rain. We borrowed a huge umbrella and went out on the roof. A breeze was blowing strongly as we leaned on the parapets and watched the East River ripple in the wind. He stood behind me with his arms around my shoulders; I rested my head on his bicep. He stroked my face as he talked; warmed and comforted was I by his deep voice, his body so close, his breath on my ear as he mixed anxiety with hope, his passion with anger at the cruel hand he had been dealt and concern that he might not find the courage to play it.

I excused myself on the way to our table and I pondered: what does happen to the mind and spirit of individuals like us after experiencing 300 years of the trauma of enslavement? Is it possible to pick cotton from dawn to dusk, be slopped at a pig's trough for dinner, sleep on clay floors barely covered with filthy rags, be humiliated by word and deed to be compliant, subservient, obedient to abusers of your flesh, your sexuality, your intelligence, and emerge with your humanity intact? These learned behaviors are not so easily dispelled. I remember Mark Twain's "Puddin'Head Wilson's" child-to-the-manor born who was switched for a slave girl's baby. He bowed and scraped, and stepped off the sidewalk to let white folks pass even after Puddin'Head's heel print proved his identity as the white patrician. Would it be possible to forget the lash and its enforcer though the keloids snaked across your back; or would the victim subjected to such cruelty for any real or imagined infraction grow up seething with submerged anger, biding his time for an opportunity to grasp and slash the cat o' nine tails across his tormenter's torso?

After generations as observer and recipient of brutality, despite hopelessness, the man would still want to live. His broken spirit would find ways to cope: He would avoid the eye, bow the head, and shuffle the broken body through years of the endless toil. We laughed as children at Stepin Fetchit at the Saturday matinee. Yet, I can remember a catch in my throat as I did; you did not hear the raucous guffaws from our segregated side that resounded from across the aisle in the white section of the movie house. There was Stepin, servilely saying, "Yassa Boss," as he moved at a snail's pace, finding the longest route for the shortest task, knowing that there was no fair remuneration for work efficiently and well done. The Negro kids related to Stepin, and saw their and their parents' reality in his antics. Their history posed the question, "Why strive for excellence?"

I said very little at dinner. I listened, and, at appropriate moments, I took his hands in mine across the table and kissed them. I was silently saying, "Our love would give him strength not to succumb to the Stepin Fetchit syndrome, but to triumph despite the negatives in his past." Instances of insults to his psyche peppered our walk to the car and the ride to Brooklyn. I don't think I had agreed that I would go home with him, but there seemed to be tacit agreement that this night we had to be together.

When we reached the apartment, he ushered me in, removing my jacket. I sat at his desk to take off my shoes. Ah hah, he had been reading about some of the issues that were the focus of our evening talk. DuBois and *The Crisis* were there and several articles from the *Nation* and *New York Times Magazine*, with passages underlined or pages clipped. I questioned him about his reading selections, to which he said studying finance and business didn't allow much time for sociology and history, so he had to catch up. Having to contend with my interest in those subjects, and getting this invitation to the UN, he thought he would bring himself up to snuff. He was pleased that the reading had aroused personal thoughts in him, made him realize how much the Negro people in this country still carried the scars of enslavement and that systems, customs and laws exacerbate them and are designed to reopen the wounds, keeping us second-class citizens. I had never seen him so inspired as if making a stump speech. He caught himself, as if a little startled at what he had said, removed his tie, unbuttoned his shirt and turned to complete his disrobing as he walked to the bedroom. I followed him like a disciple, still inquisitive, intrigued and probing to know more of his thoughts.

It was not to be; he began to disrobe me and smother my questions with kisses. In a second I was nude and he fondled away all thought of what the brain was conjuring with his ardent caresses. It seemed he was stronger, more intense in his love making that night than I had ever known. Following one episode, he murmured some thoughts about the importance of satisfying a woman as being part and parcel of the whole structure, and how much loving me was making his life more fulfilling. I whispered my response into his chest, so he could barely hear me; he lifted my face, nuzzling my eyes, and urging me to say again how transformative his love had been for me.

Oh, my god, we had forgotten the condoms, but OK, OK, this is not the time I am ovulating. I reassured myself on the way to the bathroom and checked my calendar in the early morning light. Nothing shall cloud the wonder of this night for me. I gazed at his completely relaxed body in the crumpled bed, a slight smile on his face, not a line of care: smooth, even breathing, handsome, hairy chest heaving lightly; I beheld health and well-being over his entire body. As I sidled next to him, he raised his arm to let me cuddle closer and in harmony with him, I fell into a blissful sleep...

♦ ♦ ♦

The Discovery

I knew, I knew it, the moment I woke up that morning. I had been feeling lightheaded for the last couple of days, having a kind of hollowness in my throat, belching up food polyps that had a wretched, rusty taste. Now I was feeling really dizzy; my stomach was churning, and I hadn't eaten a thing that would give me indigestion last night. As a matter of fact, I was not very hungry and could hardly get a bowl of chicken soup down. As I turned to get out of bed, I regurgitated a slimy wad of half-digested food; I picked up the wastebasket to catch it as I gagged and spat it out. I fell back on the bed, wiping my mouth on my nightgown, staring at the ceiling in disbelief. So, this is it.! Yes, my darling, we practiced using the condom but forgot, and now the horse is out of the barn. It happened so quickly, in these few months. Like my mother said, she was pregnant with another baby the moment she stopped nursing. Her contraceptive was a sponge soaked in vinegar that never worked. Fertility runs in the family. What's next? I know I can't go through with this. But, I closed my eyes, and whispered, "I like the feeling of carrying his child." I gagged again. "I can't have a child now. Stop it, stop the sentimentality; get moving." I will call my sister and tell her, she would know what I should do. It's far too late for the vinegar douche and I will not submit to the clothes hanger.

I had an extension phone in my room, and my landlady, Golda, never snooped, so I thought I'd better make that call as soon as possible. I dialed my older sister, who answered groggily. "Sorry to call you so early, but I have to talk with you." I said. "Really, it sounds urgent, and unless you were hit by a car, or need money you sound like it can only be one other thing. How many weeks?" she said in her usual know-it-all tone. "It can't be more than four, I had my period last month." "What does the guy say? I mean, does he want to marry you?" "Oh I don't know, I couldn't have a shotgun wedding, that would be the pits, and I just don't have the nerve to tell him." "Well I don't know why, he's just as responsible as you, although you were pretty stupid to have unprotected sex." "Look, look, I'm not feeling too well, and not in the mood for sermonizing. Do you know anybody who could help me?" "Sure I do, you should know somebody yourself; but you're the sanctimonious virgin, I guess you thought you'd never have to stoop to dealing with such people. So you come to ask me to find your sinful savior." She was teasing me, but I was having none of it. "Look, I need help and I need it quick. You're a married woman, you know all the ropes, and could help me." "And I will, I know an MD who does the work on the side, and a person who will house you during the procedure, but it's not cheap, and this boyfriend should pay the bill."

At first, I started to continue my argument about why I couldn't tell him, but decided I would agree with her that he would pay, and I would tell him, so I said, "I know he wouldn't want the burden of fatherhood at this juncture; he's just getting a business started, and rah, rah about what he wants to accomplish, so I'm sure he'll foot the bill."   "Is this the guy Mom was so enamored of last summer?" "Yes," I said, "he's the only guy I've been dating for almost a year." "Hmm, it seems like you should try to land him," she said. "Oh, well, maybe, but not this way, for all kinds of reasons, we both understand, I would not want a guy I bamboozled into marriage. Please, what's the plan?" I asked. "Well, bring about 1,000 bucks, I will contact them. It should be done as soon as possible. I would say this weekend. Friday?" "Call me on my job, as soon as you get everything squared away, and speak discretely, I can arrange it whenever you say." "Ok, I'm sorry, this is never easy, so don't think it's going to be a walk in the park for you. I don't think I will get to see you, but I'll arrange everything, and you know the woman where you'll be housed, so don't be afraid she'll talk as this is business for her and she's not about to be gossiping." "Thanks so much, call me at work and let me know."

I hit the wall several times as I tried to walk erectly to the bathroom to shower and get myself to work. Golda was still asleep, thank goodness, when I left. I was happy to smell the fresh air, and walk fairly soberly to the subway. How will I tell him? No, I won't tell him. I will lie. I'll say I have to go to my mother's sister's funeral on Friday; I will return late Saturday, I won't stay for all the formalities, so I can see him on Sunday. My sister said I won't feel well after the procedure, but I can say I always feel this way this time of the month, and he will have to understand that I won't be up to sex. Religious guys like him believe it's a sin to be intimate when a woman is having her menses, and no amount of amorous desire can supersede that dictum. I will tell him that I will call him, as I don't know where I will be, at the funeral parlor, the church or my aunt's house. What time will he be home on Saturday? I will call him as soon as I arrive back in New York. We can have a whole day together Sunday. Mother's Day. How apropos! He will want to spend it with his mother, I'm sure.

I told my boss the same lie about my aunt's death; I felt terrible. My mother's only sister had died years ago in the 1918 flu epidemic; I never saw her, and she never even knew I existed. I hated lying to my boyfriend, we were at such a sublime place, I trusted him completely, and I think he would believe anything I would tell him. We were at the point in our relationship that we could sense things about each other. I must admit that I care deeply for him, and feel sicker every time I think of the lie I am concocting. He might be at the place where he can see through my deception; I am glad this will be a telephone lie, God knows I don't want him to say he will come over to take me to the train. I'll wait until I am at Penn Station before I call. Ooh God, deceit is so difficult, the whole thing is difficult, tragic, awful, I wish … but you don't wish, this is the path you have chosen and you will walk down this road to wherever.

◆ ◆ ◆

Frida's place

We would not be able to get a train out until the next day; there had long been switching problems and they were working on the tracks to utilize a new system that would not require men to stand out waving lamps. Electronic switching was coming to Mexico, and techniques perfected during the war and in use all over the United States and Europe would be employed here. And the day we were slated to leave was the day it would be done in Mexico City.

We had counted our pennies, determining just how much we had to take us back to the States, at least until we got to South Carolina and Eve's aunt's house. We would have to spend another night's rent at this hotel, and lounge around the garden and maybe take a walk to one of the museums to fill our day. We could not do any shopping since the budget would not allow more extravagant purchases. I had to dig into my tiny contingency fund.

I determined that I was going to Frida Kahlo's house. I explained again to everyone who she was and asked if anyone wanted to go with me. Lou gave a yowl and an emphatic no indeed, to the idea; the others rolled their eyes. "Another wild excursion with you, no, thanks." My failed adventure there with Lou had made me more determined; I would take another route. I scoured the pamphlet PR had given me. I was absolutely fascinated by her dedication to the Revolution, her bravery, her determination to paint and to make a statement about women's rights despite her illnesses and an unfaithful husband.

The hotelier said it was not far, but we might not be able to get in. I was not to be deterred. This would be a highlight of my trip, to pay tribute to this woman artist; would that I could learn to assert myself as she has done despite all the obstacles thrown in her way.

She was the companion of Diego, a brilliant woman whose work both EF and PR had told me I must see. Both had contacted Diego to ask permission for me to visit the house, so I was sure I would be admitted. Taxis cost the equivalent of 50 American cents, so even in my precarious financial state, I could afford it. Lou was adamant: "Why do you have to be going somewhere all the time where no one else wants to go?" "Look, we agreed that we all would not like the same things, this is what I dearly want to see, so I am going. I will be back by 2 or 3 o'clock, the train won't leave until 5." They all looked angrily at me, "We will be on the Ferrocarriles Nacionales de Mexico at 5 p.m. with or without you."

The concierge called a cab; the driver was a friend of his, so I asked him to take me and wait, I would be no longer than an hour. He was amenable and told me it would cost two American dollars. I was off to "The Blue House," that was all I wanted to see, if I only made it to the grounds that would be good enough. I knew I would not see all of her paintings since they were scattered all over the place. Some still at the gallery, some purchased by Delores Olmedo, a friend, who was working to make a museum of Kahlo's oeuvre. But *La Casa Azul* is where Frieda Kahlo died on July 13; her countrymen were still mourning her passing. On the phone one night, PR said he had attended the funeral, as had a good many of her students. He had seen her last year at the first solo exhibition of her works at the Galeria de Arte Contemporaneo. She was taken there by Diego in her bed. She was gravely ill, but she said she was triumphant because she was able to attend and feel that she was finally being recognized.

Frida was ready to die and it was rumored that her death may have been a suicide. She was deeply depressed and the pain from her last back operation was unbearable. She was only able to paint lying in bed, using a special easel Diego had made for her. She knew her work was suffering: heretofore the intricate lace and delicate jewelry in each portrait was painted with precision, and now an unsteady hand held the brush, obfuscating much of the detail. Her love for the Revolution and freedom for the indigenous people of Mesoamerica was still fervent, even as she weakened. The gallant Kahlo took part in a protest against the CIA in Guatemala while suffering from pneumonia, a few of weeks before she died. A procession with her coffin aloft took place in the streets and her body laid in state at the Palacio de Belles Artes.

Her house was in Coyoacan, a suburb of Mexico City, on the other side from Xochomilco. The scenery was dry and the trees and plants browning and dusty from the end of summer heat. It was in a rather poor residential section; I knew immediately when we came upon it. The house was of stucco, painted what I would call a Gauguin blue, with the windows framed in flamingo pink. There was a small garden, with a chair and some paints just as she had left them. I was greeted by a servant, to whom the taxi driver spoke to explain the purpose of my visit. He went inside and returned with a young woman who said she was a cousin, and that they were expecting me. I expressed my delight in my best Spanish, but she spoke much better English, so we decided to converse in that language. There were just a few people there, seemingly members of the family dressed in black, who smiled pleasantly as I passed, but said nothing.

I was shown into the studio just off the garden; it was light and airy, with a wheelchair before a standing easel, her palettes, brushes and pots of paint and linseed oil neatly arranged on several tables. There were some paintings standing unframed on a table. The most fascinating one was on metal, and showed a black-faced woman holding an infant with Frida's adult face, and nursing. I was taken by the breast. The mammary glands had been carefully delineated showing that they were not virgin breasts but capable of producing milk for the baby to suckle. Drool fell from its mouth. I was told by my guide that Frida painted this picture because she had a wet nurse when she was an infant. I held my hand to my breast, immediately thinking how the body changes to accommodate the newborn child, months before it is born as my breasts had done ... but don't let me start thinking of that.

There was a painting which I thought rather primitive of peasants on a bus, and in the little hallway, a portrait of Frida's family. The coloring of each person was interesting; her father and paternal grandfather very white (they were German) and her mother's side considerably darker, especially her maternal grandfather, who was indigenous. The living relatives, her sisters and stepsisters, were sepia to light brown. There was a painting of her father, which she had done when she first started painting, praising him in an inscription for his stand against Hitler and his courage in continuing to work, although he suffered from epilepsy. I was looking for the self-portraits for which Kahlo was famous. She said she painted herself because she was the person she knew best, but most of the faces were stoic; only the surroundings gave an inkling of what she was thinking or experiencing. I had seen one with her and monkeys at the museum before we went to Cuernavaca and thought surely there would be many here, but there were none. There were several paper sketches, sketch books, and then the horrible painting, with a banner floating over it carried by what looked like a raven: "Unos Cuantos Piquetitos! – A few little pricks." I stopped and stared, and my guide explained that Frida was going through a difficult period, very hurt by her marriage and illnesses. She took the image of a man who had killed his wife with small cuts, and likened it to her own situation, where she was inflicted by constant painful incisions physical and mental. The body, the bed, the man and the picture frame were splattered with blood.

I went next into the bedroom where Frida had done so much of her painting which was just as she had left it. There was a four-poster bed, and on the bottom of the canopy was a full skeleton, and around the sides, artifacts that she could look at from her prone position. On the headboard were many photographs of family and friends and of herself with Diego. There was drapery around it, but the famous easel that she used to paint on was not there. It was perched against the wall on a table and on it stood the painting of Frida at the Henry Ford hospital in Detroit with her body bloodied from a miscarriage. There were votive images of a fetus, her pelvis, a snail, and her torso. On the wall next to it, was a lithograph of Frida's abortion, showing a fetus in stages of development. I was mesmerized by these works, literally moving from one to the other, inspecting them; the fetus was much larger, the votive images not associative to my experience, and yet, abortion is universal, the pain and horror of it is global. Why did I have to know it; pregnant when I was first experiencing the joy of sex, why me?

Suddenly the votive images were off the canvass, whirling about me; I was desperately trying to push them away. Then I was in the tailspin, I felt myself dropping from a great height, then falling hard against what was actually the floor in front of the bed but it seemed like the highest point of the Sierra Madres.   I clawed at the mattress and strained to see through the darkness. A sliver of light fell across the bloody woman stretched nude on the counterpane; the grimacing tear-stained face was mine. That was me on that bed, not Frida!

◆　◆　◆

In a dizzying moment, I was at a house in a pleasant section of Philadelphia, having arrived from North Philadelphia station. I had walked the cavernous underground tunnel from the Pennsylvania station to the Reading line, and taken the train to Pleasant Avenue Station. There I got a taxi to the address my sister had given me. The woman, whom I knew, was waiting for me. I entered quickly and was escorted to a bedroom upstairs. She told me to rest, and asked if I would like something to drink or some soup. I settled for a cup of tea and looked out the window at the greening trees.

I was remembering my mother's life with the tyrant. She read her Bible and believed the man was the master to whom she was to submit in all things. Wife-beating enforced his control. Control, the lack of which haunted him subconsciously as a residual from our enslaved past. Unresolved trauma from the time when a Black man had no control over anything: not his waking, nor sleeping; not his own body nor that of the woman he would call wife. A woman whom he could not marry and with whom a white man could be intimate whenever he pleased. My father's childhood with the foster mother who was cruel to him, who made him eat table scraps, reinforced his emotional memory of enslavement and deprivation, filling him with hatred of anything that would impede his access to gratification. My mother's family forced him to marry her, depriving him of his bachelorhood when he was finally in control of his life.

To reinforce his dominance, my father would take any infractions we committed out on our mother. "I support her; she does not work outside the home," he would boast (ignoring her endless toil inside it) and therefore her job was to rear his kids. She was blamed if we didn't toe the line. To save her skin, we were blackmailed from adventure, from romance, fearing having a child out of wedlock – the ultimate sin, for which my mother's life had forever been made miserable. I am doing this illegal act for which the physician, the nurse and I could be jailed. Abortion was illegal in Pennsylvania and everywhere else in the United States. I am doing this to save my reputation and, subconsciously, for the love of my mother.

I sighed as I felt my stomach; I could feel nothing moving inside me, yet living tissue was there, an egg now inseminated with sperm was growing there. I began to undress. The woman returned and told me she was giving me a mild laxative, and started to prepare me for the operation, washing me carefully with antiseptic. I blurted out, "I don't want to be shaved." She said that wouldn't be necessary. When she left, I fell asleep, and was awakened at around 4:30 in the afternoon. She took me to the bathroom and asked me to evacuate as much as I could.

When I returned, the doctor was there. He said hello, put on a smock over his shirt and tie, went to the bathroom to

wash his hands and returned to assemble the instruments lying in a basin of disinfectant. The woman who was now assisting him gave me a sedative, and whispered, "Don't worry,
for you it will be like a D and C," meaning the dilation and cu-
rettage pelvic procedure given to women who have excessive
uterine bleeding or other ailments. "With the sedative, you
won't feel anything." I was moved to a small portable operating table. I felt him poking around my stomach, then I opened
my legs and put my feet in the stirrups. I felt the cold steel
of the speculum he put inside me, and the clamps he used to
hold the cervix in place. Even though I was in a kind of twilight
sleep, I could hear them talking faintly, I could feel the pressure in my uterus as the instruments were brushed against its
walls removing pieces of the fertilized egg and placenta. After
the excavation, he did a light scraping and cleansing of the
cervix with antiseptic and without inflicting pain; I knew when
the tissue was gathered because I heard her say, "There it is,
not very much at all, would you say, just about four weeks?"
The doctor, who I learned was a devout Christian, responded
with, "Uh huh, not yet a living soul."

I heard the clinking of instruments on a steel basin; he
went in again to be sure every scrap of the tissue was removed; all over in less than 10 minutes. So, simple for me, so
horrid for Frida. The assistant packed my vagina with cotton,
and they moved me to the bed covered with rubber sheets. I
fell into a deep sleep, and was awakened when the assistant
came in to ask how I felt, to take my temperature and pulse
and to be sure I was bleeding properly, she took me to the

bathroom to check, removing some of the packing. She was very competent and kind, never a harsh word for the dastardly deed we had done.

I awoke about dawn and rushed to the bathroom, I thought I was hemorrhaging, as I felt a surge of blood to my head, and the need to urinate. I removed the packing and was frightened by the dark clotted blood that splattered about me. The same blood that covered Frida's bed: fetal blood, the remains of what might have been Diego's, no, my boyfriend's and my child. Poor Frida, she wanted a child so much that she risked unprotected intercourse numerous times to have a fetus in a womb that could never grow to hold a full-term child; those broken hips could never allow an infant to mature there; her injured spine requiring that her torso be encased in steel must have caused her excruciating pain as her uterus grew heavy with or tried to expel her unborn child. She delineated the deformation of hip and spine in her paintings. Mine were built for childbearing, that Harvard doctor had told me; getting pregnant was easy, too easy.

The assistant came into the bathroom and helped me clean myself and the mess I had made on the white tile floor and commode. She changed my gown, went to see that I had not soiled the bed, and urged me to get more sleep. She brought me some soup and crackers, and I went back to sleep, knowing that I had to catch a 3 o'clock train. I asked her to awaken me at about noon so I could prepare and get a taxi to the station. She said I was cutting things rather short, that I should stay at least until 5, giving myself a good

24 hours before attempting anything as strenuous as walking to the train. But that was not to be, I had to get back. I know my boyfriend would be calling me, and I could not risk discovery of the lie I had told him ….

◆ ◆ ◆

Frida's cousin and my taxi driver were dabbing my face with ice when I emerged from my swoon. My first words were, "What time is it?" They were asking if I was OK; I shook my head and, holding on to the arm of the chair, stood up. I knew there were more paintings to see, but I gasped, "I must be going, I'm going to be late. I am so sorry, but I was overcome with the pathos of it all; thank you so much for the tour. I don't know what happened, I never faint, but I'm fine, and so appreciate your showing me around the house," I said, grasping her hands. I stumbled out, holding on to the taxi driver. He said, "Don't worry, you'll get back in plenty of time." "What did I do?" I asked. "You passed out, overcome by the paintings. It happens sometimes," he said as he whirled the car around and started off toward the hotel.

When I got back, Lou was waiting. Showing her absolute disgust, she said, "Here she comes again, looking like she has been hit by a truck. What in the world happened to you? … Go wash your face, at least! You've been crying and you're all ruffled up, what happened?" "Oh, all is OK, I was overcome by the paintings and her life story; it was so sad. She was able to illustrate what she felt: the disappointment of a philandering husband, several severe operations, an accident, polio, abortions and miscarriages. I empathized with the tragedy of it all. I understand what Diego meant when he said that she painted a woman's pain."

Part 2
A Train Ride Times Two

I was subdued and contemplative on the way back to Monterrey. I was on the train in Mexico, but it reminded me of the one from Philadelphia to New York. I was as nauseous and as grief-stricken as I was then. The impact of my visit to Coyoacan compounded the horror of the actual event, and the double whammy kept washing over me:

On the Train with Bruce

How tired I was that day, how anxious to be alone. I struggled to carry my small bag into the terminal, and was afraid to close my eyes as I waited less I miss my train. I had plenty of time before the train and most of that was spent in the restroom, making sure I was fully protected from accidents. I should have stayed the entire 24 hours, as my nurse had urged, but I had to get back to Manhattan and his telephone call.

I boarded the train to return to New York. I fell into the reclining seat and stared out of the window. I was slightly dizzy and not in the mood to have to talk to anyone, so I hoped the seat next to me would stay empty. I put my coat on the seat and my bag on the floor to discourage would-be seat companions, but it didn't work. The coach car was filling up fast, and the conductor came along and offered to put my luggage on the rack above, as, he said, these items don't have a ticket. I closed my eyes and laid my head against the window frame.

I wanted sleep but that was not to be. Someone called my name; oh, my stars, Bruce, the husband of a friend of mine, Carol, from high school I hadn't seen in years. Bruce was babbling on about how glad he was to see me, and when had I seen any of the old crowd we used to party with when I was fresh out of high school. I sat up, and in my most courteous tone asked about his wife, with whom I had been close. "She's fine..." then he hesitated, "I can tell you, she's really not so fine. She just lost our second baby, and she is heartbroken." "Oh my god, I am so sorry. I must write her; I didn't get to come to your wedding, but I spoke with Carol last year and she was happily pregnant." "She lost that one, so we tried again, with the same unfortunate result." "My condolences to you, and give Carol my love, there is yet time, and the doctors can do so much now, I'll be praying for you," I said. He was rubbing his hands together, shrugging his shoulders, and on the verge of tears. I felt like a skunk just having destroyed the fetus of a child like the one they were longing for; I tried to speak but was all choked up myself and couldn't utter a word. I wanted to change the subject, but would not dare mention any of our old friends, unless he brought it up. He seemed to want to talk on and on about his wife's ordeal, and each sigh punctured my conscience like a stiletto.

I was beginning to feel nauseous; it seemed that the bleeding had started all over again. I excused myself and stumbled to the restroom, taking my small carry-on with supplies to take care of the deluge. My sister was right: this is not a walk in the park. It is scary; suppose I start hemorrhaging on this train? I was sick to my stomach, hungry too, as I didn't stop to eat a thing, since I was sure I couldn't digest it. Luckily there was an empty restroom, and I was able to enter quickly into that uncomfortable, narrow space; to hold on to the handrails and lean against the walls to freshen myself. It took forever, I had to practically mop the floor and wipe off several surfaces to clean up my spills. I used a profusion of paper towels and tried to cover them in the wastebasket so as not to offend the next user. There was a knocking on the door, and a line of scowling people as I exited and made my way back to my seat.

Bruce stood as I approached, asking, "Are you OK?" "Oh fine, just some time-consuming rituals we gals have to do," I said. I did so wish he would lay off the conversation, but he wanted to talk about his personal experience, especially to a woman, whom he knew well, but not too well. He wanted to question me about what women feel in such a situation, as he was the husband, who felt none of the pangs of childbirth or the weeks and months of carrying a child, feeling life developing inside you. "I would hold her at night, and have the pleasure of feeling my child growing and kicking from inside her body; Carol and I would both laugh at the thought of his restlessness: Was he getting bored and anxious to come out and see this world out here?"

Luckily, I did not have to answer. Clearly, I did not have the answers; she had carried that baby to term and it was still-born. When he finally told me, he began to openly cry, and I sought to comfort him. I was crying too, my heart running over with sympathy for him and Carol and full of guilt and anguish about my own transgression. He wiped his eyes, and smiled. "I'm so sorry, but would you believe, this is the first time I have cried about our losses. I don't mean to burden you with my sorrow, I am so sorry." "Please don't be, I'm so glad I was here for you. This is a painful time for both of you." "I've been staying home with her, afraid to leave her side, but I had to come to New York for a program I have been developing and a sermon tomorrow. I hated to leave her with her mother and sisters on Mother's Day yet. I have been holding on for her sake, and not breaking down myself, and I guess being away from her turned me into this simpering child. Please forgive me." I held his hand and pressed his arm against mine, telling him that we all need a shoulder to weep on sometimes. I tried to say something religious, since he was in the ministry, but it would be hypocritical for me to pray with him, or call on God in the way of the sisters in the Baptist church. I did say that "the Lord will bring you healing," because I knew he believed that, and I was not swearing to do anything with God myself.

When we got to Penn Station, I was really weak, and he thought that his travail was to blame for my condition. I told him that I hadn't been feeling well, and asked him to hail me a cab so I could go home immediately. He was anxious now for my sake, and I leaned on his arm as we took the escalator to the street and he got me a cab on Eighth Avenue. I waved goodbye to him, asking him to be sure to give my love to Carol, and to understand that I was not permanently ill, but suffering something women do every month. He smiled knowingly and said, "I'm so glad to hear it, I won't feel guilty then. Thanks for everything."

◆ ◆ ◆

My girlfriends were passing out the lunch, and Lou nudged me, "Do you want a sandwich, you seem so knocked out," she said as she pushed my covers over and sat down beside me. She wondered why I had to go to Coyoacan; why I always had to wander away from the others to see something or do something that she felt was potentially dangerous. "Sorry, but both PR and EF had said that a visit to Frida Khalo's house would be the highlight of the trip, and it was to me. I got to understand so much about her life, how she fought despite her illness and incapacity to be an independent woman, how she asserted herself through her art. I am so glad I went."

Lou, was skeptical. "You looked terrible when you came back. What in the world did you do?" "I was greatly moved by the experience of her art; I had only seen one of her paintings – you know the one we saw in that gallery when we were making the tour. She was in one of the murals that Diego painted, too." I picked up the little booklet I had gotten at the museum. "EF insisted that she was a phenomenon in the artistic world. She suffered so much to achieve. Listen to this. Diego said, 'She is the first woman in the history of art to treat with absolute and uncompromising honesty, one might even say with impassive cruelty, those general and specific themes which exclusively affect women.' I believe I had an epiphany in Coyoacan; I have learned from her experience to accept myself and my abilities with more pride and express them despite all of the limitations and restrictions that govern our lives."

"Oh, my god," Lou said in her most exasperated tone, "What you need is a better-paying job, and to get out of all that artsy stuff you are doing, all that left-wing politics with those Africans, and go back to Abyssinian Church and listen to some good old down-home preaching to set you straight. You're always trying to do something exotic." "I think I am searching for clarity. I am going to delve deeper into my understanding of the African diaspora, for example. This trip really opened my eyes to it."

"I don't get all the African stuff; we're trying to move away from our enslavement past, and you are constantly running around with those African guys, and attending those left-wing conferences that will smear your record and make it impossible for you to get a good job." "I have a good job," I said. "And I am not a communist, but I do associate with some left-wing causes, and I admired what Diego and Frida did in Mexico around the revolution. I was moved by those peasants running to hear their president speak; I wanted to talk with the artist who was designing the silver bracelets and was involved with Diego and Frida and the revolution; these are the things that have meaning for me." "Now you have broken up with a really nice guy, one who has money too. The women are clamoring for him, and he just seems to ignore them. I bet it was all this left-wing stuff that broke you two up, wasn't it?" "You and Tom are close to him, why don't you ask him?" Lou shrugged and went back to her card playing, leaving me to my solitary contemplation.

I went to the restroom to get a good look at myself. I did look pretty bedraggled; I was so deep in reverie now, fairly shivering as I remembered dragging out of the taxi and into the apartment that afternoon:

◆ ◆ ◆

The Almost Engagement

Golda's wide eyes showed that they knew that something was amiss the minute I walked in the door; when I got to the bathroom I could see why. There were circles under my eyes as dark as a hemophiliac's who had lost pints of blood. And I, who was pretty spunky, able to walk faster than most folks, was dragging, hardly able to carry my small suitcase. She literally had to help me to my room. I said that the funeral had been a sad and debilitating experience, and I had a brutal period this time, which I seldom get. She wasn't buying it, but she was not judgmental, just helped me to the room and asked if I would like something to eat, some soup or a cup of tea, which I gratefully accepted. When she returned, I hastily ate the soup and got in bed, trying my best to sleep fast, as I knew tomorrow was going to be difficult to say the least.

I had already promised an early date to last the day, and it was Mother's Day. That meant I had to have a long conversation with my own mother, who could detect the slightest aberration in my behavior by my speech. My boyfriend would want to take his mother out to dinner and invite me to stay the night with him, I'm sure. I'd better call him, but if I sound weak he will rush over here and all will be lost. I asked Golda to say that I had gone to the store and that I would call when I got back. That might give me a few hours of rest.

He called while I was asleep, so when I awakened, I knew I had to call him. I took a very hot bath, soaked myself and used an abundance of soap as if I were trying to wash away my anguish. I stared at myself in the mirror; I did look better, and maybe if I got some more ice for my face, I would begin to look normal again. I would be dressed as lovely as possible for him tomorrow in a pink linen sheath I had made that fitted perfectly with Golda's help. I will arm myself with pads to make sure I won't have an accident, I told myself. I put my hair up in rollers and laid down on the bed again. I took a deep breath and dialed.

"Hello, so you're back and all is well?" I said in my happiest tone. "Could I see you tonight?" he said anxiously. "I am ready for bed; tomorrow is going to be a long day. You're taking your mother out for Mother's Day, aren't you?" "No, she has gone to Georgia to be with her ailing sister, and so I have the day set aside for you and me. I'd like to begin it tonight," he said. "I made myself a special outfit so she could praise me for my couturier skills, and now she's not going to see it. Are you going to church tomorrow?" "Not unless you want to. I want to make the day special for you, so we can have plenty of time together. I've rented a suite for us at a swanky hotel in Westchester. We can have breakfast, lunch and dinner there if you want. I have so much I want to say to you, we could go tonight." "I don't want you making those grand plans, it's that time of the month for me, you know." "Oh, God. I'm sorry, and I'm happy, but we can still be together, and we can talk about what happens next with us. I miss you so much. You're the only thing that makes these days with those prejudiced bastards I work with bearable. I can take their shit, because I know you will be there to give the love that strengthens me."

"What's happened?" "As I told you, we needed a loan to make the investment in the new modal transport system, and my partner brought in this uncle who supposedly would offer us a quick fix so we wouldn't have to sign half of the company away. But I knew it wouldn't work from the start. His uncle looked at me as if I were a gorilla sitting at my desk, and talked down to me. I expected any day he would ask me to make coffee or bring him his mail. He made constant digs that rattled me. He poisoned the air, creating an atmosphere that gave the staff permission to disrespect me. I was about to blow my stack."

Conditions were worsening at his company. He dearly loved what he had accomplished there, and strove to be positive about the future, but I could see the weariness in his face sometimes when I met him after work. He would shake himself, as if he were warming up after being in the cold. He was like a grasshopper molting his constricting coat and emerging vulnerable, needing to rest in a safe warm place until, larger and stronger, he was ready to face the world again. Lately he would pour out his soul to me; I could see vulnerability in him and feel him nestle his head on my shoulder, and I would bend mine to make a special place for him. He would hold me and rock my body, nude or clothed, in this position. I would not disturb him until he stirred and kissed me, smothering my mouth, my eyes, my ears with his nibbling kisses, caressing my body everywhere, until he and I were ready for the … Oh, breathless pause, he would with those long and tapered fingers deftly slip on the condom with one hand, then slip into my body and rest there. I could feel him swelling inside me; I would long for him to start to touch those exquisite places seemingly made for this instrument that was soft and hard, firm and gentle....

I almost shouted into the phone, "Yes, yes, come tonight, come quickly, I need you so, I want you so, I love you so. Come now." But I squelched my breath, I gasped and said, "I want so much to see you tonight, but I am dead tired, and I am in curlers and pajamas, and *sweetheart* I had planned to be at my best tomorrow just for you. I will wait, can you?" "You called me *sweetheart,* did you mean it? I think you are falling in love with me, darling, I think we are almost there. I can wait, although I probably won't sleep tonight dreaming of tomorrow. May I come at 1 a.m. or do I have to wait until 7?" "Come at 9 and we can have brunch together." "I shall be waiting outside your apartment, or shall I come up to get you? I want to see where you live, and with whom. I think it's time for you to move to Brooklyn, but we'll talk about all that tomorrow. Sleep tight, and remember, you mean the world to me. I love you, darling."

The tears just wouldn't stop flowing and I let them tumble down my face and off my nose and on my sheets and clothing. Why was I so tortured? I had done what had to be done,

I had taken control of my body; I had made it possible for me to plan my future. "Momma." I shall not be like you, whose husband forbade you to protect yourself from pregnancy, declaring he wanted every child he produced so he could boast to his mostly childless friends, "I've got a house full of children here, enough to make our own food, grow our own flowers, mow our own lawn; we are just about self sufficient." And you, slaving every day to make the perfect home, to can the vegetables and preserve the fruit. And he, bashing you regularly to be sure you would fear him and toe the mark. And his house full of kids, cringing in fear too, slavishly following his every command to avoid his wrath, and sobbing with you, our Madonna, who was our source of affection and humanity.

I awoke to a bed askew, pillows everywhere, showing that I'd had a tumultuous night. I must have wrestled with all of my demons and called out to them in my sleep. I stretched and felt refreshed, and went to the bathroom to behold a face plumped, no sunken eyes; ready to smile, and laugh and be loved. I stepped in front of the full-length mirror. Yes, I adored my body because he adored it. My derriere was not too big, he grasped the cheeks with such tenderness; my breasts were not too small; he reveled in my brother's and his frat brothers' dictum: All over a mouthful was wasted. I painted my toe and fingernails; I pulled out my loveliest lingerie, and maybe I would take that slinky white nightgown as a total surprise for him. I would take an overnight bag with lotions and such and my supplies for possible relapse. I was hungry; I went to the kitchen and got a bowl of cereal with bananas and raisins and was smiling and laughing with Golda, who said as she came tottering in in slippers and robe, "What a transformation!" "Happy Mother's Day," I said, "Did you get my card?" I had brought her one that said, "Like a mother to me," which she was; so protective, so anxious that I should look just right in my made-to-order dresses, so interested that I should take the left-wing point of view in all matters political.

I looked out the window to see that he had arrived, took one last turn in the full-length mirror, picked up my bags and descended to the street. He got out of the car to greet me. "Wow, you are so lovely, I really do wish my mom could ogle over you and this dress. You will wear it for her another day soon," he said, giving me a nuzzling kiss on the neck so as not to paint his lips with my lipstick, and escorted me to the car. We rode to Westchester in conversation continually punctuated lavishly with innuendo about his sexual prowess, my total surrender to his manliness, and what he expected to do to me the next time.

When we arrived at his chosen place, we got out of the car and an attendant took the keys to park us, asking if we wanted to drive down to the river. We decided to walk down the stone steps, through the copse of trees interspersed with shade-tolerant bluebells and dogwood; ferns unfurling their fronds in the darker spaces. There was a fragrance of damp leaves and pine; birds were darting about and forest creatures scurrying. It was not such a good idea for me, as I was wearing heels and the steps were mossy in spots. He loved the idea that I was a little helpless, and had to lean on him for support, rewarding himself with extra kisses all the way to the patio. What a lovely place! The Hudson had never looked so blue; you couldn't believe from this perspective that it was becoming polluted. It sparkled in the sunlight, and I thought it was as Henry Hudson first saw it, "beautiful and clear, with silver fish jumping at every turn."

My boyfriend was the happiest I had ever seen him, pleasantly giving our order to the waiter, rubbing my knees under the table, toasting with mimosas to our continued love and happiness. He asked me if I could live with him, if I could weather his moods, which he knew could be dark and foreboding. "You've had the easy life, a father who provided for you; I never knew my Dad. I've been taking care of my mother since I was a kid." "Don't think it was all peaches and cream for me," I said. "My father was a brute; that gentle lady you met last summer has sustained much misery at his hand." "But she was so kind, so attractive and nice, it's hard to believe she was not a cherished wife." "Well, looks are deceiving, I'm not exactly a coddled child myself, you should know. I'm dragging much baggage from a troubled childhood, but admittedly not a hungry one, and one who, despite everything, and because of that little woman, had lots of pleasant days to remember." "You'd never guess it. Sometimes you can be a spoiled brat, kinda snobbish too, used to getting your way in all things. But I have succumbed to giving in to you, because that is where my pleasure lies, watching you become overwhelmed with serene happiness and fall asleep in my arms," he said as brunch arrived.

He was staring at me, and I was blushing; I knew I was in love with him and it was showing. As we ate he kept repeating softly, "I love you so much, it must be you and me together, forever."

Uncharacteristically he started to talk about the business. "I had a long talk with Paul yesterday. I visited him at the hospital, and went over every aspect of the new project, how I was setting it up with his friend so we could be one of the first companies to experiment with the new system. We don't have the money to buy all that it will take to establish it, but we could get in and possibly merge with one of the big boys." "Oh, this is why you're so relaxed today, you have made a deal that puts you in the driver's seat again!" "Not quite, I didn't want to tell him the gory details, he was looking at me with all the hope he could muster; those watery bloodshot eyes were asking, are you going to be OK with my uncle and the company's future? But I know I couldn't live with that situation. Have you ever read the poem 'If' by Rudyard Kipling?" "Oh gosh, where did that come from, of course," I said. "Well, I like the part where he says,"

> *If you can meet with Triumph and Disaster*
> *And treat those two impostors just the same;*
> *If you can bear to hear the truth you've spoken*
> *Twisted by knaves to make a trap for fools,*
> *Or watch the things you gave your life to,*
> *broken,*

And stoop and build 'em up with worn-out
tools

I said almost nothing as we ate, I kept thinking: No, he couldn't have given it all away, what kind of incident broke the camel's back? He would grasp my hand every few minutes, and bend to kiss it gently as I reached for my glass or spoon. Then he would recite another part of the poem:

If you can make one heap of all your winnings
And risk it on one turn of pitch-and-toss,
And lose, and start again at your beginnings
And never breathe a word about your loss;

He was putting on a brave face, I've got to help him through this and see where he is financially, I thought; that hotel venture will not substitute for the trucking industry; that was his dream fulfilled, now it has been destroyed by racism. Oh my god, I feel so inadequate, so powerless to help. I can see he is struggling to gain his footing; to be a man, to be manly, not to succumb to cowardice shrinking before Mr. Mafiosi, slinking away like a beaten dog, a spineless "nigger."

When we finished eating, I thought he would bolt for the bedroom, but no, we would amble around the river path, stopping at the stone benches tactfully tucked into clusters of azalea and rhododendron offering splendid views of the river, but hidden from the glaring eyes of passersby.

If you can fill the unforgiving minute
With sixty seconds' worth of distance run,
Yours is the Earth and everything that's in it,
And—which is more—you'll be a Man, my son!

"You have sold your business, haven't you?" I said, holding his face and looking him straight in the eye. "Partially, I'll still be a major shareholder, but I won't be running it; I didn't give it away." he said, and then returned to nuzzling me, and telling me how lovely I looked. By this time, all the lipstick was gone, and kisses on the mouth were abundant and endless. Breathlessly, I asked if I could have a restroom break; he laughed and said that was a perfect segue to go up to our rooms.

With his arm around me we signed the guest register as Mr. and Mrs. and entered the elevator to the 10th floor. The bellhop had brought our luggage, which I opened and moved quickly to the bathroom. He was serving our drinks when I returned: champagne, iced and poured ceremoniously in stemware. He fell on one knee and said," You know I love you, and want you with me always. Will you marry me?" And the tears born of remorse came, flowing. It might not have looked like a shotgun wedding, if it would have happened within three months; as a friend of my father used to say, "The first child is always premature."

I dropped to the floor beside him, held his face in my hands and said softly, "Yes." Between kisses, he removed my dress, carefully laying it over the chair. He said he loved the scent of my silky pink lingerie; he kissed the bodice, before removing it, and prepared to remove the bra. My nipples were very sore, and I got up, saying how uncomfortable this was crammed between the sofa and coffee table. He agreed, removing his tie, and hastily disrobing, dropping garments as he ushered me to the bedroom.

I would make him wait a minute longer while I adorned myself in the white satin nightgown I had bought to wear. I kept my panties on so he would remember my condition, but he steadied himself, and began to kiss me with such hunger that I thought he would discard his religious convictions. He pulled down the spaghetti straps of the gown and resumed his kissing. Frustrated, he lifted the gown, saying in muffled tones how lovely, but how useless it was, making a scarf around my neck. With eyes closed, I was breathlessly awaiting his soft lips and moist warm tongue to sooth my aching breasts. He began to kiss and fondle them, and then drew back. He had the slim tapered fingers of a physician and with that dexterity, he pinched my breasts clinically around the nipples, I gasped in pain as he rose up and looked me squarely in the face. I opened my eyes realizing that he had stopped his foreplay. He said, "How was the funeral; what else did you do besides bury your aunt?" I was startled at this change of demeanor. He was breathing hard, but not in an amorous way. He moved a face toward mine that was angry and I pulled away. "You had an abortion," he said. "You lied to me, you had an abortion." My eyes widened, how did he know?

Those were the hands of the surgeon he had wanted to be; those tapered fingers knew about pregnancy and the growth of mammary ducts that soften the aureole and made tender and enlarged the nipple. I decided not to lie, "Yes, yes I did," I said. "You destroyed my child. You never asked me if I wanted it. You had no right to destroy my child without asking me," he spat out the words as curses, in a tone and from a mouth and countenance I had never seen before. He stood up, looking down at me, "How could you do that, you knew I loved you, you knew that I would never deny my child," he said, using the past tense.

I rolled over, and sat on the edge of the bed weeping audibly. "I couldn't let my family know I was going to be an unwed mother; life would have been unbearable for my mother; shotgun weddings are just not allowed in our family. My mother had one, and all her married life she paid for it. I couldn't," laying my head on to his leg, "I couldn't, although I would love to have carried your child." I grasped his waist, his torso, then his shoulders as I stood up to go to the bathroom. He grabbed both of my arms and wheeled me around, "What was it, a boy or a girl?" In a dismissive, impatient tone that must have galled him, I said, "How would I know, I never saw the 4-week-old fetus, a mass of protoplasm of undetermined sex." He glared at me with a fury festering with past insults and present denials. His body seemed to grow huge like a monster's. With a force that startled me, with both hands he pushed me away, then slapped me with his left, and punched me with his right, making my head spin. I fell reeling to the floor. I put my hand to my mouth, which was bleeding; with eyes blinded by disbelief and breathing hard, I crawled to the bathroom.

My gorgeous nightgown was stained with facial and fetal blood. I beheld my face in the mirror. My left eye was blackening, my lip was cut and bleeding, the right side of my face was swelling. I stumbled from the bathroom, enraged; he was dressing, putting on his shirt and trousers. He sat down to put on his shoes. I picked up a wrought iron floor lamp and swung it toward his face. He was unprepared to block it, and it cut him, leaving a gash on his jaw. I screamed, "No man, for no reason, at no time is going to abuse me. I have seen enough, endured enough when I was helpless, now I am not. Get out of my life. I never want to see you again. Brutalize some other woman, but never this one." I fell into the armchair, "I bet this was why your former girlfriend left. A wolf in sheep's clothing," and then to insult him, I said, "A weakling around white men; a brutal caveman with Black women."

The tears started flowing again. He moved toward me; he was crying too. I raised the lamp, "Get away from me, or I will call the house detective." I was not Mom ready to forgive. No, I could not accept his brutality because he suffered the vestiges of enslavement and Jim Crow and reacted to insults to his psyche by inflicting physical pain on those closest to him. What subconscious memory of the lash, white overseer's whippings to enforce obedience or fear of imprisonment on the chain gang compelled him to strike with ferocity when hurt? His sperm the initiator, but my body the instrument of incubation; only his masculinity is challenged, my reputation would be sullied, my job in jeopardy; I was the loser, not he. His struggle to assert his manhood in the workplace is gargantuan; I admire him for that; he has chosen the most arduous route; a Black man trying to make his way in a business that is shielded from Negro intrusion by both Mafia and WASP strongmen. I cannot, I will not be his punching bag and accept physical blows from vicarious injury he feels on a job or even a relationship where he does not have absolute sovereignty.

What was he thinking as he glared down at me? Was he filled with remorse that without his knowledge, something that should have been his was taken away from him; something that he wanted, something he made in partnership, but did not control? His sorrow at losing his offspring was compounded by, but not unlike, what was occurring with his authority in his business which was being taken away without his consent. Yes, Mamma, I did empathize with this man whose love had begun to define my life. Now he seemed as conflicted as I, full of sorrow, sympathy, disgust and pain, mindlessly dabbing his bleeding face. I left him standing in the living room as I rose and hobbled to the bedroom. I fell sobbing on the sheets, bloodying them with my soiled gown and fresh cuts. I heard the door slam soon after, and he was gone.

I am thankful I can sleep through stress and feel that healing will come in the morning. I awoke at sunrise and knew that it was Monday; that I had to go to work, but not in this condition. I would have to lie again, there is no way I could concoct a story to explain the way I looked. My full lips looked like sausages, my blackened eye was half closed, and there was a cut on my left cheek.

The menses was just about over; I felt strong in that department, but I had this new burden to contend with. I would dress and get out of here by train or cab or whatever I could get to take me. I would swallow my pride and go down to the concierge and ask about transportation, and then see about the bill. I certainly didn't have money to pay for this expensive suite.

The concierge stared at me, and I said, "Yes, my husband and I had a spat. How can I get back to Manhattan?" He looked at his books, and said, "The room bill is paid and a car has been ordered to take you to Manhattan. Do you need any other assistance?" I was so relieved: that would be his way, to fulfill his obligations, not to leave me stranded.

Strangely as I rode along the winding parkways, I was in a dilemma; my face ached and I dabbed at my cheek and eyes with ice I had put in a hotel towel. My senses longed for him: his scent was in my nostrils; his touch was on my hand; I could taste his saliva from kisses deep and soulful. The rational side of my brain was saying, "You have to give him up, you can't live with a man you fear. You'll move to a new apartment; you're going to get a raise and can afford it. Stay home today; tell whatever lie that will fly; let Golda in so she will nurse you back to health with her potions and get you ready to face the world anew on Tuesday."

That was the last time I saw him. He never phoned me. I, in desperation, was at the point of taking the subway to

Brooklyn and camping outside his house until he came home. I really wouldn't have to, since I had a key. I filled my days with many activities after that – I found my *pied de terre* on Manhattan's lower East Side; I spent time with Ndukwe as he wrote his thesis on U.S. Diplomacy in Nigeria since 1900.

Sometimes I would go with him to the Council on African Affairs, that shabby little office one flight up on 125th Street, where the great Paul Robeson and Dr. Alphaeus Hunton discussed world-shaking issues. They were intellectuals, prepared to move mountains without the structure or financial support to move molehills. A. Philip Randolph said they were blowing in the wind; they didn't have an organization. "Nothing moves in a democracy unless you organize," he advised. But Ndukwe was welcomed there. He received just about as warm a welcome as you could get from their imperious secretary, who always seemed too preoccupied with whatever she was typing to bother with visitors. She was Lorraine Hansberry, niece of the eminent scholar Dr. Leo Hansberry, and an excellent editor, writer of letters to the editor and of protest tracts.

Dr. Hunton would discuss aspects of Ndukwe's thesis concerning the collusion of the United States with Britain in the rape of Africa, specifically in Nigeria. Mr. Robeson and I would be auditors to their esoteric conversation. Ndukwe would be assiduously taking notes on Dr. Hunton's first-hand knowledge of historical missionary exploits in Africa. They were concerned about continuing expanded exploitation, and were trying to find avenues to get more information about rumored explorations planned to extract oil from the Ibo heartland near Port Harcourt. I wouldn't dare interject my dilatant-ish study of rubber and the Congo; it didn't have the depth or commitment of blood, sweat and tears that characterized Ndukwe's work. He was ready to die for Biafra, and it seemed to me such a hopeless cause that I felt his days upon return home were numbered. Imminent was his engagement to a girl from home who had been selected for him to marry. She would be arriving soon; they would wed before he finished his study and he would return to Nigeria ready to take up the revolutionary cause of liberation.

I would also go to the Schomburg Library or Union Theological Seminary with him. Most of the information as seen through the eyes of missionaries and the British historians was pathetically patronizing. They spoke as if they were indeed tending to the salvation of "the white man's burden" as they plundered the natural resources of the African nations. Ndukwe constantly pointed this out to me, repeating his mantra: "When the missionaries came, they had the Bible and we had the land; now, we have the Bible, and they have the land." He would laugh sarcastically, and then with soulful eyes, he would say, "You smile, but your shoulders are drooping, you laugh but your eyes don't sparkle. Can I help?" I wistfully replied, "Boyfriend and I are taking a hiatus; we'll be OK."

But he knew better, the two of them talk together over lunch sometimes and on the telephone. I want to ask, "How is he, does he ask for me? Do you think he still loves …?" I bite my tongue. I bury my head in the original manuscripts on dealings in Black indigenous flesh, even though slavery was illegal by the 1880s, the time of these writings. Automobiles needed tires, and Belgium grew rich virtually extracting natural rubber from the backs of the Congolese, killing thousands. I was researching a paper on King Leopold and the land that Stanley secured for him as his personal fiefdom for my class at NYU on African Civilizations. I wanted to know more about Black history; it had become an obsession, anything to change the subject of my grief. Ndukwe could see that my heart wasn't in it.

♦ ♦ ♦

Painting the Butterfly

I had spent many hours with Dr. Charles Seifert, Dr. Leo
Hansberry and John Henrique Clark in that little basement
library on Eighth Avenue, immersing myself in Egyptian civilization and opening my mind to the kingdoms of Timbuktu and
Benin. This was life-changing information, forever altering my
perspective on who Negroes were and what we could achieve.
Those classes had dispelled what I had learned previously,
that Negro history began with enslavement on this continent,
as we were led to believe in high school; that Africans had no
history worth recognizing, no scholarship, and no art; that enslavement was a boon to these forsaken people. Even college
offered little beyond praising and exploring the work of current
and recent scholars of African descent, and certainly nothing
about Black people in the diaspora including South and Latin
America that I later learned about in Mexico.   I wished I had
said more to PR making it clear to him that I knew Africans
were the first people, but not that they might have been the
first people in Mexico, too.   When I looked at Diego's paintings at the National Palace, the Totonac civilization, the people were very dark.   The hair while straight seemed course
and the noses long and hooked, distinctively Incan or Mayan.
That society predated Cortes; those complexions could not

have come from intermarriage with slaves; is it not more likely that they resulted from prehistoric admixture?

The Mexican experience was life-changing in other ways, however. We were just travelers, tourists, without difference, fully accepted everywhere we went. I felt the burden of seg-regated, second-class citizenship, often in New York, where housing was restricted, where certain establishments, al-though not blatantly displaying the signs, did not accept Negro patronage. Change was in the air, however, as such offenses made the news, as when Josephine Baker was refused ser-vice at the Stork Club. The Thirteenth Amendment is ambigu-ous, always leaving you to question whether the Constitution guaranteed that with its passage, the formerly enslaved and their descendants were first-class citizens. If you got arrest-ed, you could be enslaved again, and that's what happened to thousands of Negroes who found themselves on chain gangs. For our men especially, this was a sword of Damocles always hanging over their heads. You could be picked up for loiter-ing and jailed and sentenced and slapped in prison for years without trial by jury or any of the constitutional guarantees.

Eve and Theta thought I was dreamy–eyed over PR, and they were relentless in their harassment about how ugly the painting was that he had given me, and what a dope I was. I didn't bother to explain that indeed I was carrying a torch, I admit it. But certainly not for a casual acquaintance. While I am no angel, one-night stands were not something I indulged in. I need more than the carnal ache to be intimate with guys; too much disease, too much for a woman to endure, with unwanted pregnancy a real possibility. As birth control, all we have is a sloppy diaphragm or, to guard against disease, thin and easily ruptured condoms. Moreover, men can be casual about it and don't seem to form attachments the way women do, or certainly the way I do. We seek relationships, while they seem to be able to be ardent and passionate for the moment and then casually walk away. I certainly didn't want to be carrying any regrets with me from a sexual encounter with a Mexican I barely knew.

Or maybe I was still *painting the butterfly* as I tried to revert to my virgin days? I thought about an episode last summer when I was on an excursion with some Jewish girlfriends to a left-wing camp in Upstate New York. I loved the wooded setting, the artsy-ness of it all. Plus, the food was delicious. I especially liked the fuchsia borsht and the crusty black bread. There was a musician there, Earl Robinson, who had written some famous labor songs, one that Frank Sinatra had made his own, and that Paul Robeson sang called, "That's America to Me." I sang with this group, even though I couldn't read a note of music. The composer thought my voice good enough; he would play the songs, and I was able pick them up quickly. I felt so privileged.

Sometimes Paul Robeson would be there; not the striking, striding celebrated artist I once saw in Philadelphia, but subdued, harassed by the McCarthy hearings, hounded as a Communist and denied his passport and performance dates. His clothing was baggy, and he had gained weight, diminishing the famous physique. That a person with his intellect and talent, a Renaissance man-- who with Dr. Hunton ran the Council on African Affairs where they championed African liberation from colonialism while others, even Negro scholars, said that Black Africans were not ready to govern themselves--that he could be humiliated by McCarthy was appalling. But he sang with us and brought the audience to their feet. I actually sang with Paul: his deep basso profundo boomed:

> *On yonder hill there stands a creature, who she is I do not know. I shall court her for her beauty, she must answer yes or no.*

And I, in my pretty good contralto soloed:

> *Oh, no John, no John, no John, no.*

There were Negro guys there, but they were obviously pursuing the Jewish girls; inter-racial dating was possible with Jewish guys, too, I guess. They may have been intellectual giants, but they were not appealing to me. My father's dictum, born of their casual rapes during enslavement, may have made me subconsciously prejudge them: "All they want to do is get you on your back," he used to say callously.

We usually danced square dances and the hora, but one night, a tall, muscular, quite handsome Negro guy whom I had seen squiring a Jewish girl around, asked me for a dance when they were doing the "two step." That meant he got to hold me pretty close, and he did, practically taking my breath away. He said he had heard me singing with Earl and Paul, asked if I sang professionally, and then where I lived. I told him I lived in Manhattan, no, I was not a professional singer, and then after a few turns around the ballroom, I asked how was it that his white girlfriend let him dance with me? He was visibly annoyed, hissing that no one owned him, and abruptly ended our dance, leaving me on the floor. I smiled, said, "Bye, bye," and went back to my friends on the sidelines.

The next day I was swimming in my pink two-piece pique bathing suit; I dove off the board and discovered to my horror that the halter top had come loose and was falling into the lake, leaving me bare-breasted. I floundered in the water desperately searching for my top. I began to flail; I was drowning in the search. My dance partner to the rescue! He swam out, lifted me from the water in his arms, retrieved the bathing suit top, and would you believe, held it in front of me as he freely caressed my breasts and brought me to shore. I was mortified, but alive and thankful. He gently gave me first aid, straddling me, pumping with his arms to help me expel the water. He reached underneath my body, and gently stroking each breast, tied on the halter and straps to restore my modesty.

I only saw him at a distance for the remainder of the week, but he and his brother were on the bus back to Manhattan. He kissed his girlfriend goodbye; they seemed very lovey-dovey as he boarded.   I tried my best to be absorbed in my book, not to make eye contact with him and to be invisible to him for the duration of the trip, to no avail. About halfway to the city, he got up from his seat and without asking, sat beside me. He said he hated to see me so lonely and I said, what a pity, now his brother would be lonely without him. His conversation was pretty crude, and he seemed to be making an effort to shock me. He talked about how the dating scene was opening up; that it was not a surprise to see a Negro man with a white woman, and that white girls were not as prudish as most Negro girls. Negro girls were too afraid of their reputations, *sublimating*, not enjoying their youth. He could see that I was like that. Then he asked if I had ever read the *New Yorker*? Did I see the cover with the spinsterish woman hard at work studying a painting of a voluptuous Venus, but carefully copying the butterfly in the corner? He said the copyist was me. I feigned a laugh, how could he possibly know me, after so brief an encounter. He offered to escort me home, but I said I was taking a cab. I thanked him again for rescuing me, but could not see him again because I was practically engaged to a young man who meant a lot to me.

He gave me something to think about, however. Am I the copyist, cold and abstracted, a "culture vulture" who feigns indifference rather than embrace life's vitality that abounds about me? Have I swallowed whole my mother's turn-of-the century books, one actually entitled *Don't,* that planted the fear that as a Black woman I will be perceived as wanton if I dare enjoy my sexuality?

Immersed in my gloom, I guess I behaved like that in Mexico, too. I want to be prudent and selective, focused on developing myself culturally and intellectually, while being opened to finding the right guy. Now that I have known a man in the Biblical sense, carnal desire creeps in. Will I reject real men fearful that they will evolve into brutes like my boyfriend and settle for wimps? My companions seemed so worldly, especially Theta, who talked a mighty game about how successful she was with men, while Eve, a married woman, listened with sagacious silence. I knew much more about Lou's love life. She was seeing a guy now whom she was considering marrying, but her romantic landscape has had as many deserts as mine.

Deserts, indeed. Frida's painting was forever creeping into my thoughts. Frida only loved one man, but he betrayed her and she became promiscuous. She had numerous affairs with men; she even dabbled with women too, because she did not want to love anyone but Diego. All these months since Mothers' Day and I haven't felt one ounce of affection for anyone; with good reason, I suppose, they are not in love with me, nor are they willing to build a relationship with me and I can't separate intercourse from a meaningful relationship. Those African guys? I enjoy listening to them, I support their causes, but I am not available to overt polygamists even for a little international and maybe secretive petting. I dated one, but his aura was wrong, his approach crude; he pawed, and laughed at the wrong things. He acted as if sex was just a physical exercise that should be available to him if he sees a woman he wants; she doesn't have much say in the matter. He said of courtship that he would be a "pussy" if he didn't bed his date. I think I'll buy myself a massage wand and try satisfying myself, I feel so desperate sometimes. I just cannot slip into another guy's arms like I did with Boyfriend; the kisses seem cold and calculated, and I get nauseous at the thought of their tongue in my mouth.

♦ ♦ ♦

From the train this time, we could see more of the mountains and the towns since the trip was in daylight. When the train pulled into a station, women with baskets on their heads offered fruit and Mexican specialties like tortillas for sale. There were no students to talk with, so I pretended to sleep, dogged by my memories. I was wallowing in my reminiscences now, afraid that I would cry out in anguish; but I had to contain myself, show a blank canvas on which my companions could read nothing. I bestirred myself and joined them as we mapped out how we would get to Sumter, South Carolina, where we could eat and rest in Eve's mother's summer house or at her aunt's nearby, which would be forthcoming with replenishment of funds as well.

After offering my few suggestions, and no accessible cash, I returned to my seat and observed that rain was forming droplets on the windowpane. Just a drizzle, but accumulating like the evening we sat in UN Plaza Park and were impervious to the puddles forming around us:

The UN, Redux

I hid under my blanket, weeping quietly again, trying to make sure Lou didn't see me. So many qualities I thought I would probably never find in a man again. The nearer we got to home, the more ambivalent I became. Mamma, Mamma, I am desperately in love, how shall I extricate myself from this dilemma? Will I allow fear to menace where my deepest attachments lay? Shall it be a poontang rapist conquering whenever I am intimate? When I tremble at the lovemaking, will it be latent fear entangled with instinctive passion that makes it so exhilarating? What is next for me? I've longed for a man to love me, now I know what that means. But will I forever belong to one man only whom I fear as you have?

There have been moments when my entire body tingled, every breath was exhilarating as I inhaled my love for this man. He let me into his life and it was as if we were growing up together. That night after our UN visit, he seemed to be reaching where his deepest troubles lay, as if at a confessional. Tears fell on his face as he spoke of being abandoned by his father and having grown up without the protection and instruction from the society of men. He felt he lacked a certain toughness that he saw in Uncle CN and in Paul; it took effort to confront those white guys who wanted to belittle him on the job; he said he practiced retorts and stances so that he would seem resolute and unflappable. He lamented the fact that he could not talk about this with the Negro guys he knew; they would ridicule such utterances. They wanted to talk sports, especially about the Black men who were contesting and beating whites on the field. They bragged about arousing envy and anger in whites: how they bested them in stylish clothes and took pleasure in hearing their curses when they read front page news of Black celebrities bedding their women. They liked to be in white guys' company, go to their houses, and mistakenly think they were being accepted as socially equal. Some Black guys would curry favor with them, even finding women for out of town visitors. Most white guys profoundly believe they are superior, and think they condescend when they associate with Blacks, that they can be crude with Negroes and stoop to their lowest impulses. It had happened to Boyfriend: a white guy whom he thought was a straight shooter, with whom he had some important business dealings, whom he thought he was on par with as they discussed issues of finance and construction. This guy had the temerity to ask him to find a nice colored girl for him. In complete confidence, of course. "I have never had any Negro pussy and want to know if it is different. Is it?" he had asked plaintively.

I could see how badly Boyfriend needed to vent; how this potpourri of anguish had long festered inside him. It seemed that his talks with Ndukwe gave him license to let it all out. I was ecstatic that we had reached the level of intimacy where he felt that he could bare not only his body but his heart to me.

And then there was that night of pure ecstasy, when we reached our deepest intimacy. Nothing could cloud the wonder of that night for me.... I gazed at his completely relaxed body in the crumpled bed, a slight smile on his face, not a line of care: smooth, even breathing, handsome, hairy chest heaving lightly; I beheld health and well-being over his entire body. As I sidled next to him, he raised his arm to let me cuddle closer and in harmony with him, I fell into a blissful sleep ....

◆ ◆ ◆

And asleep I was when Lou shook me violently. "We'll be arriving in Monterrey in half an hour; get yourself together." She sniggled, "You sure are a rumpled mess, everybody else looks like they've been on vacation; but you, eyes saggy and bloodshot, look like you've been fighting demons for days. Pull yourself together, for Pete's sake." I stumbled to the bathroom for some cold water. I put on some makeup; without much effort, I could look as good as she does, I consoled myself.

A Border awakening

Eve had telephoned ahead to let the proprietor of the Royale Hotel know what train we would be on, so he met us at the train station. He had food and lodging for us for the night. He was full of questions about our trip. We told him how glad we were that we had taken his advice and ridden the train rather than drive through the Sierra Madres. He had prepared a hot soup for us with corn tortillas, which hit the spot. Without too much ado, we went right to bed and enjoyed the pleasure of stretching out on those firm mattresses and wrapping ourselves in the muslin sheets before an arduous 17-hour drive to Sumter.

The service station manager brought our car around early the next morning. The proprietor had made arrangements with him to have our car gassed up, serviced, washed and prepared for our journey, all for the pittance we were paying him. We thanked them profusely, and Eve and Lou gave him an extra tip for his efforts, which were far beyond the call of duty. They were lively and jovial with us, teasingly telling us in Spanish that we missed the mark, not having found boyfriends, that Mexican men make great husbands. I screwed up my face trying to respond to them, still relying on my phrase book to say just the right words.

We gathered the blankets and pillows we had stashed, using some of them and our clothing to wrap the bottles of tequila, statuary and other fragile items we had purchased in Taxco and Mexico City. It was nearly noon when we started out for the trip back to the border; it would be a longer trip, three and a half hours on Route 40D as we would go through Brownsville, Texas, this time. We would be riding near the gulf as we made our way up toward the Eastern Seaboard. Eve was driving, and wanted to do so at least until we got to the border, although I was willing to drive in the daytime. It was a non-stop drive; the Royale proprietor had given us plenty of water and food to snack on; we would fill up the tank at the border.

We were full of anticipation when we entered the Brownsville Customs Station at the border crossing, experiencing the thrill of being home again. We quickly pulled into the way station and ran to the ladies' room. In a half hour or so, Eve had gotten the car gassed up. She and Theta were listening to the inspectors, who were pointing out some highway construction spots along the way when Lou and I returned from the gift shop and rest room. They had unwrapped our bundles, searched our luggage and put stamps on our purchases to be sure we had no contraband and that everything was legal. Eve had shifted into her southern accent and her polite banter; she was getting along just fine with the tall Texan officer with the decided drawl. Up walks Lou; another officer greeted her with something like, "Where y'all from, and what ya been doin' in Mexico?" Lou at her haughtiest said, "We're psychologists and social workers, professional women from New York; we've been touring for a month, studying the people of Mexico." It was clear that he did not like her tone: He stepped back, mouth agape. Eve tried to butt in, reverting to her southern drawl, "She's from New York, but I'm from South Carolina, and we're going there." The two officers were incensed; we could see anger in their eyes, as they said, "OK, we're going to let you go, but you better be careful."

We jumped in the car and took off along Route I-10E, but we could feel that all was not well. Everyone told Lou that she should have gone back into servile mode the moment we crossed the border, how dare she irritate those border guards! She felt that she did not have to take their condescending manner. "Hey, it is now as it has ever been," I said. "We are at their mercy, for goodness sake, when they hold all the cards, we have to acquiesce, take low."

We had been riding a little over an hour when we saw a sign telling us we were near Kingsville. We were just settling down after the excitement at the border when flashing lights and sirens sounded. Quickly we were surrounded by two police cars and ordered to pull to the side of the road. Four burly officers emerged, and even though it was late afternoon, began shining flashlights into our car, demanding that we get out and open our trunk. We were frightened – to say the least. Four defenseless women on a deserted Texas highway; anything could have happened. Eve told Lou to shut up, and the rest of us to let her do the talking. I was perfectly amenable to that scenario. I got out as they instructed and assisted the officers with opening the bundles, smiled and stood back to let them do their search. I recognized that one of them was the guy Lou encountered, but the other three were new guys who just came along for the fun of it. They said something about drugs being transported, and asked if we had stopped along the way to meet suppliers. Eve was quick with the, "No sir, we don't know a soul out here; we are rushing to see my aunt in Sumter, South Carolina." They took their time, making sweeps of our bodies and the car with their flashlights, and finally gave us the OK to get on our way, but again admonished us to be careful.

We decided to follow our secondary route, the scenic one nearer to the gulf that would take us to Galveston where Theta had relatives, even though much of our trip would be at night. If we stayed on Route I-10 these cops would probably follow us and harass us all along the way. I-10 was the better highway, but Route 77 probably less travelled and patrolled. Route 77 didn't save us; they followed us there, too. It was dusk; we had not driven two hours before there was another encounter. We saw their flashing lights, but it was quite a while before their sirens started and we moved to the gutter on this shoulder-less road so they could pull up beside us. With their bullhorns, they were calling for us to open the trunk. These cars were from a different area, Victoria, and we didn't recognize any of the men. Eve tried to be the spokesperson for all of us again as one of the burliest guys, who must have been six feet five, glared down at her and spat out his words of contempt as she rolled down her window to understand better what he was yelling: "What is it, officer, the Border Patrol has checked our purchases, is there anything else?" "You heard me, open up the trunk. We want to see what you got in that trunk, and that's what we're going to do, got it? Now open it up."

She got out of the car; they told the rest of us to stay inside. Strangely this time, they only wanted to talk to her, made her show her driver's license, and questioned her about the length of time she had been driving. We were worried sick about her, but were blocked from seeing what they were doing. We rolled down our windows to get some air and listen to the conversation. They kept their flashlights aimed at the windows, blinding us as we tried to look out- side to see what they were doing with Eve. It was all about her credentials, with questions about why four women would be down here in Texas without an escort. We could hear them yelling at her, telling her that she had no business rid- ing around down here from New York, that Texans are proud people and don't like women driving around alone when they have no idea what they might be up to. After about 40 min- utes, they opened her car door and told her she could go. She got inside, but before she could roll up her window, one of the men leaned on her window ledge: "Yeah," he said, his head cocked to one side, slyly speaking to all of us, "What were y'all gals doing in Mexico? Ain't there enough men in Harlem for ya?" The other guys laughed, but we remained silent. Eve settled herself in her seat and, as soon as we are out of their sight, I said I would take the wheel. She was visibly unnerved. They did hardly a cursory scan of the trunk.

Darkness had fallen. We were quaking in our boots, but Eve soldiered on. Lou reached across the seat and grabbed my hand. I opened my eyes wide and shook my head in disbelief that we had survived another encounter with those rednecks. They were determined to make us understand that white men are still in charge and can do what they wished with us. We were feeling as helpless as an enslaved girl on a Georgia plantation who turns 13 and the master decides that she is ready to be initiated and he as "lord of the manner" has the *droit de seigneur*. For all our assertions of having felt like first-class citizens in Mexico, we understand now that once we crossed that border, ole' Jim Crow was ascendant and we had no rights that those white men need respect. I leaned across the seat, touching Eve's shoulders and asked her if she was OK, observing that she was perspiring profusely and coughing after that last encounter. She blew her breath out forcefully and said, "I'm OK, they didn't touch me. I just want to get the hell out of here as quickly as possible."

Eve asked Theta to turn on the radio, hoping to get a station with some good jazz or popular music that might be soothing as she drove. But country, static and redneck commentary was all she could find on the AM stations. We decided to sing some camp songs to take our minds off the present; each person remembering one they used to sing. I sang:

*"If you m-e-e-t meet me in the p-a-r-k park, I
will k-i-s-s kiss you in the d-a-r-k dark,
If you s-a-y say that you will be m-i-n-e mine, I
will l-o-v-e love you all the t-i-m-e time."*

Eve soon was laughing and we were reminiscing about those outings as the tires slapped the road and huge bugs splattered against the windshield. Without intermittent arms and blades, the wipers did a poor job of scooping them off, leaving, gooey streaks across the pane. When we came to a streetlight in what seemed like a safe place, several times we would stop, and one of us would quickly get out and use some of our water to wipe the windshield so the driver could see.

Lou began explaining how she spent the entire summer on the beaches, going from one town to the other around Pleasantville, New Jersey and across the inlet to Atlantic City. What a great place Atlantic City was, especially around Kentucky Avenue, which was in the Negro section. Her father was strict, but he used to let her go there with her brother, Al. Thankfully Al would be a lousy chaperone, letting her and friends go on their own as he pursued girls in the various bars. At 18 you could go to all the bars and hear Charlie Parker, Lionel Hampton, Ella Fitzgerald or any of the greats. We were admonished not to let men buy us a drink, but they inevitably would. You had to be sure that you were handed it by the bartender, that you watched the bottle being opened, so that no one handled it and gave you a "Mickey Finn." We always stayed together, no pick-up dates. We knew so many boys there, from the neighborhoods in Philadelphia or Montgomery County, but even they were never taken up on an offer to drive us anywhere or take us out on a twosome.

Lou and I laughed about the time I was visiting and the fun we had on Chicken Bone Beach. That was the crummy gray sand section near the Steel Pier set aside for Negroes. Everybody who was anybody would gather there. You could see stars like Sammy Davis Jr. or baseball players like Satchel Paige strolling along or getting more tanned on the sand. We would get our spot early, push our umbrella into the sand and spread our blanket. We would bring a lunch and buy popsicles or ice cream sandwiches from the vendors. We didn't bother to go to the cafes on the boardwalk, which were segregated. It was more fun to establish your space and have various boys come by. We would run to the water with them, jump the waves, try to avoid getting our hair wet and still enjoy the surf. We had everyone laughing as we told the tale of one boy, probably poorly endowed, who lost his sweet potato when he knelt to sit on the blanket. He had put it into his bathing suit to impress the girls with the size of his erection.

For about two hours we were riding along enjoying the evening air from the gulf, which blew fresh and moist, without dust, into our partially rolled-down windows. We talked about ways we might protect ourselves, but we knew we were helpless against these strong, armed men. In desperation, we decided that we would get out our fingernail files and scissors from our makeup kits and stab or cut them, at least to scar them if they tried to sexually assault us. Theta said she bet that those guys at the border were notifying police departments all along the route to harass us. We didn't know what the next bunch would be like. At least if we were found, our attackers would bear evidence of a hostile struggle. Despite how nervous I was, I was able to nap a little, as was Lou; a respite I needed as I would take over the wheel soon and I wanted to be up to the task.

We were on Route 59 toward Houston, and had just passed a road sign that said El Campo when the sirens sounded again. Police cars with the name of that town on them pulled up beside us, blasting their loud horns to tell us to pull over. The officers told us that they had received a warning about us and trailed us and were going to take us in for speeding. Before they did that, they would have to make a search, and made us get out of the car this time. These men entered the car, pulled back the seats and threw around the pillows and blankets. They took each of us aside and interrogated us about our drinking habits. We were terrified, but very pleased that they did not try to do a body search. The cop who interrogated me, stood nose to nose with me, breathing hard upon my face. He seemed to be trying to smell my breath, to ascertain whether we had opened our bottles and were drinking the tequila we had purchased. He was most unpleasant and smelly. They said they would take us into the station house unless we paid them the fine for speeding. We scraped together $25, with Lou coming up with the lion's share of it, and without checking the trunk, the posse drove off.

We decided that we had better get some gas in a big town like Houston, which would be, we hoped, a little more cosmopolitan and not in touch with the Border Patrol. The white attendant was jaunty and courteous; he placed the nozzle in our tank, washed our windshield carefully, and sprayed off the hood and sides of the car with the hose. We were delighted; we tipped and thanked him profusely as he expressed amazement at how difficult the carcasses of the sticky bugs were to remove. How different was his attitude from those racist cops! The toilets were segregated but relatively clean and operating. We bought cans of soda and sat in the lot to eat our sandwiches. This place was a respite, allowing us to relax a bit and prepared ourselves for the perils of the next leg of our journey.

It was obvious that the Brownsville inspectors were alerting the patrols along the way to confront us. However, as we talked about this experience, we began to feel a little relief. We surmised that perhaps we were on highways patrolled by pranksters who wanted to put us in our place but knew their limits.

Nevertheless, after driving just about three hours in this semi-content mode and having passed a town called Beaumont, from a distance we heard the unmistakable sound of sirens. Four police cars filled with redneck policemen surrounded us. They forced us into a ditch on this road without shoulders. Certainly, this was overkill whatever our offense: four police cars with flashing lights and men yelling into bull horns. They made us all get out, and lined us up on the side of the road. Two or three cops interrogated each of us, inspecting our credentials with their flashlights and using them to scan our faces as we stood on the edge of the soggy meadow. They wanted to know what state we were from, our marital status, what kind of work we did, what we were doing in Mexico and Texas, and when we planned to leave their state. We had to show our passports and the papers approving our packages stamped at the border. They looked through the trunk, and shone their flashlights through the interior of the car. After about an hour, the cops decided to stop their harassment, probably because other drivers slowed down and the highway was becoming backed up by the roadblock their police cars caused. There was rubbernecking, and they didn't want busybodies' interference. Looking at our trembling hands and hearing our stammering responses assured them that they had put us in our place and made sure that we would not forget that white folks were still in charge.

"A Thousand Little Cuts." That's what Frida named her painting of the pain of infidelity. That's how Jim Crow is: a thousand little slivers of flesh scraped from the most exposed cutaneous layer are those wounds to the psyche that make you flinch. You don't bleed from the minor affronts; a little lymph oozes out; you won't die from it; you hardly miss a beat, but the pain is excruciating. You touch it, gently tamping, trying to make it well; a smile, a joke is your bandage to cover and to heal. But there will be a reminder, a psychological scar from these encounters at the mercy of white supremacists.

Eve skillfully pulled the car out of the ditch, and with sighs of relief, we were on our way. That was the biggest and scariest encounter yet. Although Theta had friends and family in Galveston, we were so far behind schedule we decided we would not make the detour to the harbor. She would call her family at the next public telephone to tell them we could not stop. Let us get out of Texas pronto!

The gulf at this point would have been magnificent, but it was 3 a.m. We passed a town called Lake Charles, and, thank God, we were in Louisiana, almost to Baton Rouge. We would have skirted this town had we not been running low on gas. It had taken us 10 hours to make a trip we should have done in seven; three hours behind schedule. We didn't have enough gas to get to Biloxi, more than four hours away, and we decided that the larger cities were where we might find an Esso station. We pulled off at Baton Rouge; just off the highway, we spotted a Texaco station. Warily, we drove in and without incident got the gas and were on the road again.

Dawn was breaking so I took over the wheel, with Eve completely exhausted by the drive and the irritation of the events along the highway. It was beautiful as we cruised toward the gold and lavender sunrise. I was enjoying the driving and I was doing it well; Eve trusted me. She could sleep when I was driving. I would not wander off in reverie while at the wheel, thinking of all those days that my boyfriend instructed me in vacant parking lots on how to judge distances, apply the brakes gently when slowing down; to measure my speed so there would be no jerky stops. This was the largest car I had ever driven. Boyfriend's Bel Air was a two-door; this was four, but the gearing was the same. It was more difficult to turn, even though it had the new power steering, but I got the hang of it quickly, keeping to the 40s or low 50s on a straight road, even while Texans flew by at 60. I was driving long distances, as I had never done before, on highways with detours, reading signs and referring to our maps.

The scenery soon changed to a sandy beach with greenery and beach houses along the way. We were nearing Biloxi, Mississippi, a 10-hour drive from there to Sumter. I spotted a sign indicating that the Jefferson Davis mansion was a few miles down the road. Perverse curiosity was telling us to see it. Behold, this was Jefferson Davis' last residence! Dare we stop and enter like any other tourist would traveling this road? Were there "colored" and "white" accommodations defining our second-class status, or would we be denied entrance entirely to the president of the Confederacy's mansion? I drove into the compound and pulled into a parking space.

We couldn't enter the plantation house because it was under repair, being converted from a Soldiers' Home to one of the National Historic places. In 1941, the main house had been opened to the public as a confederate museum. Against the wishes of my comrades, I ran to the house and peered in the windows, and walked around among the Spanish moss hung trees. This was a small plantation with a white cottage-type "Big House" and no sign of the slave cabins that had once been the heartbeat of the place. Mississippi would preserve this place to remind them of the glory days when the Confederacy ruled; when slavery was the law of this land; in Mississippi it still was, as they had not yet ratified the 13th Amendment outlawing slavery. Never mind, this was our country, we would explore this National Historic site, without restrictions. Symbolically the last residence of the president of the Confederacy meant that he and the whole slavery ethos should be dead. We ran down the slope, took off our shoes, felt the lovely soft white sand between our toes and waded in the clear water of the Gulf. It was so pleasant here, and we needed the complete relaxation this lovely spot offered. The beach had a dilapidated wooden fence around parts of it, probably to hold back the dunes. We saw people waving and yelling at the top of the hill, perhaps signaling to us to be gone, but we ignored them. Eve stretched out, let the sun fall on her face and napped for over an hour. Each of us napped in turns, and one stayed awake as a lookout. We sat on the dunes, ate our brunch, and marveled at how beautiful the United States was. Stirring inside, I felt the resolve that I should from this day forward seek to make it fully mine.

I was comfortable as I was leisurely driving along, and Eve continued to rest. I knew I couldn't drive those 10 hours to Sumter, 650 miles. But I felt confident; assured that I am the auxiliary driver, no, I am the back-up driver, the second, the trusted, the reliable number two driver. I am in second place as we make our way as second-class citizens through these Jim Crow states, always figuratively driving in second, cautiously, as we never know what terror might befall us in hooded robes, police uniforms, or sharkskin suits with Dixie accents ready to arrest us for an imaginary infraction. We rejoiced at the Mexican side of the border where we could walk as free women, as whole women, where women of our color consort legally with men who are in charge. We were relieved but cognizant and not blind to inequities there.

I was completely at ease with the stick shift, never a screech or jerk as I maneuvered the terrain; none of the lurching that annoyed Eve so much when Lou was at the wheel. The highway was relatively flat and there were few crossings, but ample need to be wary of stray animals along the way. Automatic transmission was the hottest thing; Eve said she didn't want it, the stick saves gas. Boyfriend felt that way too; I'd had plenty of practice with the stick in his 1953 Chevy. I learned to drive in a relaxed mode, and felt so luxurious on the leather seats and competent leaning back and managing the gears smoothly and reveling in his hugs and kisses at a drive well done. Oh, please, let me not reminiscence about him; no, no, focus, focus! "Driving, you make me focus on the task at hand, concentrate on the terrain and traffic, discard distractions…."

We decided that we should not stop again until we were in South Carolina, but we were not able to keep to that schedule, as nature called. Nature called about six that evening, so we had to stop in Evergreen, Alabama. Where were we? Three hours from Biloxi, not far from Montgomery, and we knew some weird tales about that place. Mobile was near on the map, not far were we from Angola, that horrid prison where Negro men were serving long prison sentences, working on chain gangs from dawn to dusk for vagrancy and other minor or trumped up crimes. They were used as contract laborers where they received no pay, but the state was paid for their labor by Bessemer Steel and the plantation owners. Regardless of the aura of Jim Crow all around us, we would have to pull into that no-name gas station down the road and use the facilities. We prepared ourselves for a hostile encounter. We would not get food, just quickly tend to our needs, get gas and depart.

The "Colored Women's Toilet" was a cesspool; not a dog would use it; the stench confronted us as we approached that outhouse; excrement was just about touching the seat. We fled from it. Our Mexican experience had emboldened us; we all went into the "White Ladies' Room." It had a spotless flush toilet. Eve used it first, then returned to the car and was talking with the attendant as he filled the tank. However, when he realized that we were using the white restroom, he gave a hoot and a holler. There was an uproar. Angry curses and threats were hurled at us by him and by the rest of his family who emerged from several doors of the house. He set the gasoline hose, ran to the ladies' room, flung open the door and jerked me from the room. Luckily by that time, I was washing my hands. He was shouting, "Niggers are not allowed in this here bathroom." Eve replaced the hose and said, "Hey Mister, here's your money," dropping it on the window wiper stand as I ran to the car. We jumped in and took off, Eve at the wheel and speeding.

We each took inventory of our feelings. What misery to live in this nation and be treated as if you had no rights that the white man need respect, just as in Dred Scott. We still make jokes about how we avoid the wrath of white men, but why should we? We are law-abiding, well-educated, moral people, and yet, we were treated like pariahs: second-class citizens in a nation that our ancestors built with their unpaid labor. The prosperity, certainly in this part of the nation, depended on the Black enslaved who suffered endless toil to build it.

Evergreen was seven hours from Sumter, South Carolina, up I-65N. Eve pulled over near a roadside campsite so I could resume driving. But after driving three hours, Eve said she had driven these roads before, and knew the way to her mother's house. We would get gas in Atlanta, another cosmopolitan area without incident, but didn't linger or sight-see, as time was of the essence. We hoped to get into Sumter where we could do some grocery shopping before dark, because on Sunday everything would be closed. Soon we passed through the city and tree-lined paved streets. We went across the tracks, down the unpaved road to the section redlined for Colored people.

Eve's mother's house was a well-maintained clapboard cottage, with white curtains at the windows; there was a lawn with a magnolia tree and attractive bushes and flowers along its edge. Four tired women entered; we flopped on the couches. Eve made some iced tea and, revived, we were ready to go shopping for the good meal we could cook that evening. Eve called her aunt. She told us to forget about cooking and come over to her house; she had enough for all of us. We showered, brought in our luggage, decided where each would sleep, and prepared to go to dinner. On the way, we stopped by a store to purchase some breakfast food. We would wait until Monday to get some items for sandwiches for the trip to Washington, our next major stop. We arrived with anticipation of a great meal at Eve's Aunt Eve (for whom she was named) and we were not disappointed.

The Decision
Deciphered

Aunt Eve was delighted to see us. When Eve had called, she told her where we had been, so Aunt Eve invited several of her friends over. There was a party to greet us; everyone seemed to have brought something delicious to add to the buffet. There were questions galore about the travails with the border guards, which they all understood. They had anecdotes of a similar nature about the taboo of Black folks having a too new or luxurious car, lest envy and resentment bring out the police with charges of speeding or other infringements. We told them about Little Rock and the Supreme Court decision, and wondered if there was any movement in South Carolina toward obeying the law. They were members of the NAACP and they knew about the ruling, which was being discussed everywhere.

A lawyer and Howard University alumnus showered praise on a former teacher, the much-respected dean of Howard's Law School, Charles Harrison Houston, who died of a heart attack a few years earlier: "He worked himself to death training lawyers and preparing folks for this; he had masterminded several lesser lawsuits honing his skills.   Thurgood Marshall was his student; Houston put the fire in him. Houston was brilliant; he designed the framework for building the case to go before the Supreme Court to fight to desegregate the schools."

Others chirped in, lamenting the fact that lots of people were afraid of the court decision. They thought it would mean the end of Negro teachers, and the closing of the Negro colleges where so many middle-class Blacks earned their livelihood.

"The people making the most fuss are the kids,"

Aunt Eve's neighbor said, and others nodded their heads in agreement. "Teenagers come to the meetings and talk about the conditions at their school and how the white schools have better equipment and nicer, newer buildings. They get to go to them sometimes to see exhibition games; we never got to go in those schools, but sometimes the kids nowadays do. They get so mad at the new uniforms and the good gyms the white kids have to play in. The kids had read about the lawsuit and agreed that their schools were separate but certainly not equal. They are right, but a whole economy has been built around the system, and the grownups are holding back because we have our stores, our businesses, our churches, our schools, and we don't want to lose that until we know there is something better."

One woman spoke about her son, who attended Morehouse College in Atlanta and was extremely militant. They were worried about him; "getting "uppity" in Georgia is not a smart thing to do. As soon as the decision was announced,

Georgia's Senator Eastland proposed a Constitutional Amendment to let the states have the right to decide whether they would implement the Supreme Court decision; there was backlash all over the South against it. This spring, they cancelled a showing of *Porgy and Bess* in Charleston because at first they said they would allow desegregated audiences in the county-owned hall, but reversed the ruling. The Negro lead actors, Todd Duncan and Anne Brown, wouldn't play to a segregated audience.

I said there was plenty of segregation still up North, and not much change since *Brown*. Negro kids in my old neighborhood still went to a segregated elementary school in Pennsylvania. When I went there in the '30s, we got the discarded curtains from the white schools, had mostly white teachers who were not as qualified, and not as dedicated to teaching basic skills as the teachers in the white schools. The kids whom I met in the integrated junior high school were much better prepared than I. Even the Negro kids who were the offspring of house servants in the upper-class restricted neighborhoods, who went to the white schools, were more proficient in math and reading than we. Bright Negro kids from the Negro school had to play catch up; the majority fell by the wayside. You were told by the junior school guidance counselor that college was not for you; even with good grades, she would "suggest" and assign you to the general or commercial courses rather than the college prep for high school.

One woman said, "I really enjoyed going to school with my own people; I don't know about this integration. I think our kids have more self-confidence than those northern kids who come down here to college. I teach them, and I see it." Eve blew a long breath, then said, "We deserve access to the whole nation, its best schools, its finest neighborhoods, our rightful share of government, not a little segregated slice they decide is good enough for us. We got to learn to compete with the best of them. I went to NYU with them, and I know they were no smarter than I was."

"What was it like as a child to go to school with them prejudice white kids?" Aunt Eve asked me. I said that associating with white girls for the first time in junior high school was exciting to me. There were none in my segregated elementary school. These girls seemed so well informed; they had read more books. I scurried to read fifth-grade Nancy Drew mysteries and the seventh-grade literary booklist so I could discuss plots with them. They read magazines and talked about the latest movies and the stars as if they knew them personally. I walked home with them sometimes, hanging behind and listening to their banter. They lived at the top of the hill, and I through the woods and across the railroad tracks in The Bottom.

I had expertise too and they were eager to listen. Compared with them, I knew a lot about jazz, about records that they vaguely heard because of the restrictive listening patterns on the radio. Negro stations were taboo for them, but they sneaked a listen. They had seen tuxedoed Negro musicians like Duke Ellington or Satchmo in fleeting moments in Bing Crosby musicals. They could sing Ella Fitzgerald's

"A-Tisket, a-Tasket;" they had hummed it for years. They liked the rhythm and the dances and wanted more than the Andrews Sisters and corny folk tunes. I listened to Symphony Sid surreptitiously late at night and heard Hampton, Basie and all the latest. My brother would bring white schoolmates by the house and wind up the Victrola to play 78s of "Cherry" and other slightly naughty hot swing numbers. I reveled in these girls' company, and one-on-one, or in small groups as we sang the hits, they accepted me. But some days without warning, a bunch of them would gather in the girls' room and poke fingers at me and sing:

> "Mammie's little baby love shortnin' shortnin',
> Mammie's little baby love shortnin' bread.
> Three little darkies, lyin' in bed, one of 'em sick
> and de other half dead.
> Called for de doctor, doctor said, 'Feed 'dem
> darkies some shortnin' bread."

They would laugh and run out of the room. I would be left alone. The discordant song was scraping flesh from my body like fingernails on the blackboard; a painful tingling, an oozing wound I must try to hide. As a 12-year-old without defenses, I grinned sheepishly as if it didn't matter, opened the door and hurried past them in the corridor.

Eve's friends were appalled; there was general agreement that those kinds of put downs would not be permitted in Negro schools and colleges. However, Aunt Eve thought for a moment, then said, "I don't know about that; if you were dark-complexioned with nappy hair, you might hear something like," and she began to sing,

"Nothing but the yellow, shall see God."

Everyone knew that old slur favoring the Caucasian-mixed, fair-skinned as the pinnacles of society in and out of school in the Negro community. Some of the guests thought that those boundaries were flexible, and were slowly disappearing, as more Negroes of every hue attained scholarship and status. But ever so slowly. Color hierarchies exist around the world. The naysayers are still around. I used to hear that the only Negroes who achieved had white blood, that quadroons were the bright ones like DuBois. Then we had Paul Robeson, definitely a dark-complexioned genius, and Marcus Garvey, and now all the Africans direct from the continent without a drop of white blood who are excelling in every field, especially in the sciences. We have to rethink what 300 years picking cotton has done to the psyche, and what kind of reparations and remediation it will take to make our kids abandon that "mark of oppression," and use their brains to become world class scholars.

Eve's cousin who preferred the status quo remarked that despite segregation, many of their teachers were well prepared; they had gone to the best universities up North and gotten Ph.D.'s and come back to maintain high standards. But still, we pay for them, so we should have the right to go to top colleges right in our own state. The way to that ideal seemed insurmountable and fraught with dangers. "Maybe someday, but not in our lifetime would there be change," she said, as others concurred.

We talked about President Eisenhower, whom they felt deserved a lot of credit. True, it seemed immigrants, and not enough Negroes, were working on the highways he was building, but he was taking a stand for Negro rights. His mother had come to this country as an indentured servant who worked right along with the slaves, so he might have gotten some empathy from her. Moreover, he observed the Negro soldiers and knew that they were capable and courageous, even though he commanded a segregated army. He caused quite a stir in February when he said that he would fight for equality wherever federal authority extends. He appointed J.E. Wilkins as the first assistant secretary of Labor and Benjamin Davis Jr. the first Negro U.S. Air Force general. Members of his party questioned whether he was going too fast in support of the Negro cause, but not the Negro Lincoln Republicans who had remained loyal despite Roosevelt's innovations.

The guests were adamant that even this *Brown* decision did not reverse *Dred Scott*. The lawyer said, "Adam Powell has been fighting a case down here since last year when some Negro soldiers were fined for making a disturbance on a bus because one of them refused to give up his seat next to a white girl. The judge said there was nothing in the constitution that bars segregation in interstate travel, and indeed there isn't. This ruling only pertains to the schools, and it's not being enforced." There was much trepidation about back-lash and fear of a resurgence of KKK activity. Despite this ambivalence among Southern Negroes concerning the deci-sion, you could sense their hunger for equality.

We said our goodbyes, with lots of hugs and kisses all around, as if all of us were treasured relatives. Aunt Eve pre-pared a basket of food, making superfluous the provisions we had gathered at the grocery store.

Four weary women, stimulated by the conversations of the evening, moved quickly to flop into bed, delighted to stretch out in single-bed comfort. However anxious we were to discuss what had been the most elucidating discussion of our trip, rest was the imperative of this moment.

That next morning, as we ate a hardy breakfast, my friends and I examined our commitment and declared where we stood. We resolved that in the North we should go full steam ahead. We thought that the opposition would be stron-ger in the South, and that Northern ways of complying would be less fraught with hostility. But Eve said it may look like all is well up North now, but when you scratch the surface, whites have subtle ways of keeping Negroes from getting top jobs and use redlining to keep us in dilapidated sections of the city with poor schools. We agreed that she was correct.

We can't condemn them, because just like the profes-sionals in the South, we must decide whether we would be activists, as we would be called upon to be, or just sit on the sidelines and protect our jobs. Eve's husband was in the real estate business. She said he felt that to some degree the infusion of Puerto Ricans was breaking down some housing barriers in New York City; the fair-complexioned spouse would rent the apartment, and then the darker husband and children would arrive. Mayor Robert F. Wagner had to enforce the fair housing laws in those cases where possession couldn't be reversed. However, landlords were using these blockbusting techniques to get whites to run from their rent-controlled apartments, so they could gouge higher rents from new Hispanic arrivals. I felt this wouldn't help Negroes much; those neighborhoods became *el barrios* and fair-skinned Puerto Ricans did not welcome Negroes.

I walked around the garden and began to pull weeds; it was a reflex action so accustomed was I to doing this task at my mother's home. In an hour or so, I had tidied up the flower beds, and was looking around for a place to dispose of the pile of broken branches, leaves, scraps of paper and weeds I had accumulated. I called Eve, who was amazed, and showed me where the trash cans were. She opened the garage door and pointed to some garden tools to assist me to complete the job. She didn't offer to help; she and the other women who peeped out of the door, apologized, declaring that they just weren't into gardening. "No matter," I said as I raked the lawn, "Eve, you can tell your mother what I did; in a small way, I feel I have repaid my host for her hospitality."

The Past is Alive

When I went inside I felt invigorated from the exercise in the fresh air. While the others were still reclining, I surveyed each room of Eve's mother's summer house. I admired the authentic plantation-style furnishings, the Civil War-era tin-types and photographs that hung in oval convex frames on the walls. "Say Eve," I asked, "Tell me who all these ances-tors are. You are so fortunate to have photographs, don't let them get stolen while your mom is in New York. They should be protected. Who is this handsome guy?" "Ugh, that's my grandfather, a tyrant," she replied. "I'm surprised she even proudly displays a picture of him." "Why," I asked as everyone turned to see who this tyrant was. "He looks like a preacher," Theta said. "He was, and he felt that gave him the right to be sanctimonious, and practice his particular brand of corporal authority. He used to beat Mother regular-ly and all of her siblings, and her stepmother too. He would line them up and chastise them for any infraction against him and God." "For real, that's why your mother cut out of here at 16," Lou laughed. "You better believe it," she said. "He tried to come after her, but she was working in Virginia and studying for the ministry too, so he sort of let her go because she had a *calling*."

"What's this about beating your stepmother?" I asked. "She was much younger than he, so he treated her like a child. He was quick with the slap, even when they were out. She was talkative and still liked to hang out with folks her age, and the old man didn't like it, I guess," Eve said. "You know, traditionally Negroes do a lot of hitting, like it's the only response to agitation or anger. They don't talk much about feelings, or try to settle differences by conversation. And parents still think it's God's way: that you don't spare the rod, or you will spoil the child," Lou said, waxing philosophical. "So many of the kids at Children's Center are victims of parental beatings," Eve added, "and it's not always because the parents are on drugs. This Black mother said, 'I just picked up the bat 'cause it was handy and hit him; he don't talk to me like that.' She nearly killed her son. Now he's in foster care and blind in one eye."

"What do you think the connections are between corporal punishment and enslavement?" I asked rhetorically. "The slave master or overseer did it to get absolute obedience; they would assemble the whole plantation to watch a cat o' nine tails beating until the victim's back was bloody and his body weak with pain to plant fear for the all-powerful master in the minds of the slave," Eve said. "Well, I don't think it works; the victim becomes more prone to violence himself; that is why our men are so physical. That's the kind of discipline they knew, Mamma and Papa would hit, at the least provocation, and threaten, 'I'm going to kill you, boy, if you don't' ......whatever," Theta rose from her magazine to offer. "It's the kind of discipline that assures the Negro will carry on the brutality learned under enslavement, although parents say they hit to save their kids' lives from the evils in the streets," I added. Eve was thinking deeply about this, because she was a child who had never been struck. Her mother declared she would never hit her, nor allow anyone else to strike her child. Eve was pensive as she said, "Mom had been humiliated by her father; he used to say he would beat the starch out of her, which literally meant destroy her backbone. Inside Black people lay a 'sleeping terror,' that's what James Baldwin called it; dormant fear of lynching and lashes that made some Black folks react violently to insults to body and mind."

"I believe that, but we can teach conflict resolution through conversation. There just wasn't any time to sit and discuss things for people picking cotton from dawn to dusk. They never gained the vocabulary for it. Moreover, danger was everywhere; you had to learn behaviors that were cowardly and cowering to save your life," Lou offered.   I said. "I think allowing the hitting response to continue for our kids is preparing them for servitude, not leadership; we don't want them to cower and be servile, to learn that submission and obedience is their proper behavior. I wish you social workers would find a way to stop our parents from using the brutal whipping response." With a loud sneer, "Oh it's all on us, huh?" was the choral response from Lou and Eve.

After dinner, we retreated to our couches and beds to get a good night's sleep. The physical punishment discussion made me regurgitate the reasons why avoiding it was paramount in the tangled web of methods I used to approach relationships. Psychologically, childhood memories of brutality were churning inside my brain until this very day, impeding or perhaps negating any healing with Boyfriend or indeed making impossible other meaningful attachments. I turned to the wall and thought about my mother and a particularly vicious fight:

♦   ♦   ♦

I was coming home from elementary school and as I entered the driveway, I heard shouts about a man named Holmes. Father was accusing Mom of having an affair with him, and she was denying it vehemently. I was the first child home as he seldom fought her in our presence. I did not go inside, but lay down on the bench under the grape arbor and covered my ears. I could hear his cursing and yelling. "I'm right up there in that bay window, and I heard the conversation. Making arrangements to meet him, when I go to work, weren't you?" (Slap) "Weren't you." "Oh, stop, that is such a miserable thing to say; I never, we never said anything about meeting." "Liar, always playing the innocent, liar," he snarled. (Slap) "You had him come here to fix the stucco, and we were talking about the job, Herbert, for God's sake," she stammered. "Uh-huh, and he could hardly work for you out there flirting with him, I heard it, you thought I was asleep, didn't you, but I heard it." (Slap, and she hit the wall, or the furniture with a thud, and pots banged on the floor.)

Pleadingly, she said, "Why in the world would I be making plans to go out with someone," she sobbed, "Right here, with you here; why don't you use common sense?" (Slap) And then as if gagging she yelled, "Stop it, please, go back upstairs and sleep off that anger you brought home from work; you know nothing is going on between Mr. Holmes and me. Please, Herbert, the kids will be home soon, they don't need to hear this foolishness." "You better watch yourself, woman," he sneered as he went back upstairs to complete his nap before his night shift job, and before he would come down and make all the kids miserable around the dinner table.

When all was quiet I entered. Mom was sobbing in the kitchen, washing her face with ice to stop the swelling, preparing to fix dinner. She tried to hide her face from me, and said cheerfully, "How was school today, sweetheart?" but she was choking back tears, and I ran to her, holding her around the thighs, sobbing, "Mommy, what happened, are you OK?" She laid down the washcloth, sat down and held me close to her, rocking me in her arms. "It's all right, he was angry about something else, and when he is, he takes it out on me. I'll be all right," she said bravely. "But Mamma, why do you let him treat you like that? Why don't you go away?" She laughed, "And where shall I go with six children, and what shall I use for money to take care of you?" "I would work, Mom, and so would all of us, we hate when he is mean to you," I offered. She kissed me, and said, "He is a good provider, you and all of us have everything we need; I guess I don't mind being the brunt of his anger sometimes when there are other benefits, especially for you," she said wistfully. Then she stood up, and without another word, began to fix dinner. I was setting the table. As each child came in they would sob and kiss her, and she would tell them not to worry, that everything would be all right, she would see to that.

As I grew older, there were other physical reprimands. He treated her like she was a person over whom he had complete dominion, a slave whom he had the right to control. One evening, when I was a teenager, I called the police to come and stop a noisy fight. When they arrived he was dumbstruck, his eyes were wide, and he was cowardly apologetic, saying, "We were just having a family discussion here, officer." And she, face beginning to swell and her eye already bloodshot, said, "Oh, yes, officer, there is no problem here." The policeman said that he knew of my father's cruelty to his wife, and the next time it happened he would be arrested. "A citizen like you, who does so much for our community, and yet, you can hurt the mother of your children who has made a home for you for years. We will be watching."

I had crept into the house through the front door, and saw my father, the bully, cower, be the supplicant as another man chastised him; like a child he had pleaded not to be arrested. I had watched his feet of clay crumble and my backbone stiffened. My mother, the ever-supportive wife, came to his rescue. My sister tried to shelter me from the debacle, telling me to go upstairs and get in bed, so he would not suspect that I had called the police. He was sweating and visibly frightened, playing the host escorting the policeman out. He left the room as soon as they were gone; I heard his feet padding quickly on the stairs. I buried myself under the covers, afraid that he was coming for me. He went into his room, which was next to ours, and slammed the door. The altercation and threat of jail made him cease the physical abuse for quite a while, although the verbal and psychological abuse continued.

He learned somehow that I had called the police, and threatened to expel me from the house. I was in my senior year in high school, and the trauma of that incident and its aftermath wreaked havoc with my school work and depressed the happiness I might have had at graduation. However, he never touched me; I stared him down as he made threats to physically assault me. Whatever threat he made, I knew it was bogus; bullying, but without courage to back it up. I vowed that I would get out as soon as possible and never come back. I told my mother of my plans; she begged me to forgive him and not abandon our home. She said he had had such a miserable childhood – his mother worked in a private family managing a big estate, only seeing him once a week; his father had been killed in a train wreck, and he lived with a family who mistreated him verbally and physically. His friends always cited this upbringing as the reason for his brutality. I couldn't see the logic of his childhood making him behave so viciously toward my mom, however. He would buy her lovely things and make such boastful remarks about his family: "My family comes first," he said. "No one eats my food before my children are fed." He was referring to the fact that he had to eat the potato peelings and the backs of the chicken after the preacher and guests left his foster family's table.

That trauma would affect him, I thought, in other ways, but why would he hurt her for it? His mother was his idol; he showed much respect to women who had been her friends and who would visit us. So I asked my mom what in the world she ever did to make him hate her, and reduce her to taking such abuse from him? She said that I was young and didn't understand; actually, he didn't hate her. At times, he was very affectionate. "Negro women had to understand their men; some are difficult to live with; they experience so much frustration and segregation in the outside world; they are belittled by their white superiors, even though they know they are smarter and more capable, like your father. So he is often filled with anger, and I try to assuage it." "He is often filled with alcohol," I said, "and you have settled into the role of being his whipping boy, Mom, you don't have to do it." "You children are my happiness," she said, "And whatever it takes to keep you warm, well-fed and happy, I will do it. He works two jobs to be sure we never want for anything. I appreciate that."

"Do you think living with him, in fear for what he will do to you, makes us happy? I visit kids who live on welfare, and there is so much laughter in the house, with their father and mother and uncles and aunts, no one is walking on eggs because of an ogre is sleeping upstairs. I can't wait to get away from here." She had a beautiful, kind face, which smiled as I spoke. I saw that my words touched her deeply, and there was sadness and suddenly a worn, tired aura about her: Her shoulders sank and she rubbed her hands together in a hopeless gesture. "You are such a wonderful mom," I said, holding her close to me as if to warm her from the chill that filled the room. "I hate to leave you alone with him." But to hear him or see his car approaching brought anxiety. I could never become the woman I wanted to be with such loathing hanging over my every effort. I would plot my escape.

I know now why she took his abuse from the day of her marriage; I had pressed her first cousin, Pauline, for the history, and she told me. It was why he hated my uncle and all of her family. They made him marry her because she was pregnant with a baby that she lost. She prayed to God that she could accept his anger as her just desserts for having broken her vow of chastity before marriage, and was always thankful that he had married her and saved her from the disgrace of being an unwed mother.

I have a college education and adventures far beyond what my mother experienced. Yet I am hounded by my mother's life with the tyrant and am adamant that I shall not relive it. Mother talked abstinence all our lives as the only sure contraceptive, and shied away from talking about sexual relationships with boys. The only behavior worthy of decent Black girls was virginity until marriage, and those other girls were common, easy and worst of all, when they had babies without husbands, they were breaking God's laws. She made us wear girdles so that nothing was shaking seductively around boys, and admonished us not to go places where we were alone with boys whether we knew them or not. To reinforce his dominance, my father would take any infractions we committed out on our mother. She let us know that my father would be particularly cruel to her if one of his daughters was seen as slutty, and God forbid, became pregnant.

To save her skin, we were blackmailed from adolescent adventure, from innocent romance, fearing having a child out of wedlock – the ultimate sin, for which my mother's life had forever been made miserable. The one hypocritical act that she committed that I abhorred was to vociferously condemn girls who made that mistake, as if she spoke from an elevated state of being pure, married, safe and sound, with a home and husband. It was the pretense for which she paid a terrible price, and which she visited as a penance on her daughters and sons.

◆　◆　◆

On the Road Again

Eve collected some of her mother's appliances; we replenished our water jugs, filled thermoses with iced tea, stored our sandwiches and Aunt Eve's food among waterproof bags of ice, and prepared ourselves for a non-stop, seven-hour drive to Washington, D.C. Eve was driving and as we neared home, I became weepy again. I tried to stifle it, as I did not want Lou to hear me, or see me dissolve into tears. Thoughts of things we did together were crowding my brain. No one but someone who cared deeply would have behaved as Boyfriend did. Certainly no one I had met lately. Does he ever think about the night we went to the United Nations and uncovered a new dimension, a new depth of understanding of who we were and what we wanted for each other? I'm sure that was the night … the night, forgetting precautions, we were truly one; the moment, we together almost built a new life, a new being….

Eve had driven five hours and I was insisting on taking over. We decided to stop in Richmond, Virginia, because the place was symbolic of the Confederacy – the headquarters, with its red brick buildings still adorned with carvings and a museum filled with memorabilia of enslavement that did not admit Negroes. I got out of the car, went to a restroom marked "colored" but clean, in the bus station, then walked around to stretch my legs with my companions. I wanted a leisurely stroll along the James River, which held so much of my family's history, but there wasn't much time. We saw the old slave market site at Shockoe Bottom and an empty lot that was reportedly Robert Lumpkin's slave jail, called the Devil's Half Acre, where slaves were tortured into submission. Not far away was the first Battalion Virginia Volunteers Armory, or the Leigh Street Armory, constructed in 1895 – the city armory for Negro militia units.

I closed my eyes and stood beneath one of the ancient oaks; I was transported just a several miles from there where my mother's family had toiled in Halifax County on a tobacco plantation; my paternal grandfather was supposedly killed in a flaming train wreck in the 1890's, and where my maternal grandfather, while still a child, had escaped the cotton processing factories in Danville to serve with the Union Army and gone North. When he came to live with us I his old age, I tried to ask him about those days, but my mother would admonish me not to trouble him because it was hard for him to talk about enslavement. He didn't seem reluctant at all. He did tell me about his working on the Brooklyn Bridge, and how he washed his face in the cold morning in the horses' trough as he rose from his bed of straw in the stables and fetched water for the soldiers.

We have an old photo album called "The Arc" with sepia and tintype images of relatives whose faces I could not connect to the names in that big Bible with the brass fasteners. Many had left the hard life in Virginia to face a cold segregated life in Philadelphia. How would I ever know of them? There are no names on the backs of the photos. Before she died, a great aunt tried to identify a few, but her memory was fading. My mother said my grandparents, like herself, did not want to talk about "slavery times"; it was all about getting an education, doing better, living better than they did; forget the past! Walking around Richmond, seeing the slave market, brought it all back: The past is not dead, it is alive!

It was full speed ahead after Richmond: many small rivers and streams to cross, lovely green foliage from the well-watered land, and no bully cops harassing us to put us in our place. In a little over two hours, we found our way to the Southwest section of Washington, D.C., where my sister and brother had a large apartment. Both were single: my sister had been in the segregated Women's Army Corps and my brother, greatly recovered from his war injuries, had decided to live with her there. He was originally in the Negro Barrage Balloon Battalion, but managed to be in the second section, which was not sent to D-Day. Instead he was sent to the jungles and swamps of New Guinea where he suffered tuberculosis and psychosis. He had given me much of the money for college, since my father did not believe in educating women, and loved me dearly as I did him. I knew my siblings would give us food, shelter and fortify me with money enough to tide me over for the next few weeks.

My sister and brother were welcoming and questioning. They pounced on me, "How did you dare take this trip with so little money; why would you take such a risk?" But they were very glad to see me. We told them we were testing the *Brown vs Board of Education Supreme Court Decision*, to which my brother laughed heartily. He had been at Howard University before World War II, and had served as a lieutenant in the Army during the war. He knew what it meant to be in a segregated Army, how they were forbidden from using the officers' clubs at Camp Huachuca, and in New Guinea, where he nearly died in the mangrove swamps. He had protested segregation with his college friends led by Kenneth Clark way back in the '40s. (Dr. Clark and his wife Mamie had done the Negro doll experiments for the *Brown* case.) They had been chased out of many places, including the movies. He would go as a servant with friends who could pass for white; but they had spotters in the booths, usually Negroes who believed they could tell if someone had one drop of African blood, and they would often be rejected.

"Passing" for white was big in Washington, as there were many mulattos and quadroons. Newspapers frequently had stories of folks in high places who were "discovered." The mulattos, including people like Walter White, the former president of the NAACP, had been indispensable in the quest for civil rights because of their role in associating with whites and being undetectable. They were the valets, the waiters at swank restaurants, the seamstresses, the caddies who listened and informed.

My brother said there was a lot of activity around the *Brown* decision in D.C., because of Howard University's law school's involvement as its architects. The McCarthy hearings were front-page news, taking up much of the reporting that might be devoted to the action on school desegregation. Black people took courageous stands anyway knowing that if they were involved in something radical like trying to picket to desegregate the schools, they might be dubbed Communist; then their jobs and future prospects would be jeopardized. He said that a courageous Negro woman and her lawyer, George Hayes, were just on Edward R. Murrow's show. She had lost her job because McCarthy had falsely accused her of being a Communist. She didn't even know what a Communist was! McCarthy treated her horribly, wouldn't bother to interrogate her, saying that she wasn't worth his time. McCarthy's assistant lawyers were harsh and rude to her. Murrow turned his wrath on McCarthy, showed an actual hearing that made a lot of people sick of McCarthy's tactics. After that, my brother felt, McCarthy, an alcoholic, was on his way out. Nevertheless, my brother and my sister were constrained since they both worked for the federal government. He warned that I should take that under advisement before going public with my resolve to oppose segregation.

They fortified me with cash and supplies so that I could repay Lou and pay my gas share on the spot. I was their youngest sister and they habitually indulged me.

I would drive the final miles to New York telling myself that being at the wheel would force me to be alert. I would not think of my unhappiness; I had to try to stop digging up the past. We would not stop in Pennsylvania, although my mother had expressed her desire to see me in our phone call last night.

I told her that we had to prepare to get back to our jobs, but that I would visit soon. My brother's talk about Washington mulattos made me think about how Mom's mulatto friend had helped them open up the new junior high school in our neighborhood in Pennsylvania, which the Negro kids were considered unprepared to attend. The "one drop" of Negro blood rule that prevailed in the U.S. officially kept even the fairest Negroes from slipping into white society, as so many of them did in Puerto Rico, Cuba and Brazil. This meant that we would have the mulattos, with their European educations their white fathers often provided, to teach in the Black schools, to set up businesses (the few that were allowed, like funeral parlors, churches, and beauty shops) and therefore let their knowledge trickle down to their darker brothers. True they established an elite social group for their own, establishing clubs and churches that one could not enter if they were darker than a paper bag. But many dark-complexioned Black men got an education, wooed their whitest-looking daughters, and that is how some of the color-line barricades were breaking down.

What courage and fortitude it took for my mom and her friends to attend the school board meetings where their presence would prompt the white board members to leave the room to deliberate. They would return with the resolution passed, not allowing comment from the Negro parents. These slights, constantly being ignored or shunned, certainly wore on their psyches. In civic affairs -- political, medical and social -- northern Negroes in the '30s and '40s still had to depend on white intermediaries to make their case.

There was this Mr. Corrigan, an Irishman who immigrated to Pennsylvania. He would meet with my father and fellow Black Democrats; then he would take their issues to the Democratic committee. My father was not allowed to go. Our physician, a mulatto with several degrees, indeed no Negro doctors in our area, would have the right to assign or serve their patients at Abington hospital; nor could Negros be elected to serve in state legislatures, nor lawyers to practice at the bar. However, my mother's mulatto friend, Mrs. A, attended the meetings and the board caucuses and got the inside information. With the NAACP, they made alliances with liberal whites, especially Quakers, who provided the majority vote that allowed Negro kids from the segregated elementary school in Willow Grove to enter an integrated seventh grade in Abington.

I wanted to embrace my mom and tell her that I was intent upon following in her footsteps. In many respects, I wanted to be like her, but not by giving in to men who would control me. Liberation for Negro women had to disabuse them of the dictum that our men must be given a chance to be in charge, that they had been stripped of their manhood and suffered more than women under enslavement. Being used by the planters, the overseers, or any white man who fancied sex with you without the power to resist or have your man protect you was destructive of the Black female, mind, body and soul. I wanted to say to her that it wasn't fair that she had submerged her personality, stood in the shadows and taken my father's abuse in the belief that he was "her husband," the only man in her life. The vows she took were literal: she would obey, endure, be the faithful mother of his children, be understanding of his cruelty in the name of supporting and encouraging him because of the insults he received from society as a Negro man. But that conversation would have to wait for another day when I would come home and we could have that long talk.

I was driving across the Pulaski Skyway, thinking of the day I first saw this now sort of quaint iron structure, my father at the wheel, taking us to the World's Fair of 1939. There it was, the Chrysler Building still displaying its beautiful dome, and the rest of the New York skyline glistening in the sunlight. Have I grown in this adventure, I wondered? Can I take control of my life without those arms about me? What have I learned about the Negro women's right to control their own bodies, to develop their own minds, to think for themselves, to be equal to any other woman?

Now we were going through the Holland Tunnel to a bustling Canal Street and past the Brooklyn Bridge my grandfather helped to build. I am so much a part of this land, this city, this nation. I must come out of the shadows, I thought. I must assert myself using my abilities, which match or surpass so many of the folks I have met.

I pulled up to my front door and debarked, gathering my belongings from the trunk, and telling my companions that we must get together to look at the photos and analyze the substance of our trip. No one wanted to come in for coffee, since I probably had none, and they were all anxious to get home. So, we said our goodbyes, with hugs all around. With Eve in the driver's seat, they took off.

Mixing Memory and Desire

My dank apartment was a little danker, needing light, life and decoration. I turned on the radio and gathered up a few pieces of mail with a notice that I had to go to the post office to pick up my month's accumulation. I opened my suitcases, hung up some items, made a grocery list and went to the pay phone on the corner to have my telephone reactivated. Then, receipt in hand, I went to the post office. I wandered aimlessly around the streets of the East Village, familiarizing myself with the old smells and uneven sidewalks. I passed McSorley's smelling of beer from freshly uncorked kegs and wandered down near the East River and Cooper Union where Lincoln made his 1860 speech about the rights of the federal government to prevent territories from becoming slave states. These were his first halting steps toward emancipation.

I was procrastinating, not wanting to pick up the threads of my life. I quickened my gait and turned toward Fifth Avenue, and soon I was at the post office a few blocks over. I retrieved several bills and letters and a package slightly larger than a shoe box with an envelope taped to the outside. I saw that it was from my old boyfriend. I decided to delay opening it; seeing his handwriting made me extremely emotional. I wanted to digest the letter and box's contents in a quiet place. I knew a garden on East Broadway where I could sit, enjoy the balmy September day and mull over the contents of this missive. The garden was abloom with autumn flowers, including chrysanthemums recently planted, and cosmos and marigolds nodding in the pleasant breeze. I sat down on a bench and opened the bills and notices, but could not bring myself to open The Letter. I thought about Mother's Day, the last time I saw him. Immediately I was awash in tears, unashamedly weeping.

With a squinting of the eyes and a shake of the head, the evening at the United Nations burst into my consciousness. How it had stirred us to confront raw truths of our life in America! My boyfriend compared Ndukwe's generations of respect for the person and societal approval to his life where fear motivated behaviors within and outside the home. Fear of those most dearly loved: "I am going to beat the tar out of you, boy!" was a common admonition of loving mothers wielding the strap or broomstick with the expertise of generational learning. This was how the Negro child was taught to stay alive: Be wary, grin, don't assert yourself against the white man, learn to sustain pain and punishment. These behaviors would be your salvation in times of trouble. After emancipation, the end of Reconstruction and the rise of Jim Crow, Blacks didn't even consider recourse to the legal system; there was no paternal protection, no benevolent community with ancestral authority, only the church offering escape in the great bye and bye. Oh, why are these irrelevant and extraneous thoughts crowding my abstracted brain?

Forget forgetting: There he was telling his story of repression; here he is, as big as life crowding out any construction that I might fancy of life without him. What shall I do when April comes again, I wondered? It is likely that I will make the somber walk up First Avenue to those benches in the park, damp from a recent rain, surrounded by air fragrant with the scent of the tiny lime-green leaves bursting out on every tree. New life will be stirring. I will gather in my heart the whole of it; I will sit silently and I shall weep the hopelessness of tears: ***"April is the cruelest month…, mixing memory and desire…stirring dead roots with spring rain,"*** T.S. Elliot said it in that miserable poem. It was that April evening after our United Nations visit that I conceived; all was so perfect, sublime, serene. We had reached our Nirvana: the highest state of happiness, understanding each other in the deepest sense, two hearts beating as one. But oh, so briefly.

I could feel the moment when our hearts meshed on that damp bench in that cobblestone park with my arms clasped around him under his jacket, my head resting on his shoulder. He and I were one in our understanding of the life we could live together; we knew a profound truth about each other: We were second-class citizens in the United States; the omnipresent reality of this fact encumbered every step we took. Our past had been a hodgepodge of dodges and shields against fear in myriad guises. We felt, with our pleasure bond intact and growing deeper, that we could assuage the angst of daily encounters with the insults of discrimination and make possible our becoming whole persons. Had all been lost in one bloody encounter?

Finally, I opened the letter and read slowly through my tears:

> Dearest,
>
> So, you went away without telling me. I saw Lou, and she told me about the impending trip. I learned too that you had moved, and got this address from her. You needn't worry; I will not come to visit you without an invitation. I was hoping by this time you had some second thoughts about ending our relationship. I swear to you that I experienced a moment of insanity borne of my grief that will never be repeated. Please forgive me.
>
> We do have something special: that I was your first lover, and indeed, hoped to be your last; that you should be my wife and mother of my children. We have so much going for us.
>
> The Bible tells us in marriage we should "forsake all others." I know why: no other woman could reach with me the depths of understanding that we accomplished. Everything else seems so superficial; nothing is as important as building our life together. I need you and want you. What could be more liberating

for us, more in the service of our people than to make a respectable home and rear God-fearing children? Here is my phone number: Hanover 8-9704. Please call me. I want to see you again, and soon.

Enjoy the gift, until we can have the real thing.

With trembling fingers, I unwrapped the box. I treated it as if it were an explosive; I was so cautious, fumbling with the top and the tissue paper. The box contained a beautiful and expensive Negro doll, wearing an adorable matching hat and a ruffled pink dress with white shoes and socks.

I was deeply moved by the gift, but had to remember what had torn us apart – how his anger at my decision to control my own body had caused him to strike me. How I went berserk swinging a metal lamp, which gashed his face. My fear of him was profound; I cringed at the thought of that deep male voice whose resonance I had begun to find soothing. In my head were a thousand echoes of my father's angry bass. How do you become entrapped? First dependence on the loving, then control. It's the Bible that is the basis for his authority; my atheist father used the same reasoning, allowing him to inflict pain to enforce his woman's obligation to obey. Misguided, indeed, was that assumption for this day and age…. And yet he is a soulful lover, so thoughtful, so respectable, so ambitious, displaying so many qualities that I admire….

This dilemma brimmed my eyes with tears unstoppable; I missed him so much. I gazed around me wondering what other people in the park were watching me, but nobody there seemed to notice my distress. I wiped my eyes and through my tears observed the flowers and shrubbery. Perched on a bushy branch with a purple flower was a monarch butterfly. Shouldn't he be gone by now? Would he make it to Morelia before the cold set in and killed him? It was a distraction, yet I was able to dismiss my personal anguish from my mind for a moment and focus on the plight of *la mariposa*. It had an important purpose: to pollinate flowers and fulfill its destiny – endure the flight to Mexico, mate and die.

Would he have really wanted me to carry that pregnancy to term? I'll never know, but it was my body, my future, my reputation that was held in the balance. In this day and age, all would be lost for me. I should have told him, but I was afraid of what he would say; that he would reject both me and the prospect of fatherhood. My father, my prototype for what men are and how they think, never led me to believe a man would cherish me because of something as nebulous as love. He talked about his children as being valuable to him because of what they produced – their own food, the care of the home, the tasks they fulfilled. I guess he did loving things, like provide food and clothing, but this was given after complete obeisance, making sure you needed the items and that you understood how much he was sacrificing to give these "things" to you. His advice was: If you find something or someone you can't live without, give them up immediately. This worked for me with alcohol, food and drugs (which I never tried, fearing that I'd become addicted), but in human relationships, not so well. I am the descendant of enslaved women; one so fair she could have passed for white. What consent had her mother given to her impregnator? Was she snatched from the cotton field by the overseer, thrown against the hay pile and raped? Was she already "married" and did her "husband" helplessly watch the abduction while another boss man on horseback forbade him with whip in hand to leave the field? Dr. Hansberry has shown us photographs of slave families: husband, wife, four Black children and one mulatto child standing with her half siblings. That slap I received demonstrated power, force, constraint, the limiting of my rights; telling me that my reproductive capacity was the providence of the enforcer, not me. Black women, to be whole, must control their bodies; must be able to say when and with whom they will bear children, and must make sure the circumstances are right for them to do so. I can perform the pregnancy miracle, but that is not all I am; there is more to me than my reproductive apparatus. I have suffered abstinence; I have known intimacy in the deepest sense. I believe that I am entitled to the warmth and comfort that having a lover in my life offers. I must find this fulfillment without the symbolic lash.

I gathered up my package and made my way to my apartment. The East Village was becoming a more pleasant place to live as it gentrified; it was near so much that I liked: NYU, the Roundabout Theater and the Village Gate. *Mariposa* had appeared like magic; a reminder of Mexico offering a taste of equality and a symbol of having witnessed at home a rising fervor among the Negro people we met that finally first-class citizenship was possible and could be a reality for us in the United States. I must not lose sight of that image with its promise for me.

The End

Other works by Marietta J. Tanner

The Shapeup – A poem about why the Negro has not pulled himself up by his bootstraps.

Children are the Barometers – A book about Bronx teenagers' suffering during the drug wars of the 1970's and 1980's.

48397522R00186

Made in the USA
Middletown, DE
17 September 2017